P9-DYY-635

the dead and the gone

SUSAN BETH PFEFFER

the dead
and the gone

HARCOURT, INC.

Orlando ∘ Austin ∘ New York ∘ San Diego ∘ London

New Hanover County Public Library
201 Chestnut Street
Wilmington, NC 28401

Copyright © 2008 by Susan Beth Pfeffer

All rights reserved. No part of this publication may be
reproduced or transmitted in any form or by any means, electronic or
mechanical, including photocopy, recording, or any information storage and
retrieval system, without permission in writing from the publisher.

Requests for permission to make copies of any part of the work should be submitted online
at www.harcourt.com/contact or mailed to the following address: Permissions Department,
Houghton Mifflin Harcourt Publishing Company, 6277 Sea Harbor Drive, Orlando, Florida 32887-6777.

www.HarcourtBooks.com

First published in Great Britain in 2008 by Marion Lloyd Books, Scholastic Ltd., UK
First U.S. edition 2008

Library of Congress Cataloging-in-Publication Data
Pfeffer, Susan Beth, 1948–
The dead and the gone/Susan Beth Pfeffer.
p. cm.
Summary: After a meteor hits the moon and sets off a series of horrific climate changes,
seventeen-year-old Alex Morales must take care of his sisters alone in the chaos of New York City.
[1. Survival—Fiction. 2. Natural disasters—Fiction. 3. Brothers and sisters—Fiction.
4. Puerto Ricans—New York (State)—New York—Fiction. 5. New York (N.Y.)—Fiction.
6. Science fiction.] I. Title. II. Title: Dead and the gone.
PZ7.P44855Dc 2008
[Fic]—dc22   2007029606
ISBN 978-0-15-206311-5

Text set in Spectrum
U.S. edition designed by April Ward

First U.S. edition
H G F E D C B A

Printed in the United States of America

Author's note: The churches, schools, businesses, and hospitals mentioned in
the dead and the gone are all products of my imagination and not intended
to reflect any real institutions. Nor does the town of Milagro
del Mar, Puerto Rico, exist. And the last I looked, the
moon was right where it belonged.

For Janet Carlson,
Best Buzz Buddy
and
Cherished Friend

the dead and the gone

chapter 1

Wednesday, May 18

At the moment when life as he had known it changed forever, Alex Morales was behind the counter at Joey's Pizza, slicing a spinach pesto pie into eight roughly equal pieces.

"I ordered an antipasto, also."

"It's right here, sir," Alex said. "And your order of garlic knots."

"Thanks," the man said. "Wait a second. Aren't you Carlos, Luis's kid?"

Alex grinned. "Carlos is my older brother," he said. "I'm Alex."

"That's right," the man said. "Look, could you tell your dad there's a problem with the plumbing in twelve B?"

"My father's away for a few days," Alex said. "He's in Puerto Rico for my grandmother's funeral. But he should be back on Saturday. I'll tell him as soon as he gets home."

"Don't worry about it," the man said. "It's waited this long. I'm sorry to hear about your grandmother."

"Thank you," Alex said.

"So where is your brother these days?" the man asked.

"He's in the Marines," Alex said. "He's stationed at Twentynine Palms, in California."

"Good for him," the man said. "Give him my regards. Greg Dunlap, apartment twelve B."

"I'll do that," Alex said. "And I'll be sure to tell my father about your plumbing."

Mr. Dunlap smiled. "You in school?" he asked.

Alex nodded. "I go to St. Vincent de Paul Academy," he said.

"Good school," Mr. Dunlap said. "Bob, my partner, went there and he says it's the best school in the city. You know where you want to go to college?"

Alex knew exactly where he wanted to go, and where he'd be happy to go, and where he would be satisfied to go. "Georgetown's my first choice," he said. "But it depends on the financial package. And if they accept me, of course."

Mr. Dunlap nodded. "I'll tell Bob Luis's kid goes to Vincent de Paul," he said. "You two can swap stories someday."

"Great," Alex said. "Your bill comes to $32.77."

Mr. Dunlap handed him two twenties. "Keep the change," he said. "Put it toward your college fund. And be sure to give Carlos my regards. Luis must be very proud of both his sons."

"Thank you," Alex said, passing the pizza, the antipasto, and the bag of garlic knots to Mr. Dunlap. "I'll remember to tell my father about the plumbing as soon as he gets back."

"No hurry," Mr. Dunlap said.

Alex knew they always said, "No hurry," when they meant "Get it done right now." But a seven-dollar tip guaranteed that Alex would tell Papi about the plumbing problems in 12B the minute he returned from Nana's funeral.

"The cable's out," Joey grumbled from the kitchen. "Yankees have the bases loaded in the top of the sixth and the cable dies on me."

"It's May," Alex said. "What difference does it make?"

"I have a bet on that game," Joey said.

Alex knew better than to point out the game was still going on even if the cable was out. Instead he turned his attention to the next customer, filling her order for two slices of pepperoni pizza and a large Coke.

He didn't get away until ten, later than he usually worked, but the pizza parlor was short staffed, and since Joey was cranky without his ball game to watch, Alex didn't think it a good idea just to leave. It was a muggy, overcast night, with the feeling of thunderstorms in the air, but as long as it wasn't raining, Alex enjoyed the walk. He concentrated on Georgetown and his chances of getting in.

Being junior class vice president would help, but he had no chance at senior class president. Chris Flynn was sure to win again. Alex had the presidency of the debate squad locked up. But would he or Chris be named editor of the school paper? Alex was weighing the odds between them when his thoughts were interrupted by a man and woman walking out of the Olde Amsterdam Tavern.

"Come on, honey," the man said. "You might as well. We could be dead by tomorrow."

Alex grinned. That sounded like something Carlos would say.

But as Alex raced across Broadway, fire engines and ambulances screamed down the avenue with no concern for traffic lights, and he began to wonder what was going on. Turning onto Eighty-eighth Street, he saw clusters of people standing in front of their apartment buildings. There was no laughter, though, no fighting. Some of the people pointed to the sky, but when Alex looked upward, all he saw was cloud cover. One well-dressed woman stood by herself weeping.

Then, as Alex walked down the short flight of outdoor steps to his family's basement apartment, the electricity went out. Shaking his head, he unlocked the outside door. Once in the darkened hallway, he knocked on the apartment door.

"Alex, is that you?" Briana called.

"Yeah. Let me in," he said. "What's going on?"

Bri opened the door. "The electricity just went out," she said. "The cable went out, too."

"Alex, where's the flashlight?" Julie asked.

"Check on top of the fridge," Alex said. "I think there's one there. Where's Mami?"

"The hospital called," Briana said. "A little while ago. Mami said it's a really big emergency and they need everybody."

Julie walked into the living room, waving the flashlight around. "She's only been there two weeks and they can't manage without her," she said.

"She said they couldn't tell her when she'd get off," Briana said.

"Papi called while you were gone," Julie said. "He said everyone arrived safely and Nana's funeral is tomorrow. I wish we could have gone with him."

"I don't know why," Briana said. "Whenever the family gets together, you always find some excuse not to go."

"You'd better be nice," Julie said. "I have the flashlight."

"Use it to find the transistor radio," Alex suggested. "Maybe the whole city is blacked out." He thought, not for the first time, how much more convenient things would be if the Morales family could afford a computer. Not that it would be any use in a blackout.

"I bet it has something to do with the moon," Briana said.

"Why the moon?" Alex said. "Sunspots cause problems, but I've never heard of moonspots."

"Not moonspots," Briana said. "But the moon was supposed to get hit tonight by an asteroid or something. One of my teachers mentioned it. She was going to a meteor party in Central Park to watch."

"Yeah, I heard about that at school, too," Alex said. "But I still don't see why an asteroid would knock out the electricity. Or why Mami would be called to the hospital."

"The radio isn't working," Briana said, trying to turn it on. "Maybe the batteries are dead."

"Great," Alex said. "In that case, why don't you take the flashlight and get ready for bed. Mami'll tell us what happened when she gets home."

"It's too hot without a fan," Julie whined.

Alex didn't know how Mami and Bri put up with Julie. She was Carlos's favorite, too. Papi actually seemed to think she was cute, but that was because she was the baby of the family. A twelve-year-old baby, in Alex's opinion.

"Do you think everything is okay?" Briana asked.

"I'm sure it is," Alex said. "Probably a big fire downtown. I heard a lot of sirens."

"But Mami works in Queens," Briana said. "Why would the hospital need her there if the fire's downtown?"

"A plane crash, then," Alex said, thinking of the people pointing to the sky. "Remind me to tell Papi that twelve B has a plumbing problem, okay. And go to bed. Whatever the emergency is, it'll be gone by morning."

"All right," Briana said. "Come on, Julie. Let's pray extra hard for everybody."

"That sounds like fun," Julie grumbled, but she followed her big sister to their bedroom.

Mami kept votive candles in the kitchen, Alex remembered. He stumbled around until he found one and matches to light it. It cast only a small amount of light, but enough for him to make his way to the room he had once shared with Carlos.

Originally the two rooms had been the master bedroom, but when they'd moved in, Papi had built a dividing wall, so that the boys and the girls each got a small bedroom. He and Mami slept in their own room. Even without Carlos, the apartment was crowded, but it was home and Alex had no complaints.

He undressed quickly, opened the door slightly so he could hear Mami when she got home, blew out the candle, and climbed into the lower half of the bunk bed. Through the thin wall, he could hear Briana's *Dios te salve, María.* Papi thought Bri was too devout, but Mami said it's just a stage fourteen-year-old girls go through.

Somehow Alex didn't think Julie would go through that stage when she turned fourteen.

When Alex had been fourteen, three years ago, he'd thought for a couple of days about becoming a priest. But Bri was different. Alex could actually see her becoming a nun someday. Mami would love that, he knew.

Sister Briana, he thought as he turned on his side, his head facing the wall. My sister the sister. He fell asleep grinning at the thought.

Thursday, May 19

"Alex! Alex! Let me in!"

At first Alex thought he was dreaming. He hadn't slept well all night, waking up several times to see if the electricity had come back on or if Mami had returned. The hot, muggy weather hadn't helped. The dreams he'd had all had to do with sirens and crashes and emergencies he was somehow involved in but helpless to prevent.

"Alex!"

Alex shook his head awake and looked out the window. It was still dark outside and the streetlights were out. But he could make out a man's face. It was Uncle Jimmy, crouching at the window.

Alex got out of bed. "I'll meet you at the door," he said, tossing on his robe, then making his way through the apartment to the outside door.

"The buzzer's not working," Uncle Jimmy said. "Everything's blacked out."

"What time is it?" Alex asked. "What's going on?"

"It's four-thirty," Uncle Jimmy said. "I need you to help at the bodega. Wake up your sisters and get dressed as fast as you can."

"What's happening at the bodega?" Alex asked, but he did as Jimmy told him, banging on his sisters' bedroom door until he was sure they were awake.

"I'll explain it all later," Jimmy said. "Get dressed. And hurry."

In a matter of minutes, Alex, Briana, and Julie were fully dressed and standing in the living room. "Come on," Jimmy said. "I have the van here."

"Where are we going?" Briana asked. "Is everyone all right? Is Mami home yet?"

"I don't think so," Alex said. "She couldn't have slept through this. Uncle Jimmy, how long are we going to be gone?"

"As long as it takes," Jimmy replied.

"What about school?" Briana asked. "Will we be back in time?"

"Don't worry about school," Jimmy said. "Don't worry about anything. Just come with me."

"What if Mami calls?" Briana asked. "Or Papi? They'll be scared if no one answers the phone."

Alex nodded. "Julie, come with us," he said. "Bri, you stay here in case anyone calls." He would have preferred Bri's company, but it was safer to leave her alone than Julie.

"All right," Jimmy said. "Let's get moving."

Uncle Jimmy had left his van double-parked in front of the building, but Alex supposed at that hour of the morning no one really cared. They piled in and Jimmy began driving crosstown through the park and then the twenty blocks uptown to the bodega. There was a lot more traffic than Alex would have expected so early in the morning, and he could still hear sirens in the distance.

"What's happening?" Alex asked. "Do they know what caused the blackout?"

"Yeah, they know," Jimmy said. "The moon. Something happened to the moon."

"Moonspots," Julie said, and giggled.

"Nothing funny about it," Uncle Jimmy said. "Lorraine couldn't sleep all night. She's convinced the looters will hit the bodegas at first light. Last night it was the liquor stores and the electronics stores, but in the daylight they'll start going for the food. So we're unloading the bodega, moving all the food out, back to the apartment. I need you to pack and lift."

"What about us?" Julie asked. "Do we get any of the food?"

"Yeah, sure," Uncle Jimmy said. "Where's your mother?"

"At the hospital," Alex said. "She worked all night, I guess. Papi's still in Puerto Rico. Uncle Jimmy, what's going on?"

"I'll tell you the best I know how," Uncle Jimmy said.

"Some big thing hit the moon last night, a planet or a comet or something. And it knocked the moon out of whack. It's closer to Earth now. Tidal waves. Flooding, blackouts, panic. Lorraine's hysterical."

Aunt Lorraine was prone to hysteria, Alex thought. Papi's nickname for her was *La Dramática,* and Mami still hadn't forgiven her for the scene she'd made when Carlos announced he was enlisting in the Marines: *"You'll die! They'll kill you! We'll never see you again!"*

"Can't they move the moon back where it belongs?" Julie asked.

"I sure hope so," Jimmy said. "But even if they can, it'll take a while. In the meantime, Lorraine says we might as well have the food and not let strangers steal it from our babies' mouths." He pressed hard on the horn at the sight of a car cutting across Third Avenue. "Idiots," he muttered. "Rich people, pulling out at the first sign of trouble."

"I don't see any cops," Alex said.

Jimmy laughed. "They're off protecting the rich people," he said. "They don't care about nobody else."

Uncle Jimmy seemed to have a little *dramatica* in him as well, Alex decided. Life with Aunt Lorraine probably did that to a person. Their kids sure had tantrums, but they were still little and Alex could only hope they'd outgrow them. Not that Aunt Lorraine ever had.

"Good," Jimmy said. "Benny's here." He pulled his van over to the front of the bodega. "Get out," he said. "Alex, you and I'll load. Julie, you assemble cartons. How's it going, Benny?"

The large man standing in front of the bodega nodded. "It's been quiet," he said. "We should have no problems." He pulled a gun from his belt. "Just in case," he said.

"Benny gets paid first," Jimmy said. "Beer and cigarettes."

"The new currency," Benny said with a grin.

Alex began to wonder if he was still asleep. None of this seemed real, except for the reports of Aunt Lorraine's hysteria. Uncle Jimmy unlocked the steel gate. Alex and Julie followed him into the bodega while Benny stayed on guard by the door.

Jimmy handed Julie a flashlight and told her to sit on the floor behind the counter and assemble boxes. He showed Alex where the cartons of beer and cigarettes were, and as Alex carried them to Benny's car, Jimmy filled empty boxes with milk and bread and other perishables.

Benny told Alex to load his trunk first, and then the backseat. It was remarkable how many cartons of beer and cigarettes the car could hold.

Finally the only room in the car was the driver's seat. "You know how to drive?" Jimmy asked Alex.

Alex shook his head.

"Okay, I'll drive the stuff to Benny's," he said. "Benny, you stay out front. Keep that gun where people can see it. Alex, start packing cartons for my family. Tell Julie to use the plastic bags for your stuff. I'll be back in half an hour."

Benny stayed outside while Alex joined Julie in the bodega. Uncle Jimmy locked the steel gate, leaving Alex with the uncomfortable sensation of being a prisoner, even though he knew he and Julie were safer if the store was locked shut.

"Uncle Jimmy's crazy, right?" Julie asked.

"Probably," Alex said. "You know Aunt Lorraine. She's only happy when the world's coming to an end." He noticed all the cartons Julie had assembled. "You've really been working," he said.

Julie nodded. "I figured I'd better," she said. "Otherwise

Aunt Lorraine will have a fit if we take any stuff for ourselves. And if we don't, Mami'll get mad."

"Good thinking," Alex said. "Uncle Jimmy says to use the plastic bags for our stuff."

"Sure," Julie said. "They'll hold less."

"It's his food," Alex said. "He's doing us the favor. Why don't you fill as many bags as you can while he's gone."

Julie nodded and began stuffing bags with jars and canned goods. Alex did the same with the cartons. As he worked, he tried to figure out just what was really going on. The moon was responsible for tides, so it made sense if it was closer to Earth, the tides would be higher. How quickly could NASA solve the problem? The distant rumble of thunder unsettled him more.

He jumped when Julie broke the silence. "Do you think Carlos is okay?" she asked.

"Sure," Alex said, silently laughing at himself. "He must be pretty busy. I don't know when he'll have a chance to call."

"Mami, too," Julie said. "With all the looting and everything, the hospitals must be full."

"And Papi's safe in Milagro del Mar," Alex said. "We're all fine. By Monday everything'll be back in order."

"I wonder if they've called off school," Julie asked. "I have an English test I haven't studied for."

Alex grinned. "You're safe," he said. "Even if Holy Angels is open, they'll probably cancel the test."

Julie continued filling the plastic bags with as much as each could hold. Alex did the same with the cartons. It was nice to tell Julie things would be back to normal by Monday, but he thought that was unlikely. The more food they had at home, the better.

"How are you doing?" he asked Julie.

"I've packed twenty bags," she said.

"Good," Alex said. "Keep on. You know the kind of stuff Mami gets."

"Better than you do," Julie muttered.

Alex laughed, but the truth of the matter was he couldn't remember the last time he'd been to a supermarket, and he certainly couldn't remember Papi or Carlos going to one. Groceries, cooking, cleaning—all that was done by Mami, Bri, and Julie. Alex kept his room tidy, and Carlos used to help Papi out occasionally, but it was Bri and Julie who knew how to sew and iron and cook. Even when Mami went back to school, first to get her GED and then to learn how to be an operating room technician, she and the girls did all the housework.

Not that Alex had ever heard Mami complain about it, or Bri. Julie certainly did, but if Julie were a crown princess, she'd complain about the crown.

Right on cue, Julie whined, "My arms ache. And I can't reach stuff on the top shelves."

"Then just take stuff from the shelves you can reach," he said. "Be sure to take canned mushrooms. Papi likes them."

"I already have a bag," Julie said.

"Good," Alex said, and went back to packing and thinking. NASA was most likely consulting physicists and astronomers from around the world about the quickest way of getting the moon in place. Things would eventually get back in order.

By the time Uncle Jimmy returned, Alex had filled all the empty cartons. He and Jimmy loaded the van while Julie returned to assembling the few remaining boxes. Then he and Jimmy filled those boxes and whatever bags remained.

"Julie, you stay here," Uncle Jimmy said. "Benny'll be outside. Alex and I'll empty this stuff at my place, and then we'll come back and drive you home."

Alex wasn't crazy about leaving Julie alone in the store, but he supposed she'd be safe locked in with an armed guard standing watch. "Behave yourself," he said to her.

Julie glared at him. Alex pitied any looters who might make it past Benny.

Jimmy swiftly drove the four blocks back to his apartment. "Lorraine'll help us unload." he said. "But it's going to take a while to carry all this stuff upstairs."

Jimmy and Lorraine lived in a second-floor walk-up. Jimmy unloaded the cartons from the van to the first floor, and then Alex carried them upstairs, where Lorraine met him and brought the cartons into her apartment. Alex could hear his little cousins screaming in the background, but that was nothing new. Lorraine said nothing, just grunting occasionally as she pushed the heavier cartons into her home.

When they finally finished, Lorraine looked up at Alex. "Thank you," she said. "You've helped save my babies' lives."

"Things'll work out," Alex said. "Give the scientists some time and they'll figure out what to do."

"This is too big for the scientists," Lorraine said. "Only God can save us now."

"Then He will," Alex said.

"Come on, Alex!" Jimmy called from downstairs. "Let's get going."

Alex gave Lorraine an awkward hug, and raced down the stairs.

Jimmy drove them back to the bodega, where Alex noticed Benny was no longer standing guard. "Dammit," Jimmy said. "I told him to stay until we got back. Julie, you okay?"

"People were banging against the steel door," Julie said, crouching behind the counter. "I heard gunshots."

"It's all right," Alex said. "We're going home now."

"Okay," Jimmy said, still looking annoyed. "I'll finish packing what's left on my own. Come on, let's load up your stuff."

Alex was impressed with how many bags Julie had filled and how heavy the bags were. They'd certainly have enough food to last until things got back to normal.

Jimmy helped them bring the food into the living room, then went back to the bodega. Alex, Briana, and Julie carried most of the bags into the kitchen. Whatever didn't fit there stayed in the living room.

"The phone rang while you were gone," Briana said. "I think it was Papi, but I can't be sure."

"What do you mean you can't be sure?" Alex asked, every muscle in his body aching. All he wanted was a hot shower and four more hours' sleep.

"There was a lot of static," Briana said almost apologetically. "But I heard a man's voice and I'm sure it was Papi's. I think he said something about Puerto Rico."

"Well, that's good news," Alex said. "If he called, he must be all right. He probably called to say he won't be coming home on Saturday."

"I told him we're all fine so he won't worry," Bri said.

"They left me alone," Julie said. "People tried to break in. Someone could have killed me."

"Are you all right?" Bri asked. Alex could see the worry in her eyes.

"Of course she is," Alex said. "We all are."

"Can we call Mami?" Briana asked. "We can tell her about the groceries and that we heard from Papi."

"We shouldn't bother her at work," Alex said. "She'll call

us when she can, or maybe she'll just come home. Look, how about making us some breakfast. We'll all feel better after we've eaten."

"I can make scrambled eggs," Briana said. "The stove's still working. I checked."

"Sounds good," Alex said. "I'm going to take a shower. After breakfast we'll go to school."

"I'm not going anywhere," Julie said. "Not in the blackout."

"I don't want to go, either," Bri said. "Can't we stay here until Mami comes home?"

"All right," Alex said. "But I'll go out after breakfast and see what's happening."

He got into the shower only to find there was no hot water. He got in and out as fast as he could, then dressed in his school clothes.

"There's no hot water," Alex told Bri.

"You don't think the people in the apartments will blame Papi, do you?" she asked.

"No one will blame Papi," Alex said. "It's not just this building. The whole city is probably blacked out. Where's Julie? Did she eat already?"

"She went back to bed," Briana said, putting scrambled eggs on Alex's plate. "I hope the orange juice is still okay."

Alex took a sip. "It's fine," he said. He hadn't realized how hungry he was until he smelled the eggs. He'd just finished gobbling down the food when the phone rang.

"Maybe it's Mami!" Briana cried, and raced to answer it. "Hello? It's Carlos! Hi, Carlos. Is everything okay where you are?"

"Give me the phone, Bri," Alex said. "Carlos, this is Alex. How are you?"

"I'm okay," Carlos said. "I can only talk for a minute. We're being deployed. I don't know where we're going, but they told us all to call home. Is everything okay with you?"

"We're fine," Alex said. "Papi called this morning and spoke to Bri. And Mami's at the hospital. How are things where you are? Is it blacked out?"

"No, we have electricity," Carlos said. "Is Julie all right?"

"She's sleeping," Alex said. "Jimmy had us empty out the bodega. She worked really hard. You want me to wake her?"

"No, that's okay," Carlos said. "Look, Alex, you're in charge now until Papi gets home. Mami's going to be depending on you."

"I know," Alex said. "Carlos, have they told you anything about how long before things get back to normal?"

"Nothing definite," Carlos said. "Just that it's going to take a long time and we should expect lots of trouble."

"Well, we're okay," Alex said. "We got a lot of food from the bodega. And Jimmy's around in case we need any help until Papi gets home."

"Good," Carlos said. "I'd better get off. There's a long line here. You take care, Alex, and take care of Mami and the girls. You're the man of the house now."

"Don't worry about us," Alex said, but before he had a chance to say good-bye, he heard Carlos hang up.

"Who was that?" Julie asked, coming out from her room. "Mami?"

"It was Carlos," Bri replied. "He called to make sure we were all right."

"Carlos?" Julie said. "Why didn't you let me speak to him?"

"He was in a hurry," Alex said. "He's being deployed. See,

Bri, there's nothing to worry about. The Marines are on the job."

"Mami'll be so glad we heard from him," Briana said. "Julie, do you want any eggs?"

"My stomach hurts," Julie replied. "I was so scared at the bodega, I ate a bunch of candy bars."

"Well, that was real bright of you," Alex said. His head was pounding, but he knew it had nothing to do with candy.

"You don't know what it was like," Julie said. "I was all alone there and I could hear people shooting."

"People are shooting?" Bri asked. "Are we safe, Alex?"

"Of course we are," Alex said. He could have killed Julie. "You know what it's like uptown. We're fine here. I'm going to go to school and see what I can find out."

"But you'll come right back?" Bri asked. "Even if school's open?"

"All right," Alex said. "Don't worry. Everything'll be all right. I promise."

"You can't promise that," Julie said, but he chose to ignore her as he left the apartment.

The chaos on the streets before dawn was nothing compared to the madness he encountered. The traffic was worse than he'd ever seen. The side streets were like parking lots, and so were West End and Amsterdam Avenues, where the traffic went uptown. Broadway was limited to emergency vehicles, and they were flying down the avenue, their sirens screaming. With the traffic lights not working, the drivers made up their own rules about when to go. No one stopped for anybody, and Alex raced each time he crossed the street. There were few other people walking, and the stores all had their steel gates locked in place. But even without pedestrians, the noise from sirens, honking horns, and screaming drivers was overwhelming.

Vincent de Paul was on Seventy-third and Columbus, and unless the weather was really bad, Alex walked. The skies were threatening, but the thunderstorm he'd been expecting since last night had yet to arrive. Sweat dripped down his brow, but he couldn't be sure whether it was from the heat, the running, or fear. Julie was right. He couldn't promise anything.

When he got to the multistory, brick school building Alex found a sign on the door. CLOSED UNTIL MONDAY.

Alex wasn't surprised, but he was disappointed. School had always been a safe haven for him, and he'd counted on finding someone there who could give him a better idea of what was going on. Not that he was so sure he really wanted to know.

He turned away from the door, and almost immediately the rain began. Lightning bolts flashed and thunder clapped. He cursed himself for not having brought an umbrella, for going out in the first place. He couldn't even be sure the subways were running in a blackout.

He walked to the Seventy-second Street station and found a chain across the stairwell. A soaking wet cop stood nearby, watching the ambulances fly down Broadway.

Alex gestured toward the subway station.

"Closed," the cop said. "The tunnels flooded."

"Thanks," Alex said. He wondered what had caused the flooding, but it was raining too hard for conversation. He ran the mile or so back home, and was drenched by the time he got into the apartment.

"School's closed until Monday," he said. "Did Mami call?"

Briana shook her head. "Julie went back to bed," she said. "You're soaking."

"Yeah, I know," Alex said. "I'm going to dry off and go to sleep. Wake me up before Monday, okay?"

Briana laughed. "Go to sleep," she said. "By the time you wake up, I bet Mami'll be home and everything will be okay."

"I bet you're right," Alex said, but he knew that was a fairy tale. As he hung up his wet school clothes and changed back into his jeans and T-shirt, he thought about the tunnels flooding. The subway Mami took to Queens went through a tunnel. But that had been last night, and things must have been all right then. Still he knew he wouldn't feel at peace until they heard from her.

Bed looked very inviting. But first he got down on his knees, made the sign of the cross, and prayed for the safety of his mother and father and brother, for the safety of his sisters, and then for the safety of his country and the world.

God, show us mercy, he prayed. And give me strength.

Only then did he allow himself to escape into sleep.

chapter 2

Friday, May 20

He was awake when his clock began blinking 12:00, 12:00. Alex checked his watch. It was 6:45 AM.

He could hear the whir of the refrigerator turning back on, but there were no other sounds in the apartment. Throwing on his robe, he tiptoed into the living room, not wanting to wake Bri or Julie. All the grocery bags scattered around looked ridiculous now, a crazy extravagance during a crazy day.

Alex turned on the TV, lowering the sound as quickly as he could. He sat close to the set, keeping the volume as low as possible so his sisters wouldn't be disturbed. Only a couple of stations came in, but he wasn't looking for variety, just information. Both stations were doing news broadcasts, focusing exclusively on the emergency.

On one station the broadcaster was talking about conditions in Europe, but Alex knew that could wait. He switched to the second station. At first that one talked about how things were elsewhere in the United States. No word of survivors on the Carolina barrier islands. Terrible conditions in Cape Cod.

It took about fifteen minutes of terrible news around the country before the newscasters began focusing on New York. Alex sat there, absolutely still, the sound so low he could barely hear. The words and pictures assaulted him anyway. Horrific loss of life. Lower Manhattan decimated. Staten Island, Long Island devastated. Blackouts, looting, riots. Curfew between 8 PM and 6 AM. Tides twenty feet tall, sweeping away people, trees, even buildings. Mandatory evacuations. Plane crashes. Countless numbers of people dead in subways and in cars from tunnel flooding.

Alex hadn't thought about people being on the subways when the flooding first began.

He felt a wave of panic and had to tell himself to calm down. It would be easy enough to find out if Mami was all right. All he had to do was call the hospital and confirm that she was there. Sure, they weren't supposed to call her at work unless it was an emergency, but they hadn't heard from her in over twenty-four hours and that was emergency enough.

Mami had the hospital number written on the scratch pad she kept by the phone. Just seeing it comforted him. He picked up the phone, but it was dead.

For an instant he went crazy. The phone was dead because Mami was dead. But then he realized how foolish that was, and he began shaking with silent laughter. No wonder they hadn't heard from Mami. It was a miracle the phone service had lasted as long as it had, long enough for Papi and Carlos to call.

Alex went back to the TV and switched to the station with all the international news. Their newscaster was interviewing a distinguished-looking scientist about how long it would take before things got back to normal.

"Things may never get back to normal," the scientist said. "I don't want to be an alarmist, but I know of nothing humans can do to return the moon to its orbit."

"But surely there must be something," the newscaster said. "NASA must be working on a solution day and night."

"Even if they can come up with something, it may take months, even years, before they can implement it," the scientist replied. "What happened yesterday will be nothing compared to what lies ahead."

"You're not suggesting we all panic," the newscaster said in that calming, don't-panic voice Alex associated with TV when things were at their worst. "Surely panic is the one thing we shouldn't do right now."

Before Alex had a chance to find out what the scientist's alternative to panic might be, the electricity went out again.

Alex cursed under his breath. No phone, no electricity, two kid sisters depending on him to take care of them until their parents returned. God certainly didn't want to make things easy for him.

Or for anyone else, he thought. Floods in the subways. Devastation throughout the world. How many people had died in the past two days? Thousands? Millions? How long would it take before Carlos was back at his base? How long before Papi could return from Puerto Rico, before the hospital could let Mami go home?

Stop it, he told himself. You're starting to sound like Aunt Lorraine. One *dramatica* in a family is enough. No matter how bad things were, he couldn't allow himself to be frightened. Not as long as he was responsible for Briana's and Julie's well-being.

Alex went back to his bedroom and picked up his notebook. Knowledge was the enemy of fear. Before every debate he always wrote lists of his argument's strengths and weaknesses. He'd do the same now.

He made three columns and labeled them: WHAT I KNOW; WHAT I THINK; WHAT I DON'T KNOW.

Under WHAT I KNOW he wrote:

> *No subways*
> *Floods*
> *Moon closer to Earth*
> *Carlos all right*
> *Bri and Julie all right*
> *School on Monday*

There didn't seem much point writing down what he'd heard about Europe or Massachusetts. People there could make their own lists.

He bit on his pen and thought. Then he wrote: *Food in the apartment.*

Of course that was assuming Julie had packed things besides mushrooms and candy bars.

But Mami had Wednesdays off, and most likely she'd gone to the supermarket to buy groceries. Alex made a mental note to check the kitchen cabinets, but he doubted there was anything to worry about when it came to food.

He looked at the lists. Under WHAT I DON'T KNOW he wrote: *How long it will take for things to get back to normal.*

Apparently no one knew that. But just because no one knew didn't mean things wouldn't get back to normal. He might have had the bad luck to catch the only pessimistic scientist on TV.

And, he reminded himself, New York always survived. It had to. The United States, the whole world, couldn't manage without it. It might take a while, and there might be a lot of politicking involved, but eventually New York bounced back from any misfortune. He lived in the greatest city in the world, and what made it great was its people. He was a Puerto Rican New Yorker, strong by birth and by upbringing.

Puerto Rico. Bri had heard from Papi. He lifted the pen to write *Papi all right in Puerto Rico* under the WHAT I KNOW list until he realized he didn't really know that at all.

What exactly had Briana said? She'd gotten a phone call, there was a lot of static, she thought she heard a man say, "Puerto Rico," and she was certain it was Papi.

Papi's family came from Milagro del Mar, a small town midway between San Juan and Fajardo, on the northern coast of Puerto Rico. When Nana died on Sunday, Alex had been sad, but he really didn't know her all that well. Then again, Mami's mother had died before he'd been born and Mami had no contact with her father, so Nana was the last of his grandparents. But that wasn't reason enough for him to go to Nana's funeral. Mami couldn't leave her brand-new job, and Carlos was too far away. So Papi had gone to Puerto Rico on his own, meeting up there with his two brothers and their families in that little town on the coastline.

It might not have been Papi who called. It might have been one of his brothers. Or it might have been a wrong number, someone asking for "Peter or Ricky," and Bri just assumed the man had said Puerto Rico.

Alex told himself to calm down. Maybe it had been Papi who'd called and maybe it hadn't. It didn't matter. There was no reason to assume the worst, but it was safe to say Papi wouldn't make it home on Saturday. Even if everything miraculously snapped back to place, there'd be long delays, the same as when it snowed and flights got backed up. If New

York didn't have electricity or working phones, neither would San Juan.

The image of a twenty-foot tidal wave flashed through his mind. What defense would Milagro del Mar have against that? Could anyone survive?

He shook his head. It was as dangerous to think about that as to think of tunnels flooding and people drowning in the subways. Until he heard differently, he was going to assume Papi was safe in Puerto Rico and Mami was safe in Queens. He just wouldn't put anything about them on his list.

Alex stared at the list. He'd written nothing under WHAT I THINK. The truth was he didn't want to think. He wanted to wake up to hear Papi cursing him out and Mami defending him and Bri and Julie fighting over who hogged the bathroom worse. He wanted the moon back where it belonged and pessimistic scientists to crawl under rocks. He wanted a full scholarship to Georgetown and summer internships with United States senators. He wanted to be the first president of the United States of Puerto Rican descent.

More than anything, he wanted to know his parents were safe. He couldn't make himself think "alive and safe." They had to be alive. They were just gone, that's all. Papi was gone for Nana's funeral, and Mami was gone because the hospital needed her. Just gone for the time being, the same as Carlos. Both of them worried about Alex and the girls. Both of them trying to get home.

If the subways were out, Mami would have to get back to Manhattan by bus. With traffic what it was, that could take hours. She wouldn't like seeing all those bags of food scattered around, though. Alex decided to ask Bri and Julie to put the food away. They knew where things went in the kitchen better than he did.

It would be harder for Papi to get back, but not impossible. Planes would start flying again eventually. Papi could get a bus from the airport to Port Authority and walk the couple of miles uptown if he had to.

Alex looked at his watch and saw if he dressed quickly he had time to make the 8:15 Mass at St. Margaret's. He thought about waking up Bri and Julie and telling them to go with him, but decided it wouldn't be worth the chaos. They'd all go on Sunday, maybe Mami, too, and they could pray for Papi's safe return. But this morning he would go by himself.

He left a note for his sisters, even though they'd probably still be asleep when he got back, and walked to Columbus Avenue, praying for safety as he crossed Broadway, then up the two blocks to the church. The sun was shining brightly, but even so the moon was clearly visible, the way it sometimes was in daylight. Only it was too big. Much too big.

Alex was relieved to find the church open and surprised at the number of people there. More men than he would have assumed would be there, and not all of them old. Many people had fear in their eyes, and many others were weeping. He was glad he'd left his sisters at home.

He expected the Mass to begin as it always did, but instead Father Franco said he had some announcements to make. Alex could see that he was reading from a sheet of paper. That reassured him. As long as lists were being made, there was order in the world.

"The mayor's office and the archdiocese's office are in constant communication," Father Franco began. "Whenever the archdiocese learns something, it will inform the parish priests so that we can inform our congregants." He looked up for a moment and then smiled. "A whole new reason to go to Mass on weekdays," he said.

There was a ripple of nervous laughter.

"Very well," Father Franco said. "We've been told the subways are not yet back in service and bus service is severely restricted, so unless your work is essential to the survival of the community, you're requested to stay within walking distance of your home. No driving except for emergencies. There is a city-wide curfew from eight PM to six AM." He looked up again. "These rules may seem draconian," he said, "but as I'm sure you understand, these are very difficult times. Now I know you've been wondering about electricity. They're hoping to have most of Manhattan back on line by Monday."

"No electricity all weekend?" a man called out from the back.

"All the municipal services are doing what they can under tremendously difficult circumstances," Father Franco said. "The outages are nationwide."

"What about the phones?" a woman asked.

Father Franco consulted his list. "There's no time frame for return of phone service," he said. "Again, these are national problems. Most of the communication satellites have crashed. Let's see, what else. Airports remain closed until further notice. No decision has been made about when the public and parochial schools will reopen." He looked up again. "We'll use our bulletin board to post any information we receive from the archdiocese, so be sure to check that daily. All the churches are running short staffed. I'm sure you can understand why. But the archdiocese has declared that all its churches will be open from six AM to eight PM. There may not be a priest available, but Christ, our savior, will hear your prayers."

Alex had thought the ritual of the Mass, which he knew so well, would provide him with comfort, but his mind was reeling from all Father Franco had said. It wasn't so much that he was taken by surprise. He knew about the phones, the electricity, the subways. But he hadn't really known that everyone else knew. Somehow it had felt like the problems belonged to West Eighty-eighth Street. But it wasn't just Papi stuck in Milagro del Mar; people all over the world were affected by the airports being closed. And Mami wasn't the only person stuck at her job with no way of reassuring her family that she was all right.

Alex prayed to Christ for the wisdom to see what would be required of him and for the strength to do it. He prayed for the souls of those who were dead, and for the safe return of those who were gone. He thanked God for the Church, without which he would be lost.

He got home to find his sisters up and prowling around the apartment.

"You're back!" Bri cried as though he'd been gone for weeks, not hours. "Where were you?"

"At St. Margaret's," he said. "I left a note. Didn't you see it?"

"Yeah," Bri admitted. "We were worried you might not come right back."

"Well, I did," Alex said. "And I'm hungry. Have you had breakfast yet?"

"No," Bri said. "We didn't feel like eating until we knew you were okay."

"I'm fine," Alex said, trying to keep the irritation out of his voice. "Why don't you make us breakfast, Bri. We'll all be happier after we've eaten."

"What do we have to be happy about?" Julie asked. "We don't know where Mami or Papi are, or what's happening, or when things are going to be normal again."

"Well, you could be happy you're not in school flunking your English test," Alex said. "You could be happy because we have food in the house and we have each other. You could be happy because the sun is shining and because you got to sleep late. There are a lot of things you could be happy about if you wanted."

"Do you want to smell the milk?" Bri asked from the kitchen. "I think it's okay."

Alex went into the kitchen and took a sniff. "It's okay," he said. "Let's have cereal and milk while we can."

"What does that mean?" Julie asked. "When won't we be able to have cereal and milk?"

"Father Franco said they weren't sure when we'd be getting electricity back," Alex said. "That's all. Maybe by Monday. No point buying milk before then."

Bri put wheat flakes into three bowls and then poured some milk over hers. She took a bite and smiled. "It's okay," she said. She sliced a banana and distributed the pieces.

"What else did Father Franco say?" Julie asked.

"He said the airports are closed and phones are going to be out for a while," Alex said. "Which is why we haven't heard from Mami. I tried calling the hospital this morning, but the phone was dead. We were lucky Papi and Carlos got through to us yesterday. And they don't know when schools will re-open."

"That should make you happy," Bri said to Julie.

"I miss school," Julie said. "I'm bored. At least at school I do stuff and I hang out with my friends."

"There's stuff for you to do here," Alex said. "For both of you. After breakfast, why don't you put away all the food we got from Uncle Jimmy?"

"There may not be room for it in the cupboards," Bri said.

"See if you can find room," Alex said. "You know how Papi and Mami feel about the apartment being a mess. That reminds me. Julie, did you think to take batteries?"

Julie shook her head. "Did you?" she asked.

"I wouldn't be asking if I had," Alex said.

"We're okay without batteries," Bri said. "The flashlights are working."

"I wanted them for the radio," Alex said. "I guess it'll have to wait."

"What are *you* going to do?" Julie asked.

"I have things to check," Alex said. "You do your job and I'll do mine."

"Yes, master," Julie said.

Alex left his sisters and went into his parents' bedroom. If Mami walked in while he was going through their things, she'd kill him. But Alex figured he'd better see if there was any cash in the house. He had his tip money from Wednesday night, more than usual, thanks to 12B, but that wasn't very much.

He started with the drawers of his parents' bureau, in case there was an envelope with money under their clothes. Then he opened the drawers of their night table. No money there, either. He fingered Mami's rosary beads, wishing she had them with her.

Alex checked their closet next, rifling through his father's pants pockets. He was rewarded with a handful of coins and two dollar bills.

On his father's night table, Alex found the key to Papi's

office, where he kept his supplies. It was unlikely Papi kept any money there, but it needed to be checked out. Papi never let any of the kids into his office unless he was there, and even then only Carlos had ever hung out with him.

As Alex crossed through the living room, he found Bri and Julie hard at work. "Where are you going?" Bri asked him.

"To Papi's office," Alex said.

"Papi won't like that," Julie said.

"He'll understand," Bri said. "Especially when he sees how many cans of mushrooms you got for him, Julie."

Alex grinned at the thought of Papi eating nothing but mushrooms for the next month. He left the apartment and walked the few feet to Papi's office. It wasn't much more than a supply closet, but Papi had a desk, and maybe he kept some cash there.

There was a minifridge in the corner, and out of curiosity, Alex opened it. There were three cans of beer and an untouched six-pack. Well, if Julie drove him to drink, Alex wouldn't have to go very far.

In Papi's desk drawer he found a directory of all the apartments, a deck of cards, and two envelopes. Both envelopes were sealed, but Alex could tell they held keys. One envelope said 11F, the other 14J. 11F felt like it had money in it. Curiosity and desperation overcame fear, and Alex opened the envelope. He found two twenties and a paint chip. Apparently Papi had agreed to paint 11F and was to use the cash to buy the paint. Well, if Papi couldn't make it home for a few days, the odds were neither could 11F or 14J.

Alex put the envelopes in his pants pocket. He debated about the beer, but then decided it was safer in the apartment. Besides, Papi would want a beer the minute he got home, whenever that might be.

Between his tip money, the couple of bucks in Papi's pants, and 11F's forty dollars, Alex figured they had a little more than fifty in cash. With the food in the house they should be okay until Mami got home.

He went back to the apartment, beers in tow. "Papi's really going to kill you," Julie said.

"I'm holding them for him," Alex said. "Count them. Nine cans."

"When do you think Papi'll get home?" Briana asked.

"Late next week probably," Alex replied. "They have to get the airports open first, so it'll take a while."

"Do you think Mami'll be back tonight?" Bri asked.

"Mami may be stuck in Queens," Alex replied. "Father Franco said the subways aren't running."

"It's funny to think she's stuck in Queens and Papi's stuck in Puerto Rico," Bri said. "Like they were both really far away."

"What's funny about it?" Julie asked. "How do we even know they're okay?"

"Our Madre Santisima is looking after them," Bri said. "Isn't that right, Alex."

"Of course she is," Alex said, praying that the Most Holy Mother's arms were big enough to embrace the millions of souls, dead and gone, crying for her mercy.

Saturday, May 21

Alex knew his sisters would expect to go to Mass on Sunday, but he wasn't sure he wanted them to hear what Father Franco might say. It didn't help that the panic inside him was growing stronger and more uncontrollable by the minute. He told himself repeatedly that it had been Papi who'd called, that Bri couldn't be wrong, that it was just a matter of time before Papi made his way back home. But he couldn't shake the image of the tiny seaside town being swept away, Papi screaming as twenty-foot tidal waves carried him to certain death.

And Mami. The longer they went without hearing from her, the more terrified Alex became that they never would. Had she drowned on the subway like thousands of others?

It was only three days, Alex reminded himself, and three days was nothing when the world was in chaos and communication was impossible.

They had plenty of food. They had a home. They had the church. They had each other. They had Uncle Jimmy and Aunt Lorraine. If it came to it, they had Carlos. They were better off than millions of people. And it wasn't as though they didn't have Papi and Mami. They just didn't know how they were.

It would be all right. It had to be.

Still, before he let his sisters go to Mass, he wanted to know as much as he could about what was going on, at least in their neighborhood. So he decided to take a walk.

"Where are you going?" Bri asked with that tinge of fear he'd come to expect in her voice.

"Just for a walk," Alex said.

"Can we come with you?" Julie asked.

"No," Alex said.

"Why not?" Julie demanded. "I'm bored. There's nothing to do here. Why can't we go on a walk with you?"

Because I'm trying to protect you! Alex wanted to yell, but he knew that would only scare Bri.

"You'll be going to church tomorrow," he said instead. "Have either of you done any homework since Wednesday?"

They shook their heads.

"I expect to see it completely done by the time I get home," Alex said, the way Mami would have. "And I tell you what. If I find anything is open, a store or a coffee shop, we'll go as soon as I get back. All right?"

"You won't be gone long?" Bri asked.

"Not long," Alex said. "I promise. Now start your homework."

"Come on, Julie," Bri said. "I'll help you with your math."

"I don't need any help," Julie grumbled, but she followed her older sister to their bedroom. Alex breathed a sigh of relief. He couldn't blame his sisters for wanting to get out. But they had to be protected.

He knew he needed to check the bulletin board at St. Margaret's, if for no other reason than to see if there was a notice about the schools reopening. But instead of walking east to the church, he went west.

Alex told himself as he walked toward Riverside Drive that the Hudson River would be fine, but even so, when he got to the river, he felt a sense of relief. The river was agitated, but that could have been from the heavy rains on Thursday. New Jersey, across the river, was right where it belonged. If rivers had tides, and Alex had to admit he didn't know if they did, they didn't seem too bad.

Alex turned around and began the walk to St. Margaret's. There was hardly any traffic compared to the days before, and there weren't many people on the streets, but there was plenty of noise coming from the apartment buildings. Alex grinned. Usually when the weather was this hot, people had their air conditioners going, but with no electricity, windows were open instead. He heard quarrels, laughter, scoldings, even lovemaking, many of the same sounds he'd heard in Uncle Jimmy's neighborhood, only now in English instead of Spanish.

But for all the sounds of life on Eighty-eighth Street, Broadway felt dead. Nothing seemed to be open, not the supermarket, or the coffee shop, or the deli, or the Korean grocery, or the dry cleaner, or the Laundromat, or the liquor store, or the florist, or the Chinese takeout, or the movie theater. He saw a couple of cops but very few other people walking around. Even the fire engines and ambulances seemed to have stopped their downtown runs.

At least St. Margaret's had people in it. The bulletin board was surrounded, and it took Alex a couple of minutes before he could see everything that had been posted.

There were so many sheets that the walls around the bulletin board had been drafted into service as well. The first thing he noticed was a listing of the dead. There weren't really that many names on it: two sheets, single spaced, three columns across, alphabetical order.

Alex forced himself to look at the Ms. Nobody named Morales. His knees buckled with relief. As long as Mami wasn't on the list, there was no reason to think she was dead. That was something he could tell his sisters.

"Not many names," a man said, looking over the list.

"Most of the bodies can't be identified," another man replied. "A lot washed out to the sea. And they're still removing bodies from the subways. You looking for anyone in particular?"

"No," the first man said. "Well, a couple of people, but not family. How about you?"

The second man shook his head. "There's one friend we're concerned about but that's it. We're lucky."

Alex turned away from the list of the dead and saw several

pages of handwritten names, with phone numbers next to them.

HAVE YOU SEEN ANY OF THESE PEOPLE?
Write Down the Name, the Last Known Sighting, and Phone Number to Contact with Information

Willing his hand not to shake, Alex wrote down his parents' names, putting *Puerto Rico* next to his father's and *7 train* next to his mother's. Then he wrote their home phone number, sending up a quick prayer that his sisters wouldn't be the ones to answer the phone if anyone called with bad news.

The first man looked over at Alex and read what he'd written. "Your parents?" he asked.

Alex nodded, not sure he could trust himself to speak.

"You okay?" the man asked. "You have someone to look after you?"

Alex nodded again.

"Puerto Rico," the second man read. "By the coast or inland?"

"Coast," Alex choked out.

The second man shook his head. "San Juan was hit hard," he said. "All the coast. You and your family will be in my prayers."

"Mine, too," the first man said, gently resting his hand on Alex's shoulder. "If you need help, you know someone at St. Margaret's will be here for you. We're family here, don't forget that."

"I won't," Alex said. "Thank you."

The two men walked away, their places taken immediately by two others. Alex checked out the rest of the notices on the bulletin board. Monday was going to be a national day of mourning. Schools would reopen on Tuesday. Curfew was still in place. A Mass for the dead would be held daily at 6:00 PM until further notice.

Alex left the church uncertain where to go, but ending up on Amsterdam Avenue. What few cars were on the street whizzed their way uptown. Alex walked the two blocks to Joey's pizza parlor. The door was locked, but he looked through the window and spotted Joey behind the counter. Alex knocked on the window, and when Joey looked up, waved.

Joey walked over to the door and unlocked it. "I'm glad to see you," Joey said. "I wanted to call but no phones."

"I know," Alex said. "Are you going to open?"

Joey shook his head. "The ovens are okay," he said. "But there's no refrigeration. I've lost all my cheese. Can't have pizza without cheese."

"The electricity's supposed to be back by Monday," Alex said.

"That's what they say," Joey said. "But what if it comes and goes? And what if the phones don't work good, either? People call in for pizzas. No, I'm shot. The chains'll figure a way. Pay off the right people, get all the service they need. But us little guys, we're goners."

"I guess I'm out of a job then," Alex said.

"You and me both," Joey said. "My wife's already after me for us to move. She says this is just the beginning."

"You think so?" Alex asked. "I figure the scientists are working on solutions. And the government. If we get electricity back, that'll make things better right there."

Joey shook his head. "I'm not ready to give up, but my wife's got a point," he replied. "It's not like the tides just hit Wednesday night, like one of those tsunamis, one-shot deal.

Tides are twice a day, every day. Full moons will really be killers."

"But people will just move away from the coast," Alex said, trying to sound calm and rational, trying not to think of his father. "Lots of New York City is inland. We're not getting hit by tides here."

"That's what I said to my wife," Joey said. "But she says the whole city will erode. I guess the question is how long will it take. Weeks, months, centuries."

Alex smiled. "I'm going with centuries," he said. "The Empire State Building isn't eroding anytime soon."

"Tell that to my wife," Joey said. "Meantime, I don't see how I can stay in business, and I don't know what else to do. Become an undertaker, maybe. But since you're here, I should settle up with you. How long since I paid you?"

"Last Friday," Alex said. "I worked a full day Saturday, three hours on Monday and Tuesday, and four hours on Wednesday."

"That's right," Joey said. "You were here when the cable went out. I never did find out if the Yankees won. Okay, that's eighteen hours I owe you for. You got all your tip money?"

Alex nodded.

"Here, take this," he said, handing Alex a batch of bills. "It's all I got in my wallet."

Alex looked over the money. "Too much," he said, handing a ten-dollar bill back to Joey.

Joey shook his head. "Take it," he said. "I got cash at home."

"Thank you," Alex said. "When you reopen, I'll put in a couple of hours for free."

"Deal," Joey said. "Look, Alex, take care of yourself. You're a good kid, best worker I ever had. Kids like you, you're the future. Especially now. Pray for us while you're at it. All of us."

Alex nodded. "I'll do that," he said. "I'll see you soon, Joey."

"I hope so," Joey said. "Here's to better days."

"Better days," Alex said. As far as he was concerned, they couldn't come too soon.

Sunday, May 22

Much to Alex's relief, at Mass Father Franco made no announcements. After the service was over, Briana and Julie found friends and joined them. After a minute or two, Bri ran over to Alex.

"Kayla's mother invited us for lunch," she said. "She said you could come, too."

Alex looked over to where Julie was standing. She and her friends were giggling as though nothing had changed.

"I don't think so," Alex said. "Thank her for me, though."

"You sure?" Bri asked.

Alex grinned. "Positive," he said. "Thanks anyway. Have a good time."

He was glad his sisters had friends to talk with. It would make Monday with no school that much easier for all of them. But he was just as glad to have some time alone.

He used the free time to walk around the west side, not sure what he was looking for. There were more people on the streets, but they seemed as dazed as he was.

Just when Alex became convinced nothing would ever be open again, he chanced upon an open hardware store. He was taken aback by the sight of the normal: paint cans, screwdrivers, duct tape all neatly in place.

Alex spotted a couple of flashlights. It wouldn't hurt to have another one, he thought, in case the blackouts continued.

"Thirty dollars," the man behind the counter said.

"Thirty dollars?" Alex said. "For a flashlight?"

"I only got two left," the man said. "Supply and demand. The last one'll be forty bucks."

Alex put the flashlight away. They could live without it. But as he reached the door, he turned around. "Batteries," he said. "You have any batteries left?"

"They'll cost you," the man said.

Alex pulled out his wallet. He had fifty-two dollars on him. "I need Cs and Ds," he said.

The man looked behind the counter. "I got a four-pack of Cs for twenty bucks," he said. "Two Ds'll cost you ten."

They had food, Alex told himself, plenty of canned goods, and starting on Tuesday when school reopened, they wouldn't have to worry about lunches. But who knew when electricity would get back to normal.

"I'll take them," he said, handing over a twenty and a ten.

The man put the batteries in a bag. "You won't regret it," he said. "Next guy comes in, I'll charge twice that."

I bet you will, Alex thought. But it won't be my problem.

As he opened the apartment door, he noticed how silent it was. There was always somebody at home, with six people in the five-room apartment. Even when they were sleeping, there was the constant background of street noise, cars driving by, honking horns, people laughing or shouting. The washers and driers in the basement laundry room rumbled well past midnight, and in the wintertime, the oil burner that kept the entire building heated drowned out all the other sounds.

But now even West Eighty-eighth Street was quiet. Quiet as a grave, Alex thought.

He sat on the sofa and told himself this was the ideal time to cry, when his sisters couldn't see him. He knew there was no shame in crying. Papi had sobbed the day Carlos went off to boot camp. He'd cried just the other day when he heard Nana had died. But Alex didn't shed a single tear. Maybe it was just too quiet to cry.

He spotted the transistor radio, put the C batteries in it, and spun the dial until he got a New York station. It was good to know it was on the air, even if all the news being broadcast was horrible.

"A telephone hotline has been set up for assistance in locating missing New York City family members," the woman on the radio said. "If one of your family has been missing since Wednesday night, call 212-555-CITY. That's 212-555-2489."

A phone number. Did that mean the phones were working? Alex turned off the radio and picked up the telephone. Sure enough, there was a dial tone.

His hand shook almost uncontrollably as he dialed the hospital number. Could it be he'd find his mother alive and well in just a matter of moments? He pictured Bri's and Julie's reactions when he told them the good news.

"You have reached St. John of God Hospital. For patient information, press 1 . . ."

Alex held for further assistance, figuring someone there could help him track Mami down. But hearing music on the other end of the line was surreal. Alex listened to one song, then another, a third, and a fourth—treacly ballads, the kind Bri liked. By the seventh song, Alex wondered how much longer he'd be forced to listen. By the twelfth, he imagined Mami walking in—while he remained on hold.

In the middle of the fifteenth song, a woman's voice said, "St. John of God Hospital."

Alex's heart pounded. "Hi," he said, trying to sound calm. "My mother, her name is Isabella Morales, works as an operating room technician at St. John of God. I'm calling to see if I can speak to her."

"Impossible," the woman said. "We're keeping our lines open for emergencies. No personal calls are allowed."

"All right," Alex said, terrified that the woman might hang up on him. "I don't really need to talk to her. I just need to make sure that she's all right. She was called in Wednesday night. Can you find out if she's there, if she's working?"

"I'm sorry," the woman said. "I have no way of knowing what personnel is on duty right now."

"But someone at the hospital must know," Alex said. "She would have taken the subway around nine-thirty Wednesday night. We haven't heard from her since."

"I understand," the woman said. "But it's chaos here, and it has been since Wednesday. Everyone is working twenty-four-hour shifts. I haven't been home since Wednesday, either. I can't stop to look around for your mother."

"There's no one you can transfer me to?" Alex asked, trying to keep the desperation out of his voice. "Someone in the surgical department?"

"They're not taking phone calls," the woman said. "And I really can't stay on the phone with you."

"Just one more question, please," Alex begged. "Have your phones been on for a while? Have people been able to make calls out?"

"We got phone service back yesterday afternoon," the woman said. She was silent for a moment. "I'll pray for you and your mother," she said. "Her name is Isabella Morales?"

"Yes, that's right," Alex replied.

"Give me your phone number," she said. "If I find someone who knows anything about her, I'll call."

"Thank you," Alex said. "Thank you so much." He gave the woman his phone number, and only after he heard the sound of the phone on the other end hanging up did he put the phone down.

They'd had phone service yesterday. Sometime in the past twenty-four hours, Mami must have had the chance to call home. Alex picked up the phone and dialed for voice mail. No new messages. Just to be sure, he pressed *1* anyway, but there weren't any saved messages, either.

Mami would have called. Somehow she would have found the time.

Maybe she'd called Uncle Jimmy. He dialed the number and Aunt Lorraine answered.

"Hi," he said. "It's Alex. How are things going?"

"How do you expect things to be going?" Aunt Lorraine replied. "The world is coming to an end. My babies will never live to have babies of their own. God has turned His back on us, and you ask how things are going?"

Alex waited until he was sure she'd finished. "Bri and Julie and I were in church this morning, so there was no one home if anyone called," he said. "We haven't heard from Mami since Wednesday. Has she called you?"

"I went to church but Jimmy didn't," Aunt Lorraine said. "Wait, I'll ask him. Jimmy! Did you hear from Isabella this morning? It's Alex. Isabella's missing."

"I didn't say she was missing," Alex said, but it didn't matter. Jimmy took the phone from his wife.

"Alex," he said. "Isabella's missing?"

"I don't know that she's missing," Alex said. "She went to the hospital on Wednesday, and we haven't heard from her since. I just called the hospital, and they have no way of knowing who's there, so it could be she's been there since Wednesday and just hasn't been able to call."

"We haven't heard from her," Jimmy said. "Is your father back?"

"No," Alex said. "But he called when we were at the bodega. Bri spoke to him."

"What did he say?" Jimmy asked.

He didn't say anything, Alex thought, and it might not have been him anyway. But Jimmy had concerns of his own, and Alex was man of the house. "It wasn't a great connection," he said. "Bri couldn't make out much."

"But he called, so he must be okay," Jimmy said. "What about Carlos?"

Alex was relieved he could be honest. "I spoke to him Thursday," he said. "His unit's been deployed, but he's okay."

"Great, that's great," Jimmy said. "Luis and Carlos are all right," he yelled to Lorraine. "No word from Isabella, though."

"We'll probably hear from her before you do," Alex said. "I just wanted to find out if you'd spoken to her."

"No," Jimmy said. "Look, Alex, you okay? You looking after your sisters okay? You want to send them to us until Luis or Isabella gets back?"

Alex decided against it. Julie and Lorraine didn't get along that well, and Bri would be happier at home.

"No, we're fine," Alex said. "Thanks anyway."

"All right," Jimmy said. "Take care now. We'll be praying for all of you. And when you hear from Isabella, call us."

"Sure will," Alex said, and hung up. He walked back to the sofa and thought about making a list, putting in a neat format the arguments for and against his mother still being alive.

He looked at his watch. It was close to two o'clock, and there was no way of knowing when his sisters might get back. If he was going to do any more calling, he couldn't wait.

212-555-CITY.

"You have reached the New York City Emergency Hotline for family members of missing, presumed dead, New York City residents. If your missing family member is a man, press one. If it is a woman, press two. For children under the age of twelve, press three."

Alex almost pressed one for his father, but then realized New York City would have no way of knowing what had happened in Milagro del Mar. He pressed two.

"The following information is only for family members of female residents of New York City who have been missing since Wednesday night, May eighteenth," a woman's voice intoned. "If you are the family member of a missing New York City woman, press one."

Alex pressed one.

"If your family member is missing from Brooklyn or Staten Island, press one. If she is missing from Manhattan, the Bronx, or Queens, press two."

Alex pressed two.

"The bodies of unidentified women are being held at Yankee Stadium," the voice continued. "If you wish to go to Yankee Stadium to search for your missing family member, press one."

Alex pressed one.

"The next available viewing will be Thursday, May twenty-sixth, at eleven-thirty AM," the voice said, its tone changing with the specific time and date. "If you wish to go to the next available viewing, press one."

Almost without thinking, Alex pressed one.

"The bus for your viewing will be leaving from Port Authority at eleven-thirty AM on Thursday, May twenty-six. Please be at Port Authority one hour before. Only one family member will be allowed on the bus. Only people who arrive on the designated bus will be allowed into Yankee Stadium for the viewing. If you wish to reserve your seat on the May twenty-sixth eleven-thirty AM bus, state and spell your name."

Alex did as he was told.

The voice parroted back his name and told him to press one to confirm the information. Alex pressed one.

"Thank you," the voice said. "You have reserved a seat on the May twenty-sixth bus, leaving Port Authority at eleven-thirty AM. If you wish to make a reservation for a different bus in search of a man or child or a woman missing from Brooklyn or Staten Island, please press one. Otherwise you may hang up."

Alex hung up. What had he done, he asked himself. Why had he agreed to go to Yankee Stadium, of all places, to look for his mother, who was most likely in Queens hard at work. She was sure to come home between now and Thursday. Why would he even think she might be dead, an anonymous body lying in a makeshift morgue.

It didn't matter. If Mami returned home, or if she called, he just wouldn't go on the bus. But if they hadn't heard from her by Thursday, he'd have to look for her.

Alex realized then he was crazy not trying to call Papi, no matter how expensive it was. He found Mami's address book, and dialed Nana's number.

"We're sorry. Calls to Puerto Rico cannot be put through at this time."

That meant nothing, Alex thought. The lines to Puerto Rico would open eventually, and then he'd speak to Papi.

It will just take time, he told himself. Time and a miracle.

Monday, May 23

The electricity came back on around eleven that morning. Bri and Julie promptly fought over the remote control, only to find it was a national day of mourning and all the TV stations had memorial services on, with sermons and choirs and politicians.

"Put on a DVD," Alex told them. "I'm going out for a walk."

He left his sisters debating over which DVD to watch. He hoped they settled on something funny.

He strolled over to St. Margaret's, not knowing where else to go. The city remained mostly closed, but he supposed tomorrow things would open up again, when the national day of mourning was over.

The church was almost full, but Alex found that Father Franco was in his office. There were five people waiting to talk to him. Alex felt like he should take a number, but they were on the honor system, remembering who was there before them and who arrived after. Two women were sniffling, and one man kept staring at his shoes, as though he was waiting for them to untie themselves.

An hour later, six new people had shown up, and it was Alex's turn to see Father Franco. He found Father Franco, jacket off and needing a shave, sitting behind a cluttered desk.

"Thank you for seeing me, Father," Alex said. "I know how busy you are."

"Please, sit down," Father Franco said. "You're one of Isabella Morales's boys, aren't you?"

"Yes, Father," Alex said. "I'm Alex Morales."

"Is your mother all right?" Father Franco asked. "I haven't seen her here in the past few days."

"We don't know," Alex said. "She went to work Wednesday and we haven't heard from her since."

Father Franco winced. "I've been hearing stories like that all week," he said. "Is there anything I can do to help your family?"

"I hope so," Alex said. "I didn't know where else to turn. It's my father. He was in Puerto Rico for my grandmother's funeral, and we haven't been able to get through to him. I was wondering if you'd heard anything about Puerto Rico, how things are there."

"Where in Puerto Rico is he?" Father Franco asked.

"Milagro del Mar," Alex replied. "Midway between San Juan and Fajardo, on the northern coast."

Father Franco nodded. "I'll call the diocesan office," he said. "They might have heard something from the San Juan diocese." He dialed a number and smiled when someone answered on the second ring. "Yes, hello. This is Father Michael Franco at St. Margaret's. I need information about the town of Milagro del Mar in Puerto Rico. It's on the northern coast, east of San Juan." He turned to Alex. "It is east, isn't it?"

"Yes, Father," Alex said. His fist was clenched so tightly his fingernails were cutting into his palm.

"Yes, yes, I understand. Yes, I'll hold." He cupped the phone with his hand and smiled apologetically at Alex. "The person I'm speaking to doesn't know anything about Puerto Rico, but he's sure there's someone there who's heard something, so he's checking."

Alex nodded.

"So where do you go to school?" Father Franco asked.

"Vincent de Paul," Alex replied. He could hardly remember what the school looked like.

"I'm impressed," Father Franco said. "They turned me down. You're a junior?"

"Yes, Father."

"Your parents must be very proud," Father Franco said. "Yes, yes, Milagro del Mar, on the northern coast. Yes, I see. I understand. Yes. Thank you. Thank you very much."

"How bad is it?" Alex asked, trying to make it sound like a joke.

"That's hard to say," Father Franco replied. "Information is very sketchy. From what they can tell, the coastline of Puerto Rico was hard hit." He paused. "Very hard. Devastated. The person I spoke to didn't know about Milagro del Mar, but things are very bad all along the coast. There was a huge amount of damage to the infrastructure, so communication is sketchy. I'm sorry. I wish I could tell you for certain that your father's village survived, but there doesn't seem to be any way of finding out."

"Do they know how long it will take before things get back to normal?" Alex asked. "I mean, until there's phone service and planes leaving Puerto Rico?"

Father Franco shook his head. "We must pray for Christ's mercy," he said. "I don't know what else to tell you."

Alex stood up and tried to smile. "Thank you," he said.

"My prayers will be with you and your family," Father Franco said. "Please let me know when you hear from your parents."

"I will," Alex said, and left the office. There were ten

people in the outside office now, all with nightmares of their own. He walked over to the bulletin boards, but there was nothing new, just more names on the listings of the missing and the dead. He tried to pray for their souls, but the words had lost all meaning.

chapter 3

Tuesday, May 24

When Alex got to school the next day, he found a note posted on the front door instructing the students to report to the chapel. Alex followed the other boys in. It was a relief to be back at school. He'd walked Bri and Julie to Holy Angels first, just in case. New York City, with fewer people, seemed more threatening somehow.

Alex went to the section reserved for juniors. Talking was forbidden in chapel, but he could sense the undercurrent. Chris Flynn, seated between his friends Tony Loretto and Kevin Daley, gestured for him to join them, but Alex shook his head and sat by himself. Ordinarily he would have sat with them, but he wasn't ready to swap stories about what had happened during the past five days.

He looked around the chapel to see if there were more empty seats than usual and found there were. Not a lot, but a noticeable amount. Then he realized none of the three priests on the faculty were there. Other teachers were missing as well, but they might not be in chapel; they didn't always attend. But the priests should have been there.

The illicit buzz grew as the other boys noticed their absence. Alex noted that a few of the boys looked concerned, even frightened. A couple of the seventh graders began to sniffle, as though they'd suddenly realized something bad had happened. Alex felt a familiar wave of resentment, which he ordinarily fought to keep under control, but this morning welcomed as an old, reassuring presence. Rich babies, he thought. What did they know of missing parents, needy sisters, thirty-dollar flashlights. They were protected by their mommies, their nannies, their maids. The nannies and the maids knew, though, Alex was sure of that.

"Silence!"

The buzzing stopped. This was the voice of authority. Alex stared up at an elderly priest. He was ramrod tall, and gaunt, with thinning white hair, bushy black eyebrows, and a mouth that looked as though it had never smiled.

"Oh God," Kevin whispered. "It's the living dead."

"My name is Father Francis Patrick Xavier Mulrooney," he announced in a voice so cold it sent chills down Alex's spine, in spite of the hothouse atmosphere of the chapel. "Due to the extraordinary circumstances in which the archdiocese finds itself, I have been called out of retirement to be acting headmaster of St. Vincent de Paul Academy. Fathers Shea, Donnelly, and Delveccio have been temporarily reassigned."

Not even Father Mulrooney's rocky stare could keep the boys from reacting to the news that the three most important members of the faculty, including Father Shea, the headmaster, and Father Donnelly, the assistant headmaster, were now gone.

"Quiet," Father Mulrooney said. "Two other members of the faculty, Mr. Davis and Mr. Vanich, will not be returning. They will not be replaced for the remainder of the school term. If you have any questions about your classes, you may bring them to me during my office hours. In addition to being acting headmaster, I will teach Latin and advanced theology. Previous to my retirement, I instructed in both those subjects at St. Vincent de Paul Academy. It is quite possible I taught your fathers those very subjects."

Not my father, Alex thought.

"In addition, two members of the custodial staff and one of the kitchen workers will not be returning," Father Mulrooney said. "It has proven impossible to contact another of the kitchen workers, so it can be assumed she will not return. Since we find ourselves so short staffed, additional responsibilities will fall upon this student body. After Mass is celebrated, the class officers are asked to meet in room twenty-five to further discuss what will be required of their classmates."

Alex cast a quick look at Chris Flynn, who, sensing his gaze, glanced back and shrugged.

"It is the belief of the archdiocese that the occurrences of the past few days are but a taste of what is to come," Father Mulrooney continued. "Unpleasant though it is to contemplate, we must assume deprivation and death lie in wait." The grim expression on his face inspired several boys to begin weeping.

"Look for inspiration in the lives of the early Christian martyrs," Father Mulrooney said. "They marched bravely to their deaths, sure in the knowledge of life everlasting."

"But they died for something!" one of the boys in the sophomore section called out.

"Silence!" Father Mulrooney thundered. "This is chapel, not the Roman forum. None of us has the right to debate God's decisions."

Even the boys who'd been crying stopped, as though tears had been proclaimed sinful.

"For as long as I am acting headmaster, attendance at morning Mass will be mandatory," Father Mulrooney said. "For the remainder of this week, if you have an open class hour because of the departure of our faculty members, you are to come to chapel for prayer and contemplation. *A cruce salus.*"

Alex wondered if Father Mulrooney would say the Mass in Latin, but the priest intoned the usual English words instead. It felt good to hear them in a setting so familiar. He knew Father Mulrooney was right. It wasn't for him, for any of them, to debate God's wisdom.

"Thy will be done," he whispered under his breath. "Thy will be done."

Wednesday, May 25

At the end of the school day, Alex went to the headmaster's office. Neither of the two clerical workers he was used to seeing was there. With no one to tell him what to do, he simply knocked on the headmaster's door.

"Enter."

Alex opened the door. It felt strange seeing Father Mulrooney sitting behind Father Shea's desk. He realized with a start how much he was going to miss Father Shea, who'd encouraged his dreams more than anyone else except Mami.

"Excuse me, Father," Alex said. "I just wanted to tell you I won't be in school tomorrow morning. I'm not sure about the afternoon yet."

Father Mulrooney raised his formidable eyebrows. "If you already know you're going to take ill tomorrow, you must know when you're likely to recover," he replied.

"I'm not going to take ill," Alex said. "It's a personal matter."

"That's hardly an acceptable reason," Father Mulrooney said. "We all have personal matters, as you so dramatically put it. Regardless of what is happening right now, school must come first. Although I appreciate that you came looking for permission to play hooky, I'm afraid I cannot grant it."

Alex swallowed his anger. "I have to go to Yankee Stadium," he said. "I've made a reservation. They're holding unidentified women's bodies there. My mother's been missing since last Wednesday and I'm going to look for her." He stared Father Mulrooney straight in the eye and dared him to object.

"I see," Father Mulrooney said instead. "There's no one else in your family that can do this?"

"No, Father," Alex said.

"Very well," Father Mulrooney said. "I appreciate your giving me notice of your absence, Mr. Morales. If you cannot make it back for afternoon classes, I will understand."

"Thank you, Father," Alex said.

Father Mulrooney nodded. "I will expect to see you in school on Friday," he said. "Unless, of course . . ."

Unless Mami is dead, Alex thought. Unless I find her dead body lying there with all the other unidentified dead bodies.

"Yes, Father," he said. "Unless."

Thursday, May 26

Alex walked down from his home to Forty-second Street Thursday morning around the time he would have left for school, far earlier than he needed to, but he couldn't risk missing the bus.

He hadn't told Bri or Julie, pretending instead that he was going to school. If he found Mami, then he'd tell them. He wasn't sure what he'd say if she wasn't there. They could keep on hoping then, but he hadn't figured out whether that was a good thing or not.

New York was no longer a ghost town, but there were few signs of life. The buses, police cars, fire engines, and ambulances drove swiftly, no trucks, cars, or mobs of pedestrians to slow them down. Most of the stores were still closed, their steel gates locked and protecting whatever had survived the days and nights of looting. The farther downtown he got, the more police officers he saw. They looked aimless and bored, as if they were uncertain what they were protecting.

It was a pleasant day, but no one smiled as they walked by. Alex realized he heard almost no conversation. People walked because there was no other way to get to their destination. Eyes were downcast, as though no one wanted to acknowledge what other people might be feeling.

He could see the Empire State Building in the distance, and it reassured him to know it was still there. Alex had heard the Statue of Liberty was gone. He'd been there once on a class trip. Never gone to the Empire State Building, though. He was glad he'd still have the chance.

He hadn't felt like eating breakfast, and although there was still plenty of food left, he'd started to get nervous about when it would run out and what they'd do when it did. But the walk made him hungry, and it was then he realized there weren't any street vendors selling pretzels or hot dogs, roasted nuts or souvlaki. Strange to see a New York where you couldn't get a complete meal on the street.

When he got to the Port Authority, he saw a vendor on the street corner, selling bags of nuts. The line had to be fifty people long. Not worth it, he decided, noticing the shoving and the shouting. He'd find something after he got back.

The vendor's line only added to the chaos. It seemed like all the people left in Manhattan were fighting to get into the bus terminal. They dragged small children with them, or dogs, or cats in carriers. They carried suitcases, backpacks, duffel bags, all crammed to the point of bursting. Maybe some of them were going to friends or families who lived more inland. Maybe some of them were simply going wherever a bus might take them.

There were plenty of cops there, and Alex went to one to ask where the buses to Yankee Stadium left from.

"Around the corner," the cop said. "You got a reservation?"

Alex nodded.

"You ready for it?" the cop asked. "It's hell up there."

"I don't know," Alex admitted. "I'm looking for my mother. We haven't heard from her since it happened."

"Good luck, kid," the cop said. "Hey, you over there! Watch it!"

Alex walked around the corner. There were several cops there telling people where to stand and giving them flyers. Alex walked over to one and said he had a reservation for the 11:30 bus.

"That line over there," the cop said, and gave him a handout.

Even though Alex was early, the line for his bus was already thirty people long. People stood there, shuffling their feet, reading the handout, going through their bags. A few had something to eat. Most look terrified, or angry, or simply miserable.

Alex looked at the sheet of paper he'd been handed.

YOU MUST FOLLOW THESE RULES

1. **Do not attempt to get on any bus other than the one for which you have a reservation.** Note its number when you board.

2. You will be given a numbered ticket when you board the bus. You must show your ticket to be admitted to Yankee Stadium.

3. **At no time may you leave to go off by yourself.**

4. Once inside the stadium, walk in single file up and down every row.

5. Look carefully at every body. Pay particular attention to jewelry, as that may be the best way to identify the person for whom you're searching.

6. **If you find the person you are seeking, keep walking until you see a Police Identification Booth.** Go there and inform an officer of the approximate location of the identified body. You may only return to the body you've identified if you are accompanied by an official. **Any attempt to return on your own will result in ejection from Yankee Stadium.**

7. If you see a person in need of physical assistance, keep your place in line, and notify a police officer at the first opportunity. **Do not stop to help the person in need of assistance.**

8. No food or drink is allowed in Yankee Stadium. All bags must be left on the bus. Anyone carrying anything into Yankee Stadium will be ejected.

9. If you find the person you are looking for, you will remain at Yankee Stadium to fill out the appropriate paperwork. If you do not, you must leave on the bus you took to get there. **You will not be allowed on any other bus.**

THESE RULES ARE FOR YOUR OWN SAFETY. THEY MUST BE OBEYED.

Alex thought the rules were stringent, but they made sense, and he was relieved that what was called for was so carefully spelled out. He liked rules. Carlos was always trying to get away with something, or at least he used to be like that before enlisting, but Alex found that rules imposed a structure, and he preferred that. He always did better when he knew exactly what was expected of him.

He wished the flyer hadn't kept referring to bodies, though. He couldn't stand the idea of Mami being nothing more than an anonymous body.

He pictured Mami then, sitting at the table, working on her homework while her children worked on theirs. How proud they all were when she got her GED. He thought of her at the stove, cooking their dinner. He remembered once when he'd been sick with fever, and Mami had pressed a cold washcloth against his forehead and held his hand until he'd fallen asleep. He envisioned her in church, shushing them while Father Franco gave his sermon.

For a week he'd refused to think of her, and now he was overwhelmed by a thousand different images. What if he found Mami at Yankee Stadium? What if he didn't?

He realized then that everybody in line for the 11:30 bus, everybody waiting for whatever bus, was as overwhelmed with thoughts and memories of the people gone from their lives as he was. No wonder no one was talking. The only protection from grief was silence and rules.

Eventually they began boarding their bus. Number 22, he noted. He gave his name to the bus driver and was handed a card that said 33. He took an aisle seat, next to a heavyset woman who kept squeezing a packet of tissues.

"You all have your tickets?" the bus driver asked before they began the journey.

Everyone said yes.

"And you have the list of rules?"

"Yes," they all responded.

"Be sure to follow the instructions," the bus driver cautioned them. "Stay in place once you get there. God go with you."

Alex looked around the bus. He was the youngest person there, but a few seemed to be in their early twenties. Since only one person from a family was allowed to go, the passengers on the bus were all strangers to each other. Several of them were praying. Others stared straight ahead, or looked out the window. A few had their eyes closed, and a handful were crying.

Alex stared out the window at the apartments on Riverside Drive as the bus whizzed up the West Side Highway. The buildings looked substantial, unlikely ever to erode. As they drove past Eighty-eighth Street, he resisted the temptation to demand to be let off. He knew what he had to do, what rules he had to follow.

After a while the bus pulled into its parking space and the people were told to get off in an orderly fashion, making sure to have their tickets in hand and to remember where their bus was located and that its number was 22. Alex got off and displayed his ticket to the officer standing there. From the outside, Yankee Stadium seemed much as it always had. He remembered the half dozen or so times he'd gone to a game with Papi and Carlos, sitting in the bleachers, worrying, shouting, eating, thrilled to be there with his father and big brother. During one game—he was nine or ten—the score was tied in the bottom of the eleventh and one of the Yankees hit a walk-off grand slam. He'd felt like he'd witnessed history, he'd been so excited.

"Stay in line. Don't wander off," the officer said. "Stand in line. Don't wander off. If you leave your place, you will not be allowed in. Stand in line. Don't wander off."

Alex stood at attention, as though his posture proved he wasn't the sort who would ever wander off.

The line inched its way closer to the entrance. Two women walked from the head of the line to the foot, one holding a pot of menthol-scented gel, the other face masks and sickness bags.

"Rub the gel under your nose," the woman instructed them. "It will help with the odors."

"Wear your face mask at all times," the other woman said. "Put it on now. Only take it off if you feel the need to vomit. Use the bag, then put the mask back on. Do not leave the bag on the ground, but carry it with you until you leave."

The menthol smell was strong. People looked strange wearing face masks, like a convention of surgeons had accidentally assembled in front of the ballpark. Alex thought of when Mami had shown them a face mask and told them she'd be expected to wear one as an operating room technician. If she hadn't been ambitious to improve her family's lot, she wouldn't have gotten the training and the hospital in Queens wouldn't have called for her to come in because of an emergency and she wouldn't have taken the 7 train to Queens and Alex wouldn't be standing in front of Yankee Stadium with menthol-scented gel rubbed beneath his nose.

"Remember to stay in line at all times," a voice over a bullhorn called out. "If you see someone in need of physical assistance, inform the next available officer. Do not leave the line. Leaving the line will result in your ejection. Keep walking. Only leave the line if you can identify the body of the person you're looking for. Look at the person ahead of you in line and the person behind you. Don't ever stray from those people."

Alex did as he was told and looked at the man ahead of him and the woman behind him. The woman behind him wore sunglasses. The man ahead of him was balding.

The door opened. "Stay in line! Stay in line!" the officer shouted. Everyone shuffled forward, staying in line. They walked through the entrance, down the corridor, and finally down the flights of stairs that led to the playing field.

The noise was what attacked him first, a cacophony of screams and sobs. He could make out some cursing, some praying, but mostly the noise was just the sound of agony.

Then came the smells, unlike anything he'd ever known, a sickening combination of vomit, body odor, and rotting meat. The menthol covered the stench slightly, but still he gagged, and he was relieved that he hadn't eaten all morning. He could taste the smell as he inhaled the scent of decomposing flesh.

It was a scene unlike any Alex could have imagined. If he looked up, it was Yankee Stadium, filled with empty seats. But if he looked at eye level, it was hell.

Alex made the sign of the cross and prayed for strength. All around the playing field were corpses, lying head to toe in neat rows with just space enough for one person to walk between. How many bodies were there? Hundreds? Thousands?

Some of the bodies had clothes on; others were nude. The naked ones were covered with sheets. All their arms were out, their hands prominently displayed, their rings gleaming in the sunlight. Their faces were swollen, many to the point of being unrecognizable. They were covered with flies, millions of flies, their buzzing providing a white-noise background to the screams and the wails. His hell was a fly's heaven, Alex thought.

"Stay in line! Stay in line! Leaving the line will result in your ejection!"

Alex longed to be ejected, to be bodily lifted from Yankee Stadium, from the Bronx, from New York, from Earth itself, to be slingshotted into the soothing void of space. He focused instead on looking for the Police Identification Booths. There were dozens of them, with police officers and medical personnel stationed there. He saw priests, also, and people he assumed were ministers and rabbis and Muslim clergy.

Staying firmly in line, Alex began the death stroll. Most of the bodies couldn't possibly be Mami. They were black or white or Asian. They were too young or too old, too fat or too thin. Their hair was gray or white or blonde, too short or too long. One woman, hardly more than a girl, had green and purple hair. One was chemotherapy bald. Another was pregnant. Their eyes were usually open, and they stared up at the moon that had killed them.

Sometimes the line stopped short, when someone ahead of them needed to check a face, a body, a piece of jewelry. A scream would pierce the air as a loved one was found. A woman several people behind Alex cried, "Holy Mother of God!" and he assumed she'd found who she'd come to look for, but she stayed in line until they made the next turn, when she went off to the nearest Police Identification Booth.

Alex felt a sharp sting he was stunned to identify as envy. He hated himself for feeling that way. No matter what, it would be better not to find Mami there. As long as she was only gone, there was a chance their prayers for her return would be answered. But if she were lying there . . .

"Stay in line! Stay in line!"

Twice Alex saw women he thought might be his mother. Something about the shape of their faces, the tone of their skin, stopped him short. But one woman had a diamond engagement ring, and the other wore a Jewish star pendant. When he looked more carefully at them, he realized they looked nothing like Mami, not really. Mami would laugh if she knew Alex had mistaken a woman with a Jewish star for her. He tried to remember the sound of her laughter, but it was impossible. He told himself he'd hear her laughing again, that it was all right not to be able to remember what the sound of her laughter was like just then.

By the time he'd finished the march around Yankee Stadium, two other people from his bus had left the line to go to the Police Identification Booths. The rest walked out in the same order they'd come in. They tossed their sickness bags and face masks into the appropriately labeled bins.

No one spoke as they showed their tickets and boarded bus 22. Eventually the bus pulled out. One woman had left her Bible on her seat, and she picked it up and began reading it, her lips moving silently. A dozen or more people wept. A man mumbled something Alex assumed was Hebrew. One woman laughed hysterically. The woman sitting next to Alex pulled tissue after tissue out of its packet, tearing each one methodically to shreds.

God save their souls, Alex prayed. God save ours. It was the only prayer he could think of, no matter how inadequate it might be. It offered him no comfort, but he repeated it unceasingly. As long as he prayed he didn't have to think. He didn't have to remember. He didn't have to decide. He didn't have to acknowledge he was entering a world where no one had laid out the rules for him to follow, a world where there might not be any rules left for any of them to follow.

chapter 4

Friday, May 27

Danny O'Brien dropped a crumpled piece of paper in the first-floor hallway, as the boys began leaving Vincent de Paul for the day.

"Pick it up," Alex said. "You heard what Father Mulrooney said."

"You pick it up," Danny said. "I pay tuition to go here." He began to walk off when Chris Flynn came up to them.

"You heard him," Chris said to Danny. "Pick it up. And then apologize."

"It's all right," Alex said, bending down to pick up the paper. "I should have done this in the first place." It enraged him to think of Chris fighting his battles for him.

"I'm sorry," Danny said. "I really am, Morales. Blame it on the moon. It's making me crazy."

"Forget it," Alex said. He tossed the paper into the nearest wastepaper basket and headed out. He didn't have time to waste with people like Danny O'Brien.

But the incident continued to bother him that afternoon as he walked to St. Margaret's, and he couldn't get it out of his mind as he waited in the office for a chance to talk to Father

Franco. He and Danny were friendly. They were on the debate squad together. He'd even been to Danny's home when they'd worked on a history project together.

It had to be the moon, Alex thought. It really was driving everyone crazy.

After an hour's wait, he was allowed in to see Father Franco. The priest looked exhausted, far worse than he had just the week before.

"I was wondering if you'd heard anything more about Puerto Rico," Alex asked.

"Not much," Father Franco replied. "Conditions are very, very bad. No one's heard anything about the fishing village your father was in, but from what little I've been able to find out, all the villages and small towns on the northern coast were decimated. I'm sorry. I know you want more specific details, but information is very sketchy. I'll continue to ask. The archdiocese is used to my questions by now."

"Thank you, Father," Alex said. "Just one more thing, if you don't mind."

"Of course not," Father Franco said. "How can I help you?"

Alex didn't want to ask the question and didn't want to hear the answer. "It's about the bodies they've found," he said. "Do you know if all of them have been found yet? Like at Yankee Stadium. Is that all the bodies of women they've found?"

Father Franco shook his head. "Many bodies haven't been recovered even now," he said. "And my understanding is they keep those poor women at Yankee Stadium only for a couple of days before replacing them with others."

"So you could go there and look and even if you don't find the person you're looking for, that doesn't mean she's still alive," Alex said.

"I'm afraid so," Father Franco said.

"And the ones that don't get identified," Alex said. "Do they bury them anyway?"

Father Franco looked uncomfortable. "They're forced to cremate them," he said.

"I didn't think the church approved of cremation," Alex said.

"These are extraordinary circumstances," Father Franco said. "I'm sure God understands and forgives."

Alex nodded, willing himself not to picture his mother's body tossed into a pile of corpses in a crematorium. "Thank you, Father," he said, getting up.

"My prayers are with you," Father Franco said. "You and your whole family."

How many people was he praying for, Alex thought as he left St. Margaret's. Did he ever have time to pray for himself?

Saturday, May 28

"This place is a mess," Alex said angrily as he surveyed the living room. "Don't you girls know how to pick up after yourselves? And why are you watching TV in the middle of the afternoon? Don't your teachers give you homework?"

Julie and Bri were sitting on the living room sofa, watching an *I Love Lucy* rerun. Julie yawned.

"I'm sorry——," Bri began saying, but Julie punched her in her arm.

Alex crossed to the TV and turned it off. Julie turned it back on with the remote.

Alex walked over to Julie and yanked the remote from her. "Get up!" he yelled. "Now! And start cleaning up your mess."

"I'm not doing anything until you tell us where Mami and Papi are," Julie said. "Neither is Bri. Are you, Bri." It sounded more like a threat than a question.

Bri looked miserable but she shook her head.

"What is this, some kind of strike?" Alex asked. "You're teamsters now? Well, that isn't going to work. Stop with the TV and the whining."

"Who died and made you boss?" Julie said.

Without even thinking, Alex slapped her hard across her face. Julie cried out in pain, then ran from the living room, Bri racing after her. Julie slammed the bedroom door behind them.

"Idiota," Alex muttered. He hated it when Papi struck any of them, had vowed he would never do that to any of his children, and now when his sisters needed him the most, he had acted like the worst kind of bully.

He gave his sisters a couple of minutes to yell and cry and do whatever it was they did in the privacy of their room, and then he knocked on their door. Not waiting for permission, he entered.

Julie sat on the upper bunk bed, her cheek still red from Alex's hand. Bri stood by her side.

Alex tried to imagine Papi apologizing but couldn't. Maybe to Mami, but never to one of his children.

"I'm sorry," he said. "I shouldn't have hit you."

Julie turned her head away from him.

"Where are they?" Bri asked. "Why haven't we heard from them?"

"I don't know," Alex said. "I don't, I swear."

"Have you even tried to find them?" Julie demanded.

"Yes, of course," Alex said, shuddering at the memory of the rows of bodies at Yankee Stadium. "They're just gone. I'm not saying they're dead. But I don't think we should count on them ever coming back."

"No!" Bri cried. "I don't believe that. I won't. I spoke to Papi. He was alive. He said Puerto Rico. I heard him!" She began to weep.

"Look," Alex said, feeling helpless and alone. "Bri, even if that was Papi, he can't get out of Puerto Rico. Planes aren't flying anymore. And the phones aren't working there. I've tried every day, first thing in the morning and last thing at night, and I can't get through. Maybe you're right and you did talk to Papi, but we can't count on him coming home. Not for a long time."

"What about Mami?" Julie asked. "Why isn't she home?"

"The subways flooded that night," Alex said. "I called the hospital days ago, and they didn't know if she was there. I think if she was, she would have called us, but I don't know for sure. I have looked, Julie. I took a bus to Yankee Stadium on Thursday and looked at hundreds of bodies there, but none of them was Mami."

"Then she must be alive." Bri sobbed.

"Maybe," Alex said. "But I think she'd call if she was all right."

"So we're alone," Julie said.

Alex nodded. "When Carlos calls next, we'll tell him," he said. "Maybe the Marines will let him come home. But until then, it's just the three of us. So we have to pull together. We have to act the way Mami and Papi would expect us to. We have to go to school and keep the place neat and attend Mass. But I swear, I'll never hit you again, Julie. Never."

Julie turned around to face him. "What's going to become of us?" she asked. "What if social services finds out about us?

Can we stay here if Papi isn't here? Do we have enough money? Who's going to take care of us?"

"We'll take care of ourselves," Alex said. "We've been doing a pretty good job of it up till now. No one cares enough to report us to social services, and I think we can stay here for a while longer before anybody notices. I don't know what we'll do about money, but we still have food. I guess if things get really bad, we'll move in with Uncle Jimmy and Aunt Lorraine." He grabbed a box of tissues and handed it to Bri. "Any more questions?" he asked.

"I'm sorry about what I said," Julie said. "I just miss them so much."

"I know," Alex said. "I pray for them all the time." And for us, he thought.

Bri blew her nose, then tossed the wad of tissues into the wastebasket. "*La madre* will hear us," she said. She took her rosary beads she kept next to the statue of the Virgin on top of the chest of drawers, then knelt in prayer.

I'm sorry, Alex mouthed to Julie, but if she saw him, she didn't acknowledge it. He left the room and went into his own.

"Graceful and loving Mother, hear our prayers," he whispered, hoping she could hear him over the din of lost souls.

Wednesday, June 1

As Alex stood in front of his locker trying to decide what books to take home with him, he felt a tap on his shoulder. His immediate response was that unnerving mix of anger and panic he felt so often the past two weeks. Seeing Chris Flynn standing there didn't help much.

"I think we should talk," Chris said. "In private." He gestured to the nearest classroom.

Alex followed Chris in. He thought about how often Chris had been cited as a natural leader. Apparently even Alex was willing to be led.

Chris closed the door behind them. "I wanted you to know I'm leaving school tomorrow," he said. "It's a long story and I'll spare you most of the details, but we were waiting for my sister to make it back from Notre Dame. She's home now, so we can get going."

"Where?" Alex asked.

"South Carolina," Chris said. "My mother has family there. Dad'll be staying in the city for the time being."

"I don't get it," Alex said. It somehow seemed worse that Chris would be leaving midweek. "What about finals?"

"I've already taken them," Chris said. "That took some arranging, too, but I am now officially a senior." He laughed. "Congratulations. You're now the president of the junior class. It'll look good on your college résumé, assuming colleges still exist a year from now."

"That's what you wanted to tell me?" Alex asked. "Why the secrecy? People will notice you're gone, you know."

"I should hope so," Chris said. "Otherwise all my years here will have been in vain."

Alex looked Chris over. He had the natural arrogance of someone for whom everything came easily. They both wore the same uniform, but on Chris somehow it fit better, seemed more natural. He'd known Chris for almost five years, and for all that time, he'd been the person Alex had tried to beat. Even those times when he'd succeeded had never seemed enough. There was always another battle, another struggle to prove that Alex was as smart, as competent, as likely to succeed. Carlos had never been as powerful a rival.

"I wish you well," Alex said. "Vincent de Paul will miss you."

"Thank you," Chris said. "I'm going to miss you, actually. You bring out the best in me. But that's not why I'm telling you any of this. Not for sentimental farewells. I've been avoiding those by not telling people we're leaving."

"What, then?" Alex asked.

Chris looked uncomfortable. Alex tried to remember if he'd ever seen Chris look quite that way before. "I know what's going on with your family is none of my business," Chris said, "but you know how it is. You hear things. Your father, he's not in New York, is he."

Alex shook his head.

"That's what I thought," Chris said. "I remembered from before all this happened, you mentioned he was in Puerto Rico for a funeral. Have you heard from him? Is he all right?"

"We think so," Alex said. "We can't be sure."

"No," Chris said. "It's hard to be sure about anything these days. My father says things are going to get a lot worse. He hears things. He and the mayor are very connected, so he hears things that way. And since he works in insurance, he knows a lot. Let's just say he has a better fix on what's going on than Father Mulrooney, and he's getting Mom and my sister and me out of here."

"How are you getting down to South Carolina?" Alex asked. "Are the planes flying again?"

"No, we'll be driving," Chris replied.

"You can do that?" Alex asked. "The radio says there are gas shortages."

"There's always gas if you have enough money," Chris said. "Gas, food, lodgings. Money and connections." For a moment, Alex thought he looked ashamed. "My father says that won't last much longer, either," he said. "He says pretty soon we'll be bartering. But for now, cash will suffice. That's one of the things I wanted to ask you about. How are you fixed? Do you have enough money? Your mother, is she working?"

Alex pictured Chris whipping out his wallet and handing him a twenty. The image nauseated him. "We're fine," he said. "We're probably in better shape than a lot of the guys here."

"Good," Chris said. "I'm glad to hear it. Look, I want to give you my father's card. He knows all about you. Five years of our butting heads, and you'd better believe he's heard about you. Frankly I've gotten a little tired of the lectures about the great Alex Morales and why can't I be more like him. My father's kept an eye on you for a while now. So he told me to tell you if you or anyone in your family needs something, something big, you should let him know. Don't bother him with the small stuff. But if it's really serious, and you'll know what really serious is, you should go to his office and see if he can help. Don't tell anyone else, though. Dad has a lot to do these days, and he told me this offer is only for you. Because your dad's away. And because he wishes I was more like you."

"Thank you," Alex said, taking the card from Chris. "I'm sure I won't have to bother your father. We really are doing okay."

"Good," Chris said. "One more thing. I hope you won't take this personally." He grinned. "Well, you will, but I'll say it anyway. I've noticed you're one of those guys everyone likes and respects, but you don't seem to have any close friends here. Maybe you're close with the guys in your neighborhood and that's why. Anyway, I told Kevin to look out for you."

"Kevin Daley?" Alex asked. Kevin was runty and cynical, and Alex always assumed Chris kept him around for laughs. He couldn't imagine a less useful companion.

"Kevin knows things," Chris replied. "It's his gift. I don't know how he does it, but he always seems to know what's going on before anyone else does. Not just in school, either. Around the city. He's yours now. I won't be able to make use of him in South Carolina."

"Thanks, I suppose," Alex said. "And thanks for telling your dad about me. About my family."

"I hope Dad can help," Chris said. "Somehow I think Kevin's going to be more useful." He looked disconcertingly serious. "Well, good-bye, Alex. I hope things work out okay for you. I hope your father gets home safely. You're in my prayers."

"You'll be in mine," Alex muttered. He took one last look at Chris Flynn, the boy who had it all, put the card in his pocket, and left the room. He was president of the junior class now, would undoubtedly be elected president of the senior class, and none of that mattered anymore. Nothing mattered, he thought, as he walked rapidly to the men's room. Not caring if anyone was there, he flung himself into one of the stalls and began to sob uncontrollably.

chapter 5

Thursday, June 2

The phone rang just as Alex was halfway out the door on his way to Vincent de Paul. His heart pounding with fear and excitement, he bounded across the living room and got to the phone on the second ring.

"Luis? This is apartment three J. My bathroom sink is leaking again. You need to put in a new washer."

Die, you old *bruja,* Alex thought, slamming the phone down without saying a word.

Friday, June 3

"I have an idea about Mami," Bri said with nervous pride as she, Alex, and Julie began a supper of spaghetti and red clam sauce. "About why she hasn't called."

"Maybe the phones aren't working where she is," Julie said. "Lauren says sometimes the phones work and sometimes they don't. Maybe Mami only calls when the phones aren't working."

"Who's Lauren?" Alex asked, trying not to take too much spaghetti. They still had food in the house, but their supplies were dwindling and he wasn't sure when they'd be able to replenish them or how. They all had lunch at school every day, but with the weekend coming, and the end of the school year not that far off, he wasn't sure how they'd manage.

"She's my best friend," Julie said, and oblivious to any food shortage, helped herself to seconds.

"I don't think it's the telephone," Briana said. "I don't know if phones are working all the time or not, but that's not why we haven't heard from Mami."

"Why, then?" Julie asked. "It's not like she doesn't know our number."

"That's it, exactly!" Bri said, looking happier and more excited than she had in weeks. "Maybe Mami has amnesia."

"Amnesia?" Julie said sarcastically.

Bri either didn't hear or didn't mind Julie's skepticism. "She could have got hit on the head that night," she said. "Or maybe seeing all the awful things shocked her. I don't know. But people do get amnesia. It happens on the soaps all the time. So Mami's all right, she isn't hurt, but she can't remember who she is or where she lives or anything. You can't call home when you have amnesia, and that's why we haven't heard from her. But one day she'll get her memory back. Maybe someone will hypnotize her or maybe she'll get hit on the head again, or she could be at Bellevue and some-one from St. John of God will be there and recognize her, and then we'll hear from her. It could happen, couldn't it, Alex?"

Alex looked at Bri and couldn't bring himself to argue. "It would be a miracle," he said.

"But miracles do happen," Bri said. "So that's what I'm praying for. I'm praying to *la madre* and to St. Jude for Mami to have amnesia and regain her memory and come home."

"I'm praying to Joan of Arc," Julie said. "Don't we have any more spaghetti? I'm still hungry."

"That's it for tonight," Alex said. "You've had your fair share and then some."

"There's still a little left on my plate," Bri said. "You can have it, Julie."

"No," Alex said. "Eat what's there, Bri. So Julie, why are you praying to Joan of Arc?"

"She's a saint, too," Julie grumbled. "If Bri isn't hungry, why can't I have her food?"

Because you didn't take enough from the bodega! Alex wanted to shout. *Because Bri can't be expected to starve herself just so you don't feel a hunger pang.*

"Because you already had seconds," he said instead. "I never thought about amnesia, Bri. Probably a lot of people are wandering around New York right now, shocked from what's happened. Like shell-shocked soldiers in World War One. St. Jude must be very busy right now, interceding for everyone who's been praying to him, so it might take a while for a miracle. But the important thing is to stay strong and not give up hope."

"St. Jude must be way too busy to hear everyone's prayers," Julie said. "I think Joan of Arc is a much better saint to pray to."

"But St. Jude is the patron saint of lost causes," Bri replied. "And Mami's lost, so he must be especially interested in her. In all the people like her. People with amnesia and shell shock."

"Joan of Arc is the patron saint of soldiers," Julie said. "I did a report on her last year. I bet she's the saint you pray to if you have shell shock."

"But Mami doesn't have shell shock," Bri said. "She has amnesia."

Alex felt a wave of guilt for finding a heartfelt discussion about saints to be so stupid. "Julie, clear the table," he said. "Then you and Bri do the dishes. I'm going to my room."

"What will you be doing?" Julie asked.

"Praying," Alex replied, leaving the room rapidly so he wouldn't have to tell his sisters he'd be praying for strength to cope with them and forgiveness for not wanting to.

Saturday, June 4

The electricity was off again, but even in the basement apartment there was enough late-afternoon sunlight so that no candles or flashlights were needed. Bri and Julie sat on the sofa looking at a magazine while Alex sat in the easy chair, the transistor radio broadcasting the news. Lower Manhattan, up to Houston Street, had been evacuated because of constant flooding. The bodies of 112 men, women, and children had been found in a church in Northridge, California, the third apparent mass suicide in and around Los Angeles in the past week. Food riots in Tokyo had claimed at least eight lives, and there were rumors of a revolution in Russia.

"Do you really like him?" Bri asked Julie. "You really think he's cute?"

Julie nodded. "I thought you did, too," she said. "I remember when we saw him on TV and you liked him a lot."

"Not that much," Bri said. "Besides, I was a lot younger then."

"What?" Julie said, her voice rising. "You saying I'm a baby? You saying only babies like him?"

"Do you mind?" Alex said. "I'm trying to listen to the radio."

"I do mind!" Julie shouted. "I mind a lot. Why do you have to keep listening all the time? I hate the radio. I hate it." She stormed off to her room.

"What?" Alex said as Bri gave him a look.

"Nothing," she said. "It's just it upsets Julie to hear what's going on in the world. I don't mind so much because I know someday God will return Mami and Papi to us. But Julie doesn't feel that way. She doesn't want you to know, but she's scared. She's been having awful dreams lately."

It seemed to Alex that Julie was a lot more upset by Bri's not liking some actor than she was over food riots and revolutions. "It's important that I know what's going on," he said.

"Why?" Bri asked.

Alex wasn't sure he could explain. When everything had started, he'd been just as happy not to know what was going on. But lately he felt a desperate need to know, and right then the radio was his only means of finding things out. The bulletin board at St. Margaret's only reported on things in New York. But there was a world out there, a world Alex had dreamed of exploring.

Even if he could explain his feelings to Bri, she'd think protecting Julie was more important. She might even be right.

"Fine," he said. "I'll only listen to the radio at night in my room."

"We can hear it when you do," Bri said. "I know you don't have it on very loud, but the sound comes through the wall."

"Great," Alex muttered.

"Maybe there are earphones," Bri said. "I could look for them if you want."

Alex nodded. "You do that," he said. "I'll go talk to Julie." He left Bri searching through the kitchen drawers and went into his sisters' bedroom.

Julie was sitting cross-legged on her bunk bed. "You come to hit me again?" she asked.

"No, of course not," Alex said, fighting the temptation to do just that. "I didn't know the radio bothered you so much. You never told me."

"You wouldn't care," Julie said. "No one cares what I want except Carlos, and he isn't here."

"Bri cares," Alex said. "She says you've been having bad dreams."

"Aren't you?" Julie asked. "Isn't everyone?"

Alex burst out laughing. "Only sane people," he said. "Okay, maybe not Bri. But everyone else is."

"Are things going to get better?" Julie asked. "Is that why you listen to the news all the time, because someday things are going to get better?"

Alex shook his head. "That's not why I listen," he replied. "That's why I pray but not why I listen."

"Do you think God listens?" she asked.

"Bri thinks so," Alex said. "Father Franco thinks so."

"All those people killing themselves," Julie said. "And in a church."

"I need to know what's going on," Alex said. "For all our sakes. Bri's looking for the earphones. If she finds them, I'll use them whenever I listen."

"And you won't tell me what's happening?" Julie asked.

"Not unless you want me to," Alex said.

Bri came into the bedroom. "I haven't found them," she said. "But the radio has a place to plug them in, so they've got to be somewhere."

"Come on, Julie," Alex said. "If we all look, we'll find them that much sooner."

Tuesday, June 7

"The government knew," Kevin Daley said. "They must have. They just kept it to themselves, how bad things were going to be."

"But why not give people time to prepare?" James Flaherty asked. "No, I think it was a true act of God and the scientists were taken by surprise, same as everyone else."

Alex sat between his two companions at the cafeteria table and listened while they argued the same argument he'd heard almost daily for the three weeks. At this point what difference did it make? Alex gratefully finished each bite of the lunch Vincent de Paul provided for him, a lunch he'd noticed that Kevin and James complained about. They must still have food in their homes, he thought. Otherwise they'd be grateful, same as he was, for anything nourishing.

He felt a tap on his shoulder and looked up to see Father Mulrooney standing there. All the boys at his table rose.

"Sit down," Father Mulrooney said. "Mr. Morales, I have a message for you from Father Franco at St. Margaret's. He asked you to come see him at his office as soon as possible."

"I'll go now," Alex said, his stomach twisting. Father Franco must have heard something about Puerto Rico, about Milagro del Mar. It was good for Alex to learn the news first.

That way he could figure out just how to break it to his sisters.

Father Mulrooney raised his eyebrows. "Do you have permission to leave school?" he asked.

"No sir," Alex said. "But I'm leaving anyway."

Kevin snickered.

"I do not care for the attitude some of you are taking," Father Mulrooney declared. "This is a school, not a social club. You cannot come and go as you please."

"I'm very sorry," Alex said, "but I have to go. I'll come back if I can. Now if you'll excuse me." He grabbed his books and walked out of the cafeteria, aware that the eyes of the other students were on him. Alex Morales, who had never missed a day of school, who had never talked back to a teacher, let alone a priest, had just defied the headmaster. Well, let them look. What did they understand? Even Father Mulrooney, who knew about Mami, had no knowledge about Papi being gone as well.

Alex rammed his books into his locker, then left the school building and began running to St. Margaret's. He paid no mind to the traffic lights, since there were hardly any cars on the streets. It had been an unusually hot spring, and Alex was sweating by the time he reached the church, but that didn't matter. What mattered was that Father Franco knew something. After three weeks, there was finally word.

As always there were a half dozen people sitting in the outer office, waiting for their chance to speak with the father. Alex took his place resentfully. If what Father Franco had to tell him was so urgent, why did he have to wait for an hour to hear what it was?

He should have looked at the bulletin board first, he told himself. If he got up now, he'd lose his place and add a half hour or more to his wait. He should have brought at least one schoolbook with him, since he had nothing to distract himself with except looking at the suffering faces of those who sat with him. Distraction would have been welcome, because he found he was beginning to hope. Maybe Milagro del Mar had been spared the tidal waves and Papi was all right.

Or maybe Bri was right and Mami had suffered some kind of accident and only now was able to tell people who she was and where she lived.

Or maybe Father Franco had gotten word about Carlos, through his Marine chaplain. There were as many good possibilities as bad ones, but Alex knew the good ones were more dangerous. It was one thing to say "Don't give up hope." It was another to have hope dashed time after time.

Eventually his turn came. He prayed for the strength to hear what Father Franco had to tell him.

"Alex," he said. "I thought you'd come after school."

"Father Mulrooney said I should come as soon as I could," Alex replied, sitting down. He'd seen Father Franco at Mass just two days earlier, but already the priest looked years older. "Have you heard something?"

"Yes," Father Franco said. "Oh, you mean about your father. No, son, I'm afraid not. Nothing new, at least. There is some communication now between San Juan and the mainland, but the fate of the little villages still isn't known. No, that's not why I asked you to come."

Alex waited for the next body blow, that his mother's body had been identified. But Father Franco surprised him.

"It's about your sister, Briana," he said instead. "Good news for a change."

Alex tried to smile. "I'd like good news," he said.

"There's a small convent in upstate New York," Father Franco said. "Really quite a remarkable place. There are six sisters and they have a working farm. They've decided to invite ten Catholic high school girls to stay at the convent indefinitely. The girls will work on the farm, but they'll also be educated by the sisters, sort of a summer camp turned into boarding school. Most of the girls they've invited come from families who have connections to the convent, but I happen to know one of the sisters, and I told her I know a perfect candidate. I wasn't positive how old Briana is, but I said fifteen and going into her sophomore year of high school."

"She'll be fifteen next month," Alex said, trying to take it all in. "And yes, she'll be a sophomore."

Father Franco looked quite pleased with himself. "The sisters are only inviting girls who attend Catholic schools, but that should be no problem," he said. "Briana goes to Holy Angels, doesn't she?"

Alex nodded.

"Excellent," Father Franco said. "I'm very pleased for you, for your family, and most of all, for Briana. I know what a devout girl she is, and perhaps growing up in the atmosphere of a convent, she'll find she has a vocation. But even if she doesn't, she'll still have a safe place to stay, and you and your family won't have to worry about her."

"Just Briana?" Alex said, suddenly realizing that with Bri gone, he'd be left alone with Julie. "Couldn't they take Julie also?"

Father Franco shook his head. "I asked," he said. "But Sister Grace said the girls must be teenagers. Besides, they're only taking one girl from each family. Briana is the perfect fit."

"Thank you, Father," Alex said. "I'm very grateful." It would be good to know Bri at least was someplace safe.

Father Franco smiled. Alex couldn't remember the last time the priest had looked so satisfied. "The bus leaves for the convent on Thursday afternoon," he said. "Briana needs to be at St. Benedict's Church, Madison and 112th, by one. She'll need her baptismal certificate, her most recent report card, and a recent canceled check to Holy Angels. Can you find all that?"

"Yes, I think so," Alex said. "Do you mean this Thursday?"

"The sooner the better," Father Franco replied. "Imagine Briana in the fresh country air, eating eggs and drinking milk. Now here's the information about the convent, its address and phone number. Sister Grace said that for the first month you shouldn't call, since it's natural for the girls to be homesick and it will be easier for them if they're not reminded of what they've left behind. But I assure you, Briana will be in the best possible hands. When you see her next, she'll be plump as a kitten." He stood and extended his hand for Alex to shake. "Your family is in my prayers," he said. "But I like to think one prayer has been answered."

"Yes, Father," Alex said. "Thank you for everything." He left the office, then went to the nave, genuflected at the crucifix, then knelt in prayer.

Heavenly Father, teach me to accept all my losses, he prayed. And show me how to live in peace with Julie.

Wednesday, June 8

Alex watched his sisters leave for Holy Angels, then went to his parents' bedroom to search for the papers Bri would need. There'd been no electricity the night before and he was uncomfortable enough with the idea of rifling through his parents' possessions without wanting to do it by flashlight. Besides, he didn't dare risk having Bri or Julie wake up. Better to do it Wednesday morning and get to school late. He wouldn't even mind detention. The less time he spent with Bri the better, since seeing her and thinking about how long it might be before he saw her again upset him fiercely.

It's for the best, he told himself. Their food supplies were running low. Even if they skipped more meals, there was hardly enough left for two weeks. As it was, they no longer ate breakfast. With the school year coming to an end, Alex had no idea how they'd survive. This way, at least, Bri would have food, and what little remained at home would last that much longer.

Alex gritted his teeth and began going through his parents' chest of drawers. He hoped he'd find a report card, since the sisters would be impressed with Bri's grades.

The scent of his parents' clothing nearly made him sick with longing. Three weeks ago, they'd been a family. Now Alex was exiling Bri, the sweetest of them all. Would he ever see her again?

It's for the best, he reminded himself. He had to be strong, the way Papi or Carlos would be.

No report cards, no baptism certificates in the chest of drawers. He went into the kitchen and got the step stool so he could go through the shoe boxes on the top shelf of their closet. The boxes weren't labeled, but eventually he found their report cards and Bri's baptism certificate. He put the boxes back, carried the step stool back to the kitchen, and located the bank statements in a kitchen drawer. Then he took the papers to his room, hiding them under the top bunk mattress. He doubted the girls would ever go through his things, but there was no point taking chances.

Knowing he'd found the needed documents made him realize he was actually going to send Bri away.

Who died and made me boss? he asked himself. Not wanting to know the answer, he gathered his schoolbooks and decided facing the wrath of Father Mulrooney would be a welcome diversion.

Thursday, June 9

Alex had waited to tell Father Mulrooney that he'd be gone from school all day until after he'd served detention for being late the day before. Father Mulrooney had given him a ten-minute lecture on the importance of education in troubled times, but at least Alex didn't have a guilty conscience about cutting classes.

He went through his closet until he found Carlos's old duffel bag. It still had that faint smell of sweat and aftershave Alex associated with Carlos, but he doubted Bri would mind.

Alex wished he had a list of what Bri was going to need, but he hadn't been given one. This kind of packing was best done by Mami, he thought. She'd done it for their Fresh Air Fund summers. She knew how to pack, just as she knew how to cook and clean and do all kinds of things no one had ever felt the need to teach Alex. And yet here he was, going through Bri's most private things, trying to decide what she would need to have with her and what the sisters would provide.

She'd be working on a farm, he told himself, so she should have work clothes. It promised to be a hot summer, so T-shirts and shorts were good ideas. He added a couple of pairs of jeans and the oversized Vincent de Paul sweatshirt he'd given her for Christmas two years ago. Nights got cold in the country.

The girls might be expected to dress for dinner and they'd certainly have to for church, so Alex carefully packed a skirt and two blouses, as well as Bri's best dress. She had her uniform on, so that was an extra blouse and skirt. She was wearing a pair of shoes, but she'd need something more practical for farmwork, so Alex dug out a pair of sneakers he was reasonably sure were Bri's. Next came nightgowns and *la ropa íntima*. Alex grimaced at the thought of handling Bri's most personal clothing, but it had to be done. He pulled open the top drawer in the bureau, and trying hard not to think about it, threw an assortment of undergarments into the duffel bag. Nightgowns were a little less awkward, and he felt a sense of relief when he remembered that Bri would need socks, slippers, and a robe as well. He knew which robe and slippers were hers, so that was easy. Any socks would do, just as long as he left enough for Julie.

Next came the bathroom items. The nuns would certainly have toothpaste and soap, but Bri would want her own toothbrush. The only problem was Alex had no idea which brush was hers. He knew his, but Bri's could have been any of the others. Not knowing what else to do, Alex threw all except his into the duffel bag. He could always find another one for Julie, he supposed, somewhere in New York, and if Mami or Papi came back, he'd find toothbrushes for them, too. As far as anything else a girl might need, he decided the nuns could handle it.

He found Bri's diary and put it in the duffel bag. He looked around her room for something that she loved and would want to have with her. Most of the pictures she'd Scotch-taped to the walls were of TV stars, good-looking guys that Alex was pretty sure wouldn't be welcomed at a convent, no matter how open-minded the sisters might be. But the postcard of the van Gogh painting *Starry Night* Bri had gotten because it reminded her of the night skies in the country should be acceptable, so he peeled it off the wall and slipped it into the bag.

What else? A photograph of the family, he decided, but that was in Mami and Papi's room. A sweater. He found one in the closet and threw it in. A jacket? A coat? If Bri stayed at the convent past the summer, she'd need a coat. Alex felt his throat constrict at the idea that Bri might never leave the convent, that he might be sending her away from home forever. He told himself that whatever happened, Bri would be safe and healthy and he couldn't guarantee that in New York. It was best for Bri to be gone. And he'd always know where she was. It wasn't the same kind of gone as Mami and Papi. It was more like Carlos, only better, since the church would know just where Bri was and he'd be able to get in touch with her in an emergency. And she'd be on a farm, with other girls like her, protected by the sisters. It was the best thing that could possibly happen.

He rolled up Bri's raincoat and put it in. There wasn't room in there for her winter coat. He knew he should carry it but couldn't make himself. If Bri stayed on into the winter, he'd find a way of getting the coat to her, he decided. Besides, the sisters probably were prepared with coats for the girls, just in case.

Bri's rosary beads! No matter that the sisters would have extras; Bri had to have her own. They were on top of the bureau, and Alex packed them, then went to his parents' bedroom and took the framed picture of the six of them that Mami kept by her bedside. Uncle Jimmy had taken it at Christmas, right before Carlos enlisted. Alex looked at it carefully before packing it. They all looked so much younger. Had it been less than six months ago?

There might have been other things Bri would want or need, but Alex couldn't figure out what they might be. Besides, he had to get Bri to St. Benedict's before the bus left for the convent, and it would be a long walk there from the school. He went back to Bri and Julie's bedroom, gave it a quick appraisal, decided enough was enough, then went to his bedroom, and pulled the documents out from under the mattress.

He walked to Holy Angels and went into the school office. He didn't know what to expect, but things seemed reasonably normal there, busier than at Vincent de Paul.

"I'm Alex Morales," he said to a woman sitting at a desk. "Briana Morales's brother. I'm here to take her to St. Benedict's for the bus."

The woman looked at him blankly. "What grade is she in?" she asked.

"Ninth," Alex replied.

"Room 144," the woman said. "If she isn't there, try Room 142."

Alex thanked her, walked down the hallway, and located Room 144. Bri was sitting at her desk, scribbling madly in her notebook.

Alex walked into the classroom and approached the teacher, sitting at her desk. "I'm Briana Morales's brother," he said. "I've come to take her away."

The girls all looked up, Bri clearly puzzled to see him.

The teacher didn't seem all that surprised. Judging from the number of empty desks, Alex guessed Bri wasn't the first kid in class to be mysteriously called away lately.

"Will Briana be coming back?" her teacher asked.

"No," Alex whispered.

"We'll miss her," the teacher said. "Very well. Briana, get your things, and go with your brother."

Alex thanked her, and walked over to Bri. "Come on," he whispered. "We have to get going."

"Is it Mami?" Bri asked. "Or Papi? Are they home?"

"No," Alex said. "Come on, Bri. Don't worry about your textbooks."

"I don't understand," she said.

"I'll explain later," he said. "Just follow me."

Bri did as she was told. They left the classroom, and then the school. "We have a bit of a walk," Alex said. "All the way to Madison Avenue and 112th. We'll cross the park at 96th. Are your shoes comfortable? You can switch to your sneakers if you want."

"I'm okay," Bri said. "But what's going on? Where are we going? Where's Julie?"

"Still in school," Alex said. He paused for a moment. "Bri, something great's happened, thanks to Father Franco. There's a convent upstate that's taking teenage girls. Julie's too young, but you're the right age, so you can go there."

"To be a nun?" Bri asked. "Alex, I'm too young."

Alex pretended to laugh. "Not to be a nun," he said. "It's

a convent but it's also a working farm, and the sisters decided to open it up to good Catholic girls. You'll be working on the farm, but it'll also be a school. And because it's a farm, there'll be plenty of food. You like the country. You always had great times with your Fresh Air Fund family. This'll be like that, only better, because there'll be other girls your age there, and the nuns."

Bri stood absolutely still. "Is it an orphanage?" she asked. "Are you sending me to an orphanage?"

"No, of course not," Alex said. "Come on, Bri. We can't miss the van. If it was an orphanage, wouldn't I be sending Julie instead?"

"I don't know," Briana said. "Are you sending her someplace else? Or is it just me?"

"Just you because you're the right age," Alex replied. "Stop acting like it's forever and you're some kind of martyr. I wish there was a place I could go, where I'd be guaranteed three meals a day."

"There is," Bri said. "Join the Marines."

"Very funny," Alex said. "Now come on. We still have the park to cross."

Briana was silent for a while. Alex was relieved not to have to answer any more questions, and to see what passed for normal activity in Central Park. There were plenty of people riding bikes and others walking, enjoying the hot June day. No cars, but at times Central Park was closed to cars anyway. Even the cops riding horseback added to the sense of normalcy, the *clop-clop-clop* of the horses' hooves making a soothing noise.

"If I hate it, can I come home?" Briana asked.

"You won't hate it," Alex said.

"But what if I do?" Bri persisted. "What if they're mean to me? What if everyone's nasty?"

"We're lucky this place exists," Alex said. "The nuns will look after you, and you'll make lots of friends. The important thing is you'll be safe. I don't know how much longer New York'll be okay. It is now but things are getting worse. We may not talk about that, but you've got to know. And yeah, if I can find a safe place for Julie, I'll send her there. I'm responsible for the two of you, at least until Papi or Mami come back. Don't you think they'd want you to be with the sisters, out of harm's way?"

Briana remained silent.

"Answer that," Alex said. "Don't you think Mami and Papi would want you to be safe, at a convent with holy sisters looking after you?"

"Yes, Alex," Bri said.

"Good," he said.

"Does Julie know?" Bri asked. "Did you tell her and not me?"

"No, of course not," Alex said.

"She'll be angry when she finds out," Bri said.

"That's her problem," Alex said. "Besides, she won't be angry for long. Not when she realizes it's best for you. The way we have."

"I wish I could have said good-bye to her," Bri said.

Alex pictured what that would have been like. "It's better this way," he said. "I'll tell her all about the convent tonight."

They walked in silence for a while longer, Alex trying not to think about how Julie would react.

"Where are we going, anyway?" Bri finally asked.

"To St. Benedict's Church," Alex replied. "They're sending a van there to take all the girls to the convent."

"Will you wait with me until it comes?" Briana asked. "Please, Alex."

Alex nodded. "If they'll let me," he said.

"And you'll write?" she asked. "You and Julie?"

"Of course we will," he replied. "And you'll write to us. The post office is crazy these days, so I don't know how often you'll get mail, but we'll write. I promise."

"I guess it will be like the Fresh Air Fund," Briana said. "I was always scared when I left home each summer, but I had a nice time once I got used to it."

"I packed your things," Alex said. "I put in that picture of all of us that Mami had and your rosary beads and your diary and the *Starry Night* postcard."

"Thank you," Briana said. "How long have you known I'd be going?"

"Just a couple of days," Alex said.

"I hope I'll come home someday," she said. "I think I'll die if I don't ever see you and Julie again."

"You aren't going to die," Alex said. "And you'll see us again. Now come on. We still have to get to Madison and then walk uptown."

"Are you tired?" she asked. "Do you want me to carry the duffel bag for a while?"

"No, of course not," Alex said. "Just walk faster."

Briana picked up her pace, and the two of them walked more swiftly, resting only at street corners before crossing. The faster they walked, the less Alex thought about how much he was going to miss her.

By 108th Street, they could see the church up ahead. It

was older than St. Margaret's but every bit as imposing. Alex was glad. It made little sense, but it was a relief to see the church look so respectable.

As they got closer, they saw a girl about Bri's age accompanied by her mother. Alex picked up the pace, and Bri followed his lead. "Are you off to the farm?" Alex asked.

"Yes," the mother said.

Alex noticed the girl was weeping.

"She's homesick already," the mother said. "It's scary for her."

"I'm Briana," Bri said to the girl. "What's your name?"

"Ashley," the girl replied.

"I have a friend named Ashley," Bri said. "She looks a little like you. Have you ever been on a farm?"

"No," Ashley mumbled.

"I have," Bri said. "Farms are really nice. Where do you go to school?"

"Mother of Mercy High School," Ashley said. "I'm a sophomore."

"I go to Holy Angels," Bri said. "I'm in ninth grade."

Ashley's mother looked gratefully at Alex. "This has been so hard," she whispered. "But I don't know what else to do."

"I know," Alex said. "I've been telling Briana how lucky she is."

They walked into the church together, and found a sign telling them to wait in the basement. When they got there, they found the room filled with girls and their families. A lot of people were crying, and Ashley began weeping again. Alex found two seats for himself and Briana. He held her hand, but she didn't cry.

"You're being very brave," he told her. "I'm proud of you."

"I don't want to cry," she said. "Alex, I've been thinking. I need you to promise me something."

"If I can," he said.

"No," she said. "You have to promise me this. It's like a holy vow. If you don't, I'm going to get up and leave right now."

Alex thought about Bri, how few scenes she made compared to Julie's endless whining or Aunt Lorraine's dramatics. "There are things I can't promise," he said. "I can't promise the moon will return to its place, that things will ever be normal again."

"I know," she said. "And I know you can't promise me that Papi and Mami will come home. But you have to vow to me that you and Julie won't leave the apartment, that you won't disappear on me. You have to vow that you'll stay at home, so I'll always know where you are, so when Papi and Mami and Carlos come home, they'll know where you are and you can tell them where I am and I can come home then. Promise me that, Alex. I can't have you gone like they are."

"I promise," he said, hoping that if he and Julie ever did have to leave, they'd have time to let Bri know. "We'll stay there for you and Papi and Mami and Carlos."

"All right," Briana said. "You can go now. You need to get back so Julie will know what's going on."

"No," Alex said, surprising himself with his vehemence. "I can't just leave you. I have to stay to make sure you get on the van."

"I told you I would," Bri said. "You can trust me."

"It's not that," Alex said. He didn't want to tell Bri what he just realized, that if he left without seeing her get on the van, she'd be one of the gone and he couldn't bear that. "I have papers they need. I have to stay until the van gets here."

"All right," Briana said. "I just thought you might want to go."

"Bri, I don't like this, either," Alex said. "But it's for the best. For you, and for Julie and me. More food for us. And we won't worry, since we'll know you're being fed and taken care of."

Briana nodded. "I think I'd like to pray now," she said. "I think the holy *madre* will make me feel better."

It was almost three before the van arrived. When it did, the sniffles turned to sobs, and even Alex had to fight tears. Briana was weeping openly as she hugged her brother farewell.

Alex showed the nun Bri's baptism certificate, report card, and the canceled check. She was older than Alex had expected but she looked kind, and she smiled at Bri and welcomed her aboard. Alex loaded the duffel bag onto the overhead rack. The girls crowded in, and Alex noted that Briana sat next to Ashley. She'd already begun making friends, he thought, feeling proud. Her courage and her faith would be an example for all the other girls.

It was too late to go back to Holy Angels and find Julie, he realized as he began the walk back. Better to go straight to the apartment. He'd been avoiding thinking about Julie and how she'd feel, since the important thing was taking care of Briana, getting her to a place of safety. He knew Julie loved Bri, but he couldn't help thinking there was a part of her that would be glad to be the only girl in the household.

It would be hard for him, having Julie without Bri serving as a buffer. But Julie would learn to respect his decisions. She wasn't a bad kid, just spoiled and treated like a baby for too long. Her baby days were over. The world had no more room for twelve-year-old babies.

They'd start tonight, he decided. From now on, Julie would be making supper. She'd get to decide what they'd eat. Bri had been doing the cooking, such as it was, but now Julie would. It would mean more work for her, but more responsibility as well. And she wouldn't be able to complain about the choices if she was the one doing the choosing.

Alex felt proud of himself. He was doing everything he had to do. It was hard for him, hard for all of them, but he pictured Bri and how brave she was, and he felt a new surge of pride. Carlos would say Bri was brave because she was the sister of a Marine, but Alex was learning there were a lot of different ways of being a fighter. Even Papi would be proud of Alex. When he came back, he'd treat Alex with a newfound respect.

He was sweaty, tired, and hungry by the time he unlocked the door to the apartment. It no longer mattered to him what Julie chose to make for their supper, just as long as she prepared it immediately.

But Julie was in no state to make supper. She ran straight at Alex, and instead of greeting him with a hug, began pummeling his chest with her fists.

"Where were you?" she screamed. "Where's Bri? What have you done with Bri? I thought you were both gone forever, that you'd left me behind. I hate you! I hate you!"

Alex grabbed her wrists and held them tightly. "Stop it," he said. "You know we would never leave you behind. Stop acting like a baby."

"You're hurting me," she said.

"You hurt me," he said. "Punching me like that. Would you ever do that to Papi?"

"You're not Papi," Julie said.

"I'm in charge," Alex said. "Until Papi comes home, and

you'll respect me like you respect him. Now if you'll behave yourself, I'll tell you where Bri is."

Julie glared at him, but she kept quiet.

"Father Franco told me about a convent upstate that has its own farm," Alex said. "The sisters decided to open the convent to teenage Catholic girls. Bri is old enough so she got to go. You're too young so you're staying here. That's all. No one's disappeared on you. I would have picked you up at Holy Angels, but the van to the convent came late and I didn't have the chance."

"Is she coming back?" Julie asked.

"Not tonight," Alex said. "It's like camp, or school. Maybe she'll like it so much, she'll become a nun. You should be happy for her, that she's someplace safe, where she'll make friends and have food to eat. And I'll take care of you. But you have to obey me just like you obey Papi, because that's what he and Mami would expect of you. Do you feel better now? Do you have any other questions?"

Julie continued to look sullen. "Are you going to send me away?" she asked. "Like you sent Bri?"

"I'm going to do what's best for you," Alex said. "You're my responsibility, and I'll make sure you're safe. Maybe you'll stay with me or maybe you'll go someplace else. Either way, I expect you to be as brave as Bri. She prayed to our Holy Mother for strength, and Mary granted it to her. Bri comforted another girl who was crying. A girl older than her. Do you think you can be that brave?"

"Promise me you won't leave without telling me," Julie said. "Alex, I was so scared. Promise me that."

"I promise," Alex said. "Now how about making supper for us. I don't know about you, but even a can of spinach sounds good to me right now."

"Okay," Julie said. "Do you want some salmon with that? I think we still have a can left."

"It's up to you," Alex said. "From now on, you're in charge of the kitchen." He realized what the consequences of that might be. "But don't use up our food too fast," he added. "Maybe just the spinach for tonight."

"All right," Julie said. "I'll be careful. I promise I will be. And I'll be good. Just don't leave me again."

"I won't," Alex said. "I promise." Half a can of spinach, he thought. No breakfast, no lunch, and a half a can of spinach for supper. He could only hope that Bri would be eating more than that at the convent.

chapter 6

Sunday, June 12

After Mass, Julie asked Alex's permission to spend the afternoon at her friend Lauren's and Alex gladly said yes. He and Julie had an uneasy peace going, with neither of them saying very much for fear of provoking the other. An afternoon of not having to watch every word he said to his kid sister definitely had its appeal.

Father Franco had made a point of stopping Alex after church to tell him he'd heard from Sister Grace that Briana was making a successful adjustment to her new life.

Alex wasn't certain whether he'd tell Julie. She hadn't mentioned Bri since that first afternoon, except to complain that her toothbrush was missing. Alex found an unused one in the medicine cabinet, and that seemed to satisfy her. He knew Julie missed Bri as much as he did, but whatever pain Julie was feeling she kept to herself, for which Alex was very grateful. He had no words to comfort her, not having any to comfort himself.

The electricity was out when he got home. They hadn't had any on Saturday, either, and the apartment, which never got much natural light, was dark and unwelcoming. Alex picked up a flashlight and his chemistry textbook. Finals were coming and this was as good a time to study as any.

He was startled by a tapping on the window. Looking up, he saw Uncle Jimmy. The last time Jimmy had done that, there had been food. Maybe Jimmy had gotten a delivery and was offering to share some with his sister's children. Alex rushed to open the door.

Jimmy entered the apartment and sat down on the sofa. "You kids are taking good care of the place," he said. "Your parents would be pleased."

"Thanks," Alex said.

"I feel kind of funny about this, but Lorraine seems to think it's a good idea," Jimmy began. "The thing is, we're moving out. There's a little bit of food coming in, but I can't afford what they're charging and even if I could, my customers sure can't, so there's no point pretending I can make a go of the bodega. And Lorraine's convinced New York is going to sink. You know how she is."

Alex nodded.

"She may be right," Uncle Jimmy said. "Things are going from bad to worse; a fool can see that. I have my kids to take care of. Anyway, we're getting out while we can. Lorraine has cousins in Tulsa, *si Dios quiere,* we'll be able to get gas on the way."

"Thank you for letting me know," Alex said. "You and Aunt Lorraine saved our lives with the food you gave us. I hope you get there without too many problems."

"Me too," Uncle Jimmy said. "But the reason I came over—well, of course we wouldn't have just vanished on you—but Lorraine and I talked about it, and we'd like to take Briana with us. Ordinarily we'd offer to take all of you, or at least the girls, but it's hard to know just what's going to happen with food and everything. Lorraine's pregnant again."

"I didn't know," Alex said. "Congratulations."

Jimmy scowled. "Not great timing," he said. "Four little ones under the age of six with all this going on. Bri would be a big help, and if things are okay in Tulsa, we'd be providing her with a good home. Is it a deal?"

"No," Alex said. "I mean it's very nice of you, Uncle Jimmy, but Bri isn't here anymore."

"No?" Jimmy said. "Where is she?"

"I should have told you," Alex said. "Our priest heard there was a convent upstate that was taking in teenage girls. Bri left Thursday."

Uncle Jimmy nodded thoughtfully. "That would make Isabella very happy," he said. "Well, Lorraine might not like it, but we could take Julie, I guess. She'd be better than nothing. And I liked how she worked at the bodega that morning. Yeah, I think I could convince Lorraine to take Julie instead. How about it?"

"Do I have to let you know right now?" Alex asked, feeling a strong need to make lists of arguments in favor and against.

"Yeah," Jimmy said. "It's gonna be hard enough, me convincing Lorraine Julie'll work as hard as Bri, without me going home saying 'Alex don't know.' We're leaving first thing tomorrow. Where is Julie, anyway?"

"At a friend's," Alex said. He pictured what things would be like without Julie around, without the constant tension.

Then he thought about how it would feel to have nobody, to have his entire family gone. Maybe Jimmy would end up in Tulsa, but maybe not. Phone service came and went. The mail couldn't be counted on. Julie could vanish, the same as Carlos, the same as Papi and Mami.

And he'd vowed to Bri that he and Julie would stay home. What kind of vow was it if he broke it four days later?

"I don't think so," Alex said. "I'm really sorry, Uncle Jimmy, but I think Julie'll be better off here with me."

"I know Lorraine and Julie don't get along too good, but that'll change," Uncle Jimmy said. "You won't be able to stay here much longer. When it's time for you to go, it's going to be easier if you don't have Julie to worry about. You did the right thing sending Bri away. Now do the same for Julie."

Alex knew Uncle Jimmy was right. Sure, he and Lorraine would work Julie hard, but as long as they had food and a home, Julie would, too. And things might be better in Tulsa. He couldn't even be sure schools would be open in New York in the fall, assuming they could get enough food to make it until then.

But Julie would be miserable and Alex just couldn't do it to her. Not to her, not to Bri, not to himself. Besides, what if Papi or Mami came home, and he had no way of finding Julie?

"Thanks," he said. "But we'll manage. If it gets too bad, we'll find someplace to go."

Uncle Jimmy got up and hugged Alex hard. "You're a good boy," he said. "Isabella was always so proud of you, how good you do in school. You're not so tough, but you're strong. We'll be staying with Miguel Flores on East Eightieth Street. Maybe someday you'll make it there, all of you."

"My prayers are with you," Alex said as he saw his uncle out. What was he doing, he asked himself, sending Bri into the arms of strangers and preventing Julie from going off with family?

Oh Mami, he cried silently. Papi. Come back. I'm more lost now than you are.

Tuesday, June 14

"Before we celebrate Mass, I have been instructed by the archdiocese to take a survey," Father Mulrooney thundered. Alex remained impressed with how much sound could come out of such a thin body. "I want a show of hands. How many of you have been informed by your parents that you will be leaving New York City for good at the end of the school year?"

About a third of the boys raised their hands.

"Very well," Father Mulrooney said. "How many have been told your families will be leaving New York City by September?"

Maybe another third raised their hands.

"Just to make sure that you're listening," Father Mulrooney said. "Raise your hands if you've been told you will not be returning to St. Vincent de Paul Academy next September. Seniors, raise your hands as well."

So many hands went up, Alex began to fear he was the only student who intended to stay in the city.

"Now let me see a show of hands of those who have not been informed that they're leaving New York," Father Mulrooney instructed.

Alex reluctantly raised his hand. He was relieved to see at least some other hands go up. Some of them, he thought, probably would be gone also, but just didn't know it. And under ordinary circumstances there would be a class of seventh graders to replace the seniors. So he doubted the accuracy of the numbers.

Were any of his friends among those planning to stay? Hands went down too fast for him to be sure. But then again, did he really have any friends? Or were they all like Danny O'Brien, friendly on the outside but cold where it counted?

At least with Chris I knew where I stood, Alex thought.

After Mass Kevin Daley sauntered up to him. "Hey, Morales," he said. "I see you're planning to stick around for a while."

"That's the plan," Alex said as though he had plans.

"I'll be here," Kevin said.

"Great," Alex said. At least he'd have one runty, cynical weasel to hang out with.

Wednesday, June 15

It had been four weeks since the asteroid had knocked the moon just a little closer to earth, four weeks of untold devastation and death. Four weeks since Alex had last heard from his parents and one day short of that since he'd last spoken to his brother.

He and Julie went to the evening Mass for the dead at St. Margaret's. Two Masses in one day, he thought. Mami would be sure I had a vocation.

The church was full to overflowing. If other people there took comfort from the service, Alex couldn't tell. Julie, he noticed, looked a little bored. And he felt nothing. It was easier that way.

Saturday, June 18

"I tried calling Uncle Jimmy," Julie told Alex over what passed for lunch, half a can each of kidney beans, "to see if he had any food he could give us. But no one answered."

"He's gone," Alex replied. "He and Lorraine took the kids. They're hoping to get to Tulsa. They left a few days ago."

"Oh," Julie said.

"We'll be fine," Alex said, a shot of guilt piercing his heart. What had he condemned Julie to?

Julie pushed away her plate, even though there was still a forkful of food left on it. "No one says good-bye to me," she said. "Bri spoke to Papi and you spoke to Carlos and Bri and Uncle Jimmy, but I didn't get to speak to any of them."

"You still hold that against me?" Alex asked. "That I didn't wake you when Carlos called?" He longed to eat Julie's remaining kidney beans. It would teach her a lesson if he did.

"At school they asked how many of us are coming back next year," Julie said instead. "Most of the girls are leaving."

"Same at Vincent de Paul," Alex said. "But we're staying. You and I aren't going anywhere. Now finish your lunch."

"Some lunch," Julie grumbled, but she did as she was told.

What if we die? Alex asked himself. What if we starve to death, and something happens and Papi and Mami and Carlos and Bri all come back, only to find our dead bodies? Maybe it was the sheer awfulness of the thought, or maybe it was hunger, but Alex found himself laughing for the first time in weeks.

Sunday, June 19

Alex was sitting on the living room sofa, taking advantage of unexpected electricity on a Sunday afternoon to illuminate his Latin textbook. Finals began on Monday, and with Father Mulrooney teaching Latin, Alex was determined to ace the exam.

"Electricity really does make things easier," he muttered to himself, but that was just the kind of statement that aroused Father Mulrooney's scorn. Of course Father Mulrooney was so old, electricity probably hadn't been invented when he first learned Latin. Most likely it was Julius Caesar who taught him his declensions.

Alex was picturing Father Mulrooney in a toga when he heard footsteps coming toward their apartment. For a second his heart stopped.

Julie raced from her bedroom. "Who could it be?" she cried.

Alex gestured for her to be quiet and go back to her room. Julie pouted for a moment then did as he told her.

There was a knock on the door.

"Who is it?" Alex called.

"Greg Dunlap," a man replied. "Apartment twelve B."

Oh God, Alex thought. They had a plumbing problem. He opened the door. "Mr. Dunlap," he said, "I'm sorry my father hasn't gotten around to making that repair. It's just . . ."

"He never came back," Mr. Dunlap said. "That's been my guess. Am I right?"

Alex couldn't come up with a reasonable lie, so he simply nodded.

"We've heard a lot of stories like that," Mr. Dunlap said. "May I come in?"

"I'm sorry," Alex said. "Please. We haven't been getting a lot of visitors lately."

"Are you all right?" Mr. Dunlap asked. "I should have checked up on you, since I knew Luis was in Puerto Rico, but things kept getting in the way. That's how it is with good intentions. How is your family holding up? Have you heard from Carlos?"

Alex nodded. "He's fine."

"Good," Mr. Dunlap said. "And your mother? Is she around? I'd like to speak to her."

"She's out right now," Alex said. That wasn't a lie exactly, and it was a lot easier than the truth.

"All right, then, I'll discuss this with you," Mr. Dunlap said. "Bob and I are leaving the city tomorrow for Vermont. We have friends there. The only thing that kept us here for this long is that we've been taking care of the cat in sixteen D. Friends of ours live there and they were vacationing in Maui when it happened. They were due back that weekend, and we haven't heard anything from them, so we just kept taking care of the cat. But this is ridiculous. We're not going to die just so we can keep taking care of a cat for people who are . . . Well, they won't be coming back. We gave them a month. We'll take the cat with us."

"So you won't need the plumbing repair," Alex said.

"Plumbing's been the least of our problems," Mr. Dunlap said. "You know, I came home with that pizza and Bob was hysterical because he had the TV on, so he knew what happened. I didn't. I just remember walking home thinking it was going to rain. That was the last happy moment in my life, maybe the last one ever. Anyway, I came down here so I could give you the keys to my apartment and to sixteen D.

Bob and I have eaten most of their food, but there are still a few things left, and there's stuff we're not taking that maybe your family can use." He handed Alex two sets of keys. "Bob says it's better if the stuff goes to a Vincent de Paul man," he said. "I hope it'll help."

"Yes, thank you," Alex said. "We really appreciate this."

"I guess you're sticking around waiting for your father," Mr. Dunlap said. "I know how hard it is to give up your home. But New York is in for some very bad times. Bob works for the *Daily News*, and naturally he hears things. It's going to get very rough, and it won't get better anytime soon. Maybe never. Tell your mother she should think about making other plans, at least for your sisters so they'll be safe."

"Yes, I will," Alex said. "Thank you again, Mr. Dunlap, and thank Bob for us as well. I hope things work out in Vermont."

"I'm not sure things are going to work out ever again," Mr. Dunlap replied. "Sometimes the best you can do is postpone the inevitable. Please tell your mother that our thoughts are with her."

"I will," Alex said. "And thank you."

As soon as he closed the door, Julie ran out of her bedroom. "Let me see," she demanded as though two sets of keys were worth looking at. "Oh, Alex, can we go up to sixteen D now and get their food?"

"No," Alex said. "Not until tomorrow. Besides, Mr. Dunlap said there isn't much there."

"Not much is better than nothing," Julie said. "I don't want to wait."

Alex didn't want to, either, since the only thing he'd

eaten all day was half a can of chicken noodle soup, with half a can of mushrooms promised by Julie for supper. "Wait a second," he said, and walked to his bedroom. He lifted the mattress from the upper bunk bed, and pulled out the two envelopes that held keys for apartment 11F and apartment 14J. If either of them had ever come back, they'd made no effort to contact Papi. And if they hadn't come back, there might be food going to waste.

Was it stealing? Was it a sin? Alex thought it might be both. But Christ couldn't want them to starve when there was food available.

He walked back into the living room, his hands shaking with excitement. There was no time to waste, since the electricity came and went.

"We're going upstairs," he told Julie. "Papi had keys for two apartments, and if the people there never came back, we'll take their food."

They ran into the hallway and pressed the button for the service elevator. It had gone up to the twelfth floor and took a moment to return.

"We'll start with fourteen J," he said. "I don't know when they left or if they ever came back. We'll ring their bell and give them a minute before we open their door. If they do, look cute and apologize. We'll take the stairs to eleven F next. Okay?"

"Do you really think I'm cute?" Julie asked as they boarded the elevator.

"Compared to me," Alex said. "And maybe Carlos."

Julie giggled. She hadn't laughed, Alex realized, since Bri had gone.

There was no one in the fourteenth-floor hallway. Alex

and Julie walked over to apartment 14J. Alex willed himself to press the bell. They could hear it ring within the apartment, but there was no other sound.

"Can we go in now?" Julie pleaded.

"Let's ring it one more time," Alex said. He didn't want to knock on their door, since the other people on the floor would hear that. He gave them thirty more seconds, which felt like an eternity, then used the keys to unlock the door.

He could sense right away that the apartment was empty and had been for a while. There was a thin layer of dust on the furniture and the air was stuffy and hot.

"Hello?" he said loudly enough for anyone in the apartment to hear him.

There was no answer.

"Now?" Julie asked.

"Now," Alex said, and they walked into the kitchen.

Alex knew he shouldn't have been, but he was startled at how beautiful the kitchen was. It must have been remodeled recently, he decided. It was strange seeing how much bigger the apartment was than their own, how much airier and lighter. Same building, but totally different lives.

Still, he was alive and so were his brother and sisters. Who knew if 14J could say the same.

He opened the side-by-side refrigerator and was accosted by the smell of rotting fruits and vegetables. "They're gone," he said. "Let's take everything in the cabinets."

"Everything?" Julie asked. "Look, Alex, there are Oreos!"

Alex grinned. "Oreos and everything else," he said. He checked under the sink and found a box of trash bags. "Let's start loading."

"Maybe she has a shopping cart," Julie said. "Like Mami."

"Where would it be?" Alex asked.

Julie scurried to the coat closet, and came back with a folding cart.

Alex began loading food into the plastic bags. There were cans of tuna and salmon and sardines, two jars of herring in wine sauce, lots of cans of beans and soup, both of which he was tired of but he knew ultimately he'd be grateful for. There were jars of artichokes and hearts of palm.

"Saltines," Julie said. "Look, Alex. Peanut butter. Look at all these different kinds of jams and jellies."

"Not so loud," Alex said, ramming boxes of weirdly shaped pasta into a bag. Searching the lower cabinets, he found two six-packs of bottled water, which he put into the bottom of the shopping cart.

"Pretzels," Julie whispered as though Joan of Arc herself had materialized. "Hershey's Kisses."

Alex wished rich people ate more canned vegetables and fewer Hershey's Kisses, but he had to admit it was exciting to see candy and cookies. He located a bag of puffed rice and a box of Cheerios and threw them into a bag. They'd eat weird, but they'd eat.

The wagon was full and the cabinets were empty. Alex handed the keys to their apartment to Julie. "Go back home with the cart," he told her. "I'm going to try apartment eleven F. If I'm not back in half an hour, go there and see what's happening."

"Eleven F," Julie repeated. "In half an hour."

Alex escorted her to the service elevator, which hadn't moved since they'd taken it. He thought about taking it for the three floors down, but decided it was safer to use the stairs.

He walked down the three flights of stairs, and rang the doorbell to 11F twice before using the keys to get in. He found the living room furniture covered with sheets, as though waiting for the walls to be painted.

He looked around quickly to confirm the apartment was empty, then went into the kitchen and opened the refrigerator. Once again, he was assaulted by the glorious smell of rotten produce.

Having learned from Julie, he checked the hall closet and found a shopping cart waiting for him. He couldn't locate shopping bags, so he used trash bags instead. 11F wasn't too snobby to buy canned fruits and vegetables, he was delighted to discover. They had an especial fondness for Le Sueur green peas and apricots in heavy syrup. The sight of two big jars of applesauce made him salivate. He'd almost forgotten how much he liked it.

They'd feast tonight, he thought, and the image of Bri flashed through his mind. Would he have been so quick to send her away if he'd known there was food in the building for them to eat?

Yes, he decided. Bri was better off where she was, and so was Julie. What seemed like a lot of food now would dwindle to nothing in a matter of weeks. All he was doing was postponing the inevitable, not that he knew what the inevitable would be.

He finished loading the garbage bags into the shopping cart and said a quick thank-you to 11F and to Christ for the food that would keep them alive that much longer. He dragged the cart into the hallway, relieved no one had noticed, and found Julie standing by the service elevator, keeping the door open.

"I thought this would be faster," she whispered.

Alex grinned at her. "You're smart as well as cute," he said, and they began the ride down, back to a home with food.

Monday, June 20

"The archdiocese has requested me to inform the students at St. Vincent de Paul Academy that the school will remain open all summer long," Father Mulrooney announced before Mass. "If the longing for academia is insufficient enticement, the archdiocese wishes you to know that lunch will be served daily."

There was a murmur of excitement. Even Alex, who'd dined on pork and beans the night before, grinned. The lunches at school lately had mostly been canned vegetables and potatoes, but food was food.

"Nothing in life is free," Father Mulrooney continued. "Those students who wish to attend the summer program will be required to participate in a social welfare activity. Assignments will be made, and the students are to do their work before arriving at school. No completed work assignment, no lunch. That is the quid pro quo."

Alex spent most of the school day trying to decide whether he should skip suppers on days when he had lunch in school. He wanted Julie to eat more than once a day, but he wasn't sure how to swing that.

If things got really bad, maybe he could convince the school to let him take lunch home with him, and then he and Julie could split it.

At least Bri's eating, he told himself as he went to Father Mulrooney's office to find out his work assignment. He had definitely made the right decision. And because some food came in, it was probably the right decision to keep Julie at home. At least he hoped so.

"Ah, Mr. Morales," Father Mulrooney said. "I see you'll be staying on this summer."

Alex shrugged. "I have nowhere else to go," he said.

Father Mulrooney gave him one of his wrath-of-God looks. Alex had never known anyone to have such imposing eyebrows. "I trust one day you will appreciate the near sacred power of education," he said. "As the world collapses around us, it is learning and culture that will prevent us from becoming barbarians."

"Yes, Father," Alex said. "May I ask what my assignment will be?"

Father Mulrooney nodded. "You'll have the job of looking after some of the elderly and infirm parishioners in this neighborhood," he declared. "Every morning before you come to school, you'll check up on ten different people. You'll knock on their doors, speak to them briefly, and have them sign a sheet indicating that they did indeed have contact with you. Not a particularly onerous task, but one that calls for strong legs and heart, since many of these people live on the higher floors of their apartment buildings."

Alex pictured himself climbing the Alps on a breakfast of puffed rice. Assuming the puffed rice lasted another week, which he doubted.

"Thank you, Father," he said.

"Your finals are this week," Father Mulrooney said. "I trust you've been studying for them."

"Yes, Father," Alex said.

"Has there been any word from your mother?" he asked.

"No, Father," Alex said.

"Very well, Mr. Morales," Father Mulrooney said. "I look forward to seeing you here all summer long."

Alex smiled. It was funny to think of Father Mulrooney looking forward to anything except a hot night translating Cicero.

He walked over to Holy Angels and found Julie waiting for him. Usually when he ran late, she was sulky, but this time she was bursting with excitement.

"Holy Angels is staying open this summer," she said. "They'll feed us lunch if we work and then in the afternoon, there'll be classes."

"That's great," Alex said. "Do you know what work you'll be doing?" He wasn't going to let Julie knock on strangers' doors.

"We're all doing the same thing," Julie said. "They got permission to turn part of Central Park into a vegetable garden. Not a famous part. So we're going to garden in the mornings. Isn't that funny? Bri and I are both farmers. Then we'll go back to Holy Angels and eat lunch and have classes. Lunch! If I'm eating lunch, Alex, you can have my supper."

Alex stared at his sister. A month ago she never would have made that offer. Without even thinking about it, he gave her a hug. "Vincent de Paul is staying open, too," he told her. "I'll be checking on people to make sure they're okay. Then I'll get lunch and go to class, same as you."

"When we get home, I want an Oreo," Julie said. "To celebrate."

"Two Oreos," Alex said. "Let's live dangerously."

Thursday, June 23

With electricity pretty much gone in the evenings, Alex and Julie had gotten into the habit of going to bed early. Alex assumed Julie fell asleep right away, but he used the solitary time to listen to the radio, with the once missing earphones, and find out as much as he could about what was going on.

There were a couple of New York City stations that still broadcast, but Alex preferred the ones out of Washington and Chicago, which now came over loud and clear. He knew New York City still existed, but with all the horrible things happening throughout the world, it was comforting to hear that the rest of the United States, in spite of West Nile virus epidemics and earthquakes and blackouts and food shortages, was still surviving. He was reassured whenever the president addressed the nation to let them know the government was working hard to solve all the problems. One night he heard an interview with an astronomer about what would have to be done to get the moon back in place. Everything was still theoretical, but the brightest people in the world were working on it. Prayers, Alex was sure, would be answered.

"In New York City, the mandatory evacuation of the borough of Queens will begin on Saturday," the news broadcaster in Washington announced. "All municipal services there will end by Friday, July first."

Alex frantically turned the dial until he located a New York City station. The one he found talked of nothing else. Addresses were reeled off. Interviews with residents and city officials were played. Protests were described. It took almost an hour before Alex learned that all the hospitals in Queens were scheduled for evacuation no later than Thursday, June thirtieth.

Alex knew how implausible it was that Mami was still at St. John of God, working so hard she forgot to call her children for a month, but as long as the hospital existed, so did hope.

In a week, the hospital would be closed. In a week, Queens would no longer exist.

Did Puerto Rico still exist? Did the Morales family? Did hope?

Friday, June 24

Alex made a point of going to St. Margaret's that morning, after dropping Julie at school. He'd been avoiding reading the bulletin board there, figuring he was following events carefully enough with his nightly radio reports. But if the evacuation of Queens could slip up on him like that, he needed to pay closer attention.

Sure enough, the Archdiocese had sent out an information sheet about Queens. It was dated a week before, and it listed all the times and places for people to board buses that would take them to an evacuation center in Binghamton, New York. From there they could make their own arrangements.

Father Franco walked over to the bulletin board, armed with new information. Alex said hello.

"How are things going?" Father Franco asked.

"Pretty good," Alex said. "My sister and I will both be in school this summer." He didn't bother asking Father Franco if he'd heard anything more about Puerto Rico, or even about Bri. There was no point.

"I'll let you be the first to know," Father Franco said. "We just got the news this morning. Starting next Friday, July first, there's going to be a food distribution at Morse Elementary School, on West Eighty-fourth Street."

"You're kidding," Alex said.

Father Franco grinned. "Priests don't kid," he said. "We learn not to in our first year of seminary. It's going to be once a week, and every person in line gets one bag of free food. See for yourself."

Alex read the flyer. The distribution center opened at 9:00 AM, Fridays only. He'd miss Friday Mass at Vincent de Paul, but he could still do his work and get to school in time for lunch.

"How much food in a bag?" he asked. "Do you know?"

Father Franco shook his head. "My guess is not enough for a week's worth of meals," he said. "But any food is a blessing these days."

"And the limit is one bag per person," Alex said. "So Julie can come along and get a bag, also."

"It's set up that way so families can get food for everyone," he said. "You should definitely bring Julie with you."

A bag of food each, plus five days' worth of lunches. They wouldn't get fat as kittens, but at least they wouldn't starve.

Wednesday, June 29

The ten people Alex had to check up on lived in four different buildings between Amsterdam and West End Avenues and two on Eighty-sixth Street and two on Eighty-seventh. He was relieved none lived in his building, where he figured the fewer people knowing he and Julie were still there, the better.

The job wasn't too onerous—except for the fact that in one building the woman he needed to look in on lived on the eleventh floor and in another on the sixteenth, with electricity a novelty before noon. The people had all signed up and if they were startled or nervous because he was Puerto Rican and they weren't, they hid it well. Mostly they seemed pleased that anyone cared enough to climb all those flights of stairs. Alex made sure they were okay, asked if they needed anything in particular, and then had them sign the sheet showing he'd actually been there. It was tiresome having to smile and act interested, especially if they were chatty, but that was a small price to pay for a meal.

Julie, it turned out, loved gardening and she talked about nothing else. There was some concern because things were being planted late in the season, but most of the vegetables had gotten a head start in a greenhouse: string beans, corn, tomatoes, squash, zucchini, cabbage, potatoes, broccoli. Holes to be dug, fertilizer to be spread, plants gently bedded, watered, weeded. Marigolds to keep rats away. Sunlight, no matter how hot the day was, to be celebrated.

"And we'll get some of it," Julie said for the third time in three days. "Can you imagine? Real vegetables."

Alex couldn't imagine. He didn't even mind hearing about it day after day. It gave him something else to think about besides what kinds of food would be in the bag of groceries he and Julie would each be given on Friday.

He could see that Julie had lost weight, but he never asked her if she was hungry, and if she was, she didn't whine about it. Actually, she was whining considerably less than she had when things were normal. He guessed he had the moon to thank for that.

Thursday, June 30

Alex walked Julie to school, then raced back home. It made no sense, he knew, to sit by a phone that hardly ever worked, waiting for a phone call that wasn't going to be made, from a mother who was almost certainly long dead.

But that was what he did, just in case. Just in case on the last day that Queens, New York, existed, Mami might call her family to let them know she was still alive. He was glad he hadn't told Julie, since she would have insisted on staying home as well. This way at least she'd have lunch.

It was hard being alone in the apartment staring at an unringing phone, haunted by the food in the kitchen, which he wouldn't allow himself to touch, haunted even more by the image of his mother drowning in the subway that very first night.

He tried reading. He tried praying. He tried push-ups. He tried counting the cans of soup. He listened to the radio, using up the twenty-dollar batteries. The world was coming to an end. Well, that was nothing new.

In spite of the excruciating boredom, it physically hurt to leave the apartment, but he had to get Julie. The day was hot and sunny. The waning quarter moon seemed larger than the sun. At least it wasn't a full moon, he thought. Alex had really learned to hate full moons.

Julie's topic of the day was insecticides, their uses and history. Apparently Sister Rita, who was in charge of the garden project, felt the girls should learn as many different things as possible about the food chain. Alex was just relieved Sister Rita hadn't gotten to recipes. It was hard enough hearing all the talk about vegetables when he'd eaten lunch. But today, even moths and aphids sounded appetizing.

As soon as they got back, Alex picked up the phone to see if by some miracle Mami had left a message.

"What did you do that for?" Julie asked.

"Because I felt like it," he snapped.

Julie looked at him. "You're really weird, you know that?" she said.

Alex nodded. "Yeah, I know," he said. "It comes from living with you."

Julie smiled. "Well, I guess I'm good for something, then," she said. She went into her bedroom, leaving Alex alone in the living room with a phone that he continued to stare at, a phone that stared back at him.

chapter 7

Friday, July 1

Alex slept on the sofa just in case the phone rang.

At a quarter to seven he gave up and got dressed before
waking Julie. She would sleep until noon if she had her way,
and she inevitably woke up cranky. He hoped the bags of food
would include cereal. They were on the verge of running out,
even though all he allowed either of them to eat was half a
cup's worth.

That morning, though, Julie was too excited to eat, and
her excitement proved contagious. It wasn't like Alex had
really expected Mami to call, he told himself. Food was important. They raced through their morning rituals, and left
the apartment by seven-thirty. They'd be at Morse well before eight. It would be boring standing on line for over an
hour, but they needed to be among the first, since they had to
take the food back home and then Alex had to walk Julie to
Central Park, make his rounds, and get to school before lunch.

They walked down Amsterdam Avenue, figuring they'd
turn east on Eighty-fourth. Julie speculated about what food
they'd be given.

"Nothing'll be as good as fresh vegetables," she said. "But
that's going to have to wait."

"Anything'll be good," Alex replied. "But yeah, your vegetables will be the best."

"I wonder what Bri's growing," Julie said. "Her birthday's tomorrow. Can we call her?"

"We're not supposed to," Alex said. "No calls from home for the first month."

"If she was here, we'd get three bags," Julie said.

"But one of those bags would be for her," Alex replied. "So there wouldn't be more food for us, anyway."

"Wow!" Julie said. "Look at that line."

Alex had no choice but to look. From Eighty-fourth down to Eighty-third was a solid row of people.

"Do you think they're all here for the food?" Julie asked.

"There's a cop," Alex said. "Let's ask."

The cop was standing on the corner of Eighty-fourth and Amsterdam, bullhorn in hand. "Keep in line! Keep in line!"

Alex remembered Yankee Stadium and started to shake. He told himself this was a completely different situation, and willed himself to calm down and ask the cop where the end of the line was for the food giveaway.

"Eighty-second," the cop replied. "That's what I heard fifteen minutes ago."

"Come on, hurry," Alex said to Julie. They ran to Eighty-second, but it was clear the end of the line began south of that.

"How can there be so many people?" Julie asked as they finally located the end of the line on Eighty-first and Columbus.

"I guess everybody from the Upper West Side is here," Alex said. It certainly seemed that way. Unlike the line at Yankee Stadium, whole families stood in single file, some with little children tethered to their mothers to keep them from wandering off. Occasionally a cop strolled by and saw to it that there was no cutting ahead.

Julie stood immediately in front of Alex. "How long do you think this'll take?" she asked. "They're expecting me at the garden."

"How should I know?" Alex replied. It had never occurred to him there'd be so many people there. But even as they stood, the line grew longer, until it curved around Eighty-first Street. It was only slightly comforting to know they were no longer the last people in the line.

Most of the people kept quiet, although some of the children cried and yelled. The sun beat down on them, and Alex guessed the temperature was close to ninety. He saw an old woman faint and heard the panic from the family she was with. Eventually a man carried her off while his wife and their children stayed on line.

At nine o'clock everyone got excited, waiting for movement to begin, but nothing happened. There was no way of knowing if the distribution had begun three blocks north of them, and no one was willing to leave in order to scout ahead and report on what was happening.

Finally, at close to ten o'clock, the shuffling forward began. It took another hour before Alex and Julie reached Eighty-second Street. By then, the quiet orderly line had grown angry. Men and women screamed and cursed. The cops yelled into their bullhorns for order, which only fed the anger of the crowd.

At eleven o'clock one of the cops yelled through his bullhorn, "Everyone south of Eighty-fourth Street, go home! Everyone south of Eighty-fourth Street, go home. There's no more food! Go home! Go home!"

"What the hell do you mean there's no more food?" a man screamed, and rammed into the nearest cop. Soon hundreds of people were stampeding, swinging wildly, not caring who they hit in their hunger and their rage.

Alex grabbed Julie. "Hold on!" he yelled, terrified that she'd get carried off by the mob.

Julie clutched his arm.

"Run!" Alex screamed. The two ran in tandem, trying desperately to weave their way through the chaos. Someone or something cut his face, and he could taste blood in his mouth. He pushed and pulled alongside Julie. Then he saw a baby being trampled. Almost in spite of himself, he bent down, trying to save the child, and as soon as he did, he lost Julie.

"Julie!" Alex screamed. It was impossible to see her now. He prayed that she was where he thought she was, and threw himself into the mob.

"Grab my hand!" he yelled to her.

Julie reached out, but she was too short to reach him. Alex pushed an elderly man onto the street. He could feel the man's fingers crunch under his shoe as he grabbed Julie. Holding on to her as tightly as he could, he used her almost as a battering ram, making a path through the mob until they could run freely toward Central Park.

Julie was trembling, "It's okay," Alex said, giving her a hug. "We're safe now."

"Your face," Julie said. "It's all bloody."

"It's nothing," Alex said, running his fingers over the cut. "Are you all right?"

Julie nodded, but he could see she was badly shaken. She had the makings of a bad bruise on her right cheek, where someone must have elbowed her. Alex heard gunshots to their west. They were lucky they'd escaped when they did.

"I'll take you home," he said. "We should be okay on Central Park West."

"No," Julie said. "Take me to the garden. They're expecting me."

Alex looked at his watch. There was still time to get Julie there before they returned to school. If he didn't, she wouldn't get fed, and now there were no bags of food to fantasize about and only their limited supplies at home. "All right," he said. "But we'd better hurry."

They raced through the park, and found Julie's classmates hard at work weeding. She went to Sister Rita, who put her arms around her and held her close.

"I've got to get to Vincent de Paul," Alex said, uncertain whether he was telling the nun or Julie or if either of them cared. He went back to Central Park West, then walked south to the school, arriving there just before lunchtime.

But Father Mulrooney stopped him on the way to the cafeteria. "Where do you think you're going, Mr. Morales?" he asked.

"It's lunchtime," Alex said. "Oh, do you mean the cut? I'll take care of that when I get home. Right now I just want to eat."

"I'm sure you do," Father Mulrooney said. "But you haven't handed in your sheets for the past two days. What makes you think you're entitled to lunch?"

"Maybe I'm not entitled," Alex said. "But I'm hungry and I need to eat."

"You know the rules," Father Mulrooney said. "No work, no food. If you're that hungry, go home and eat there. Don't bother to return on Tuesday unless you have done your visiting and have the signed sheet to prove it. Now go, Mr. Morales, and spend the holiday weekend contemplating the virtues of obedience."

Alex longed to pick up the priest and throw him across the hallway. He felt the other kids staring at him, almost willing him to do so.

"Go," Father Mulrooney said.

Alex stood still for a moment. If he did anything but leave, he'd be kicked out of Vincent de Paul. Forget college, which most likely no longer existed. Forget graduating, which had lost any meaning. No Vincent de Paul meant no lunch five days a week. No lunch five days a week meant certain starvation.

"Excuse me, Father," Alex said, and did as he was told.

Saturday, July 2

"I'm calling Bri," Alex declared. "The hell with the rules."

Julie stared at him like he was a stranger. Maybe it was the cut on his cheek, he thought. It made him look like a pirate.

He picked up the phone only to find it was dead. That figured. But it wasn't like he had anything else to do. So for the rest of the day, at fifteen-minute intervals, he picked up the phone to see if it was working.

At four-fifteen, he got a dial tone. He pressed the numbers carefully, and was rewarded by the sound of a ringing telephone on the other end.

"Notburga Farms."

"Hello, this is Alex Morales," Alex said. "My sister Briana Morales is staying with you."

"Yes," the woman on the other end said. Alex pictured a nun like Sister Rita, warm and caring.

"Today's Bri's birthday," Alex said. "My sister Julie and I are calling to wish her a happy birthday."

"I'm sorry," the woman said. "But none of the girls are allowed calls from their families for another week. You'll receive a schedule in the mail telling you when you may call."

"But it's her birthday!" Alex protested. "We won't stay on long. Just wish her a happy birthday and hang up, I promise."

"I'm sorry," the woman said. "But the rules are for the good of all the girls. We can't make any exceptions."

Alex heard the click as he was hung up on. Julie looked at him.

"She wouldn't let me talk to her," he said. *"¡Maldita monja!"* Julie's jaw dropped. Then she giggled.

Alex was too angry to laugh. He could hear Father Mulrooney telling him to contemplate the virtues of obedience. He raised his hand to smack Julie into silence, then realized what he was about to do and stormed out of the apartment, not stopping until he reached Eighty-fourth and Columbus, where, standing in front of Morse, he screamed curses at the empty building.

Sunday, July 3

At Mass Father Franco instructed the parishioners to boil all their drinking water. Cases of cholera had begun to appear in the city.

"That includes the water you use for brushing your teeth," he reminded them. "And whenever you're going outside don't forget to put on insect repellent to ward off West Nile virus."

"Sister Rita always has us put on insect repellent before we go to the garden," Julie said somewhat smugly. "That's the rule."

"Good," Alex said, too hungry and too angry to care.

Tuesday, July 5

Alex returned to school with the ten signatures proving he'd made his morning calls. It had been a long, miserable weekend, not improved any with Monday being the Fourth of July.

There was very little food left. If he didn't get any on Friday at Morse, he had two choices: either to go without eating all weekend or without supper the following week. Otherwise, there'd be no food for Julie.

He never should have made that vow to Bri. He should have let Uncle Jimmy take Julie. He had little chance of surviving with her around, and if he died, what would become of her anyway?

But he was stuck with her, at least until he could find someplace that would take her in. Maybe the sisters at Holy Angels knew of something. If he could talk to one of them without Julie finding out, he would ask.

He took the list of signatures to Father Mulrooney's office. "Here they are, Father," he said.

Father Mulrooney barely looked at them. "Very well," he said. "I trust you spent the weekend in contemplation, Mr. Morales."

"I thought about a lot of things," Alex replied, trying to keep the anger out of his voice. "Including the virtue of compassion."

"Do you feel I showed insufficient compassion?" Father Mulrooney asked.

To hell with him and his damn eyebrows, Alex thought. "Yes, Father, that's exactly what I felt," he replied.

"And what's so special about you that you deserve compassion?" Father Mulrooney said. "You have shelter. You have food. You have family and friends. I'm supposed to feel pity for you because of a cut cheek?"

"You don't understand at all," Alex said. "I have shelter for as long as no one thinks about it. Once they do, once they realize my father is gone, they can throw us out. I have food only if I get lunch here. We're down to almost nothing at home, and I have to make sure my kid sister eats. She is my family right now, because my parents are both gone and my older brother is in the Marines somewhere and I sent my other sister to live at a convent with strangers. My cheek was cut because I got caught in a food riot, with my kid sister, and we ended up with no food anyway. I'm not asking you to pity me. I pity me enough for the two of us. But when one of your students asks you for food, you shouldn't say no and feel righteous about it. That's not what Christ would have done, and you know it."

"These are the worst of times," Father Mulrooney replied. "Rules are needed even more now. Without them there is anarchy."

Alex thought about the riot, about the baby, about the man he had trampled on. "Sometimes the rules don't work," he said. "Sometimes the rules cause the anarchy."

"I believe you were on the debating team," Father Mulrooney said.

"Yes, Father," Alex said.

Father Mulrooney nodded. "Very well," he said. "I'll think about what you just said."

"Thank you, Father," Alex said. "I'll think about what you said as well."

He walked out of the office to find Kevin Daley standing there. "I like your style," Kevin said.

"Thank you," Alex said. "I like it, too."

Wednesday, July 6

Kevin ran over to Alex as he was about to leave to get Julie. "I have something for you," he said, handing Alex a brown paper bag.

Alex peeked inside the bag and saw a canned ham.

"Where did you get this?" he asked.

"Don't worry," Kevin said. "No one'll notice it's gone."

"I can't pay you for this," Alex said, handing the bag back.

"I'm not asking for anything," Kevin said. "You're doing me the favor. I can't stand the stuff."

Alex couldn't begin to guess how many meals he and Julie could make from the ham. "Thank you," he said. "My sister and I . . . Well, I really appreciate it."

"*De nada,*" Kevin said with a grin, and Alex grinned back.

Thursday, July 7

Alex left Julie in the apartment and went up to check out the four vacant apartments for which he had keys. It took a fair amount of searching, but in 11F, he located a travel alarm clock. At some point he'd go through things more thoroughly, but this was all he wanted right then.

He set the alarm for 5:00 AM to make sure he had enough

time to get ready. Curfew ended at 6:00 in the morning. He didn't know how rigidly it was being enforced, but he couldn't afford to take any chances. Julie wouldn't survive if he ended up in jail or shot for curfew violation.

He knew he wouldn't sleep well anyway, since he'd be worried the alarm wouldn't go off. It would take a while before he trusted it. But it was the best he could come up with in a world with unreliable electricity. And knowing he'd done the best he could made him feel more positive about how things would go on Friday.

Friday, July 8

The clock worked. Alex dressed and left a note for Julie, explaining he was going to the food line and that she was to stay in the apartment until he got back. He was pretty sure she would. She'd gotten better about doing what she was told. Then again, he wasn't telling her what to do as much.

He left the apartment at 6:00 on the dot, and ran down the few blocks to Eighty-fourth and Columbus. When he got there, the line had already curved around Amsterdam, but it was nowhere near as long as it had been the week before. Alex wondered if it would get that way later, or if people had given up. It didn't matter to him, just as long as he got there early enough to get the bag of food. Two would be better, but after last week he wasn't going to risk Julie's life. One bag of food, he hoped, would be enough for the two of them for the weekend and for suppers for Julie for the week, if not for him. That didn't matter too much. He was getting used to being hungry. There were worse things.

The line began shuffling forward around nine-thirty. It felt good to see progress so quickly. By ten-fifteen Alex was inside the school, and twenty minutes later he had his large plastic bag of food to take home. Smooth and easy, he thought as he checked out the contents. A box of powdered milk. Two bottles of water. A can of spinach, two cans of green beans, a box of rice and another of instant mashed potatoes. A can of chicken and another of kidney beans. A jar of pickled beets and a can of fruit salad. Pretty much the same stuff he'd been getting for lunch. Enough for him to have something to eat over the weekend and for light suppers for Julie all week. She was getting creative with stretching their food, so maybe she'd get a couple of extra meals out of it for him.

He walked west rapidly, to get away from the crowd of people still waiting, and made it home without incident. He showed Julie what he'd gotten, then walked her to Central Park. On his way to Vincent de Paul he made his stops.

"See," Father Mulrooney said as Alex handed him his sheet. "I knew you could do it all."

Alex wasn't sure, but he thought Father Mulrooney actually smiled. Alex risked it, and smiled back.

Kevin was waiting for him in the cafeteria. "Where were you this morning?" he asked.

"On the food line," Alex said.

"Oh yeah, I heard about that," Kevin said. "One bag per customer, right?"

"Right," Alex said, savoring his lunch of rice and beans.

"How about if I join you next week?" Kevin said. "You could have my bag. My family doesn't need it."

"Are you sure?" Alex asked. "We have to get there as close to six as possible, then stand on line for four hours or so. And it can be dangerous. Riots. Shootings. It isn't fun."

"Fun's overrated," Kevin said. "Or hadn't you noticed."

Alex grinned. "I don't remember what fun feels like," he said. "So it's hard to tell. But we'd be very grateful for the extra bag next week."

"Gratitude's overrated, too," Kevin said. "Remember grilled cheese sandwiches?"

Alex nodded.

"Grilled cheese sandwiches were not overrated," Kevin said. "Neither were *Playboy* centerfolds. But that's about it, and I've still got the centerfolds."

"You must be a happy man," Alex said.

"I am what I am," Kevin said. "Same as I always was, only with a lot more time on my hands."

"Thank you," Alex said, thanking God and Chris Flynn while he was at it, for the peculiar gift of Kevin Daley's friendship.

Saturday, July 9

"Gin," Alex said, showing Julie his cards. "You owe me $3,870.12."

"I'm bored," Julie said. "What's happening in the world?"

"I don't know," Alex said. "What difference does it make anyway?"

"You can listen to the radio," she said. "When you use the earphones, I can't hear."

Alex hadn't turned on the radio since Queens died. He no longer cared what astronomers said, what the president said, what anyone said. All that mattered was food enough for him and Julie to survive another week. "I've stopped listening," he said. "We might need the batteries for something more important."

"Like what?" Julie asked.

Alex had no answer. "How about chess?" he asked. "I taught Bri how to play. I could teach you."

"But then you'll just beat me all the time," Julie said.

"I'll sacrifice a castle," Alex said. "A castle and a bishop and a couple of pawns, at least until you get the hang of it. Come on. It'll be something new for us to do."

"Will you get mad if I beat you?" Julie asked.

"No, of course not," Alex said. He knew he'd have to let Julie win occasionally or else she'd stop playing. And chess would give them both a way to kill time between their half cans of string beans and their half cans of corn.

chapter 8

Sunday, July 10

He and Julie spotted the man's body, curled up on the corner of Columbus and Eighty-eighth, at the same time.

"Is he asleep?" Julie asked. "Should we wake him?"

"I think he's dead," Alex said before his sister could walk over to check him out. "Leave him alone."

"Did he die on the street?" she asked. "How? Will anyone move him?"

"I don't know," Alex said. "Come on, Julie. We don't want to be late for Mass."

Tuesday, July 12

"The air tastes funny," Julie said as they walked to Central Park that morning. "It looks weird, too."

"Just cloudy," Alex said. The sky was a peculiar shade of gray. "Maybe a thunderstorm. What do you girls do if it rains when you're gardening?"

"I don't know," Julie said. "It hasn't rained yet."

"Don't stand under any trees," Alex said, trying to remember thunderstorm rules from his Fresh Air Fund summers.

"You really think it's going to rain?" she asked. "I know the sky's gray, but it doesn't look cloudy. It just looks . . ." She searched for the right word. "It looks dead," she said. "Like the sun died."

"That didn't happen," Alex said. "If the sun died, we'd be dead. Everybody instantly." He noticed a corpse lying in front of the dry cleaners, and another by the florist five doors down, rats nibbling on their faces. Alex wanted to cover Julie's eyes, but he knew he couldn't protect her forever.

"Do you think it's like this where Bri is?" Julie asked.

Alex shook his head. "She's in the country," he said. "Everything's green and pretty there. Why? Do you want to live in the country, too?"

"I want to stay with you," Julie said. "I don't care as long as we're together."

"Well, I'm not going anywhere," Alex said.

"Me neither," Julie said, linking her arm in his. "We're okay as long as the sun stays alive."

Friday, July 15

"How about those volcanoes," Kevin said as he and Alex stood on line, halfway down Amsterdam Avenue.

"What volcanoes?" Alex asked, although he knew he didn't want to hear the answer. He cursed himself for giving Kevin an opening to tell him what was happening in the rest of the world.

"Volcanoes erupting all over," Kevin said. "Millions dying."

Was that all? Alex made the sign of the cross and said a quick silent prayer for the newly dead souls. "Very sad," he muttered.

Kevin grinned. "That's what I like about you, Morales," he said. "Always thinking about others."

"What?" Alex grumbled. "They found a volcano in Central Park?"

"They might as well have," Kevin said. "Can you get your mind off of heaven and back on the Upper West Side? Look up and see the ashes."

"You mean the sky?" Alex asked. "It's gray. So what."

"So it's going to be gray for the rest of our lives," Kevin replied. "Which'll probably be over before I ever get laid."

"Well, we're talking decades, then," Alex said. "If you end up the last man on earth, you might stand a chance."

"With my luck, the last woman on earth'll be a nun," Kevin said. "Old, fat, and devout."

Alex laughed. "The air does taste funny," he admitted.

"That's the volcanoes," Kevin said.

"You're crazy," Alex said. "It's the crematoriums. They're working overtime now, all those extra bodies around. It's polluting the air."

"Great," Kevin said. "We're tasting dead body ash?"

Alex tried to decide which was better: dead body ash or volcanic ash. He voted for dead bodies. That way, at least, Bri would be all right.

"You really think it's volcanoes?" he asked, trying to sound sarcastic.

"That's what they're saying," Kevin replied. "Now that the moon's closer, the gravitational pull is stronger, so it's easier for the magma to get out. Volcanoes are erupting all over the place, even ones that were dormant, and the ash is going into the air currents everywhere. Here, Asia, Europe, maybe even Antarctica."

"Okay," Alex said. "So this is volcanic ash. How long before it leaves?"

"It doesn't," Kevin said.

There was a tone to his voice Alex had never heard before. "You're kidding, right?" he said. "You mean we're stuck with this ash for a few weeks. Great. All my shirts will end up gray. Father Mulrooney will love that."

"I'm just telling you what my father said," Kevin replied. "Volcanoes are erupting all over the world and the ash is cutting off sunlight. Sometimes in the past when there was a big volcanic eruption, the ash lasted for months or a year. Now with so many volcanoes, they think it'll be years before it clears up. If ever."

"No sunlight for years?" Alex said.

"Years," Kevin said. "But I think we'll all be dead before the sky clears up. Dad says it's going to get really cold really soon. Then crops'll die and everybody'll starve. It may take a while, but it's gonna happen."

"That can't be," Alex said. "Christ would never let that happen."

"Oh good," Kevin said. "I feel all comforted now."

"If you believe that," Alex said, "that we're all going to die anyway, why are you here? I mean right here, right now, standing on line for food you're not even going to eat?"

"Just racking up the brownie points for heaven," Kevin replied. "I figure being nice to you is my last best shot."

"If this is a joke, I'll kill you," Alex said. "You may think this is funny, but I have sisters I have to watch out for."

"Yeah, I know," Kevin said. "They're your ticket to heaven. And no, I'm not kidding. Ask Father Mulrooney. Ask anybody. You're the only person who doesn't seem to know." He turned to the woman standing on line behind him. "Excuse me, ma'am," he said. "But my friend doesn't believe volcanoes are erupting and throwing ash into our sky. Have you heard anything about that?"

The woman nodded. "It's been all over the news," she said. "They've been blowing up in the west. Lots of people died out there. I guess the worst one was in Yellowstone Park. The ash is so hot it starts fires, so people die that way, too. Fire and smoke and lava. We're lucky to be so far away, but I did hear the sky's that funny color because of it. I didn't know we were going to get cold, though, but now that you mention it, it has been chilly for July the past few days. And it was so hot up until now. The hottest summer I can remember, but I just figured that was a coincidence. I mean why would the moon make things hot?"

Alex tried to convince himself that this was a massive practical joke, that the woman who wouldn't shut up was Kevin's mother or his nanny or someone he hired for the sole purpose of scaring him.

"Not just the city," he said.

"No," Kevin said. "All over the world."

"And no more sunlight for months, maybe years?"

"Maybe ever," Kevin said.

Julie was right. Dammit, she was right. The sun had died, and with it, humanity died, also.

"No!" he said sharply. "I won't believe that."

"Okay," Kevin said, humoring him. "Maybe not ever."

"No, I mean that we're all going to die," Alex said. "All over the world there are Einsteins and Galileos. They're figuring things out." He paused as he remembered how certain he'd been that those great minds were figuring out how to get the moon back in place. Now they had volcanic ash to deal with.

"That's what I say!" the woman chimed in. "They're working on it right now. Sure, all those people out west died, and it's very sad and all that, but we've suffered, too, with the tidal waves and the cholera. The scientists are doing everything they can to make things better. *We* may not understand how—I mean, I flunked physics—but lots of people are solving all these problems. It's just a matter of time before things get back to normal."

Alex wasn't sure he knew what normal was anymore. But as long as he knew there was food enough for his sisters and himself, he wouldn't lose any sleep over volcanoes.

Tuesday, July 19

"I'm going to check the mail," Alex told Julie after school. The mailboxes were on the first floor, and for weeks Alex had avoided theirs, figuring the only mail they could possibly get was bills he didn't know how to pay. But since the sister had told him they'd be sending a schedule for phone calls to the convent, Alex had checked the mailbox daily, always finding it empty.

But today there were two postcards. "What?" Julie demanded. "What do they say?"

"This one's from Carlos!" Alex said. "No date. It just says, 'I'm all right. We're on our way to Texas.' He turned it over and saw a June 14 postmark. Over a month ago.

"Let me see," Julie demanded, and he handed her the postcard. "Do you think he's there? Is the other postcard from him?"

But it wasn't. It was from the convent, and it said, "Family members may call Briana Morales on Thursday, July 14, at 4:00 PM."

"Great," Alex said. "We were supposed to call Bri last week."

"But the postcard only got here today," Julie said.

"Yeah, I noticed," he snapped. "Let's go home and see if we can reach her now."

They went down the stairwell and entered the apartment. It was cold in there, not bone-chilling cold, but dank and lifeless. The sunlight had been faint for over a week, and Julie worried about her vegetables.

Alex walked over to the phone and was pleased to hear a dial tone. It might not be Thursday, July 14, but at least it was close to 4:00 PM. He dialed the number for the convent.

"Notburga Farms."

"Yes, this is Alex Morales," he said. "My sister Briana is staying there. I just got in the mail today a postcard saying I could call her last Thursday. I'd like to speak to her now."

"I'm sorry," the woman on the other end said. "If your appointment was to call her last Thursday, you needed to call her then. We'll send you another postcard to tell you the next time you can talk with your sister."

"No," Alex said sharply. "That's unacceptable. You're the ones who sent the postcard and you must have known how unreliable the mail is. I insist on speaking with my sister."

"The girls are all doing chores right now," the woman said. "Most likely Briana is in the stables. That's why we sent out appointment cards."

"I don't care if Briana is cleaning the stables for the birth of baby Jesus," Alex said. "Get her."

To his astonishment, he heard the woman say, "Find Briana Morales, and bring her here. Her brother's on the line."

"Thank you," Alex said. "I'll hold."

Still clutching Carlos's postcard, Julie stared at Alex. "Is she coming?" she asked.

Alex nodded.

Julie hugged him. "Let me speak to her," she said. "Please."

"Of course," Alex said. "But we probably won't have much time, so make it fast."

"I want to tell her about my garden," she said.

"Tell her you have one," he said. "Don't go into details."

It took close to five minutes before he heard anything, but when he did, it was worth the wait. "Hello?"

"Bri? It's Alex."

"Alex? Is it Mami? Is she home? Or Papi?"

"No," Alex said. "It's just us, me and Julie. We haven't spoken to you for so long, and we wanted to wish you a happy birthday and find out how you're doing."

"I'm fine," she said. "I just thought . . . I mean Sister Marie made it sound like it was an emergency, and I've been praying so hard for Mami and Papi to come home so I could, too; I guess I got carried away."

"Why?" Alex asked. "Aren't you happy where you are? Are they treating you okay?"

"Oh no, Alex, they're really nice to all of us," Bri said. "I love the farm. I love taking care of the goats and the sheep. We eat three meals a day. I even have a nickname. The girls call me Brush, because I came with so many toothbrushes. But I miss home anyway. It's like I never stop aching. How's Julie?"

"She's right here," Alex said. "Ask her yourself."

"Bri!" Julie shrieked. "Bri, is that really you? I miss you so much. I think about you always. Alex says I can't talk too long, but I want you to know I'm working in this big garden in Central Park. All of us at Holy Angels are, and I wish you were here working with me. Yeah. Really? Goats? Do they kick? And sheep? And breakfast? We don't eat breakfast anymore, but Alex gets us food every week and we eat lunch at school, so it isn't too bad. But sometimes I just hurt because you're not here. I know that's selfish and I pray for forgiveness, because you're happy and there are the goats and all that, but I still wish you were here. Yeah. Well, Alex is gonna kill me if I keep talking. No, we're getting along pretty well, actually. He lets me beat him in chess sometimes. Okay, here he is."

"You're doing all right?" he asked. "You're not hungry or overworked or anything?"

"I'm fine," Bri said. "How's everyone else? How're Uncle Jimmy and Aunt Lorraine? Have you heard from Carlos?"

"We just got a postcard from him," Alex said. "He went to Texas."

"Texas," Bri said. "Well, I guess that's closer than California. Does he sound all right?"

"You know Carlos," Alex said. "He sounds fine. Do you have classes, or is it all farmwork?"

"Oh no, we have classes, too," Bri said. "It's practically tutoring, because there are just us ten girls. We wake up at dawn and do chores, and then we go to chapel, and then we have breakfast and do some more chores. Then after lunch, we study for a couple of hours, and then it's back to working until evening chapel and suppertime. But after supper we talk and play games and have lots of fun. Some nights we sing. I don't know if I have a vocation, but I think I might. I pray for one, because it would make Mami so happy if I did. When she gets home. You haven't heard anything from her or Papi?"

"Nothing," Alex said.

"Well, I still believe in miracles," Bri said. "Talking to you is a miracle. Someday there'll be another miracle and Mami and Papi will come home."

"We tried to call on your birthday," Alex said. "We think about you all the time."

"I think about you, too," she said. "Sister Marie says I have to get off now. I still have to tend the sheep."

"Okay," Alex said, reluctant to hang up. "Bri, just one more thing. What's the weather like up there?"

"It's kind of strange," Bri said. "It was really hot and sunny at first, but a week or so ago, it turned gray and it's been that way ever since. Every night we pray to St. Medard to intercede and bring us sunshine, because without it, the crops will die and we don't know what we'll do if that happens. But it stays gray."

"It's like that here, too," Alex said. "Okay. Bri, we'll talk again soon, I promise. Take care. We love you."

"I love you, too," she said, and hung up.

Alex held on to the phone a second longer. Julie stared at Carlos's postcard.

"I wonder if the sun is shining in Texas," she said. "Maybe when Bri gets back, we should go there."

chapter 9

Monday, August 1

"Watch out for that rat," Alex said to Julie as they walked home from Holy Angels. Every day there were more dead, and the rats were getting larger and more daring.

Julie dodged the rat. "Sister Rita doesn't know what we're going to do if the sun doesn't come out soon," she said.

"She'd better think of something," Alex said. "The sun isn't coming back for a while."

"I really worry about the string beans," she said. "They're my favorites. Lauren likes the tomatoes best, because there are so many of them, but the string beans remind me of summer." She laughed. "I guess it is summer," she said. "Do you think it's cold like this at the convent?"

"Probably," Alex said. "It's probably getting colder all over the world."

"Brittany—she's my new best friend—she says her father says the strong will survive and everyone else will die and the world will be better because everyone'll be strong," Julie said. "Lauren says the meek will inherit the earth, not the strong, and Brittany says who wants the earth anyway, so the strong might as well have it."

"What do you say?" Alex asked.

But before Julie could answer, they both felt a rumbling underfoot, the way it used to feel in subway stations. Only now they were outside, and the subways weren't running anymore.

It lasted for about half a minute. Alex and Julie stood there, frozen. The few other people walking down Broadway had the same shocked looks on their faces.

"Earthquake!" a man shouted.

"You're crazy," another man said. "This is New York, not California."

"I used to live in California," the first man said. "I know what an earthquake feels like and that was an earthquake." He looked thoughtful. "Four point five maybe," he said. "Nothing serious."

"Was it really an earthquake?" Julie asked Alex as they resumed walking.

"I don't know," Alex said. "Does it matter?"

Tuesday, August 2

"Did you feel that earthquake?" Tony Loretto asked Alex and Kevin at lunch. "I was home, and my St. Anthony statue fell off the chest of drawers."

"I was on Broadway," Alex said. "My sister and I both felt it. Someone said it was an earthquake, but I didn't know whether to believe him."

"The quake wasn't too bad," Kevin said. "It's the tsunami that caused the problems."

"Tsunami?" Alex said.

Kevin shook his head. "Sometimes I think you live under a rock, Morales," he said. "The earthquake was in the Atlantic, and lower Manhattan got hit by a tsunami. Big one, too. Like the tidal waves haven't been enough to wash New York clean of sin."

"My mother works for the city," Tony said. "She says there are going to be mandatory evacuations south of Thirty-fourth Street by September. All of lower Manhattan is flooded now, and the water keeps seeping up. Big sewage problem, too. Coffins floating around. Huge health problems."

"From one tsunami?" Alex asked.

"And the tides," he said. "But they think there're going to be more tsunamis. There's a fault line in the Atlantic close to the city, and with the moon changing the gravitational pull, the earthquakes are going to happen pretty regularly, and that means more tsunamis. It isn't like Thirty-fourth Street is under water, but the water keeps moving uptown, pushing the sewage and the coffins, and things keep getting worse."

"Even the rats are drowning," Alex said.

"Nah," Kevin said. "They've been taking swimming lessons at the Y."

Monday, August 8

"So, Morales," Kevin said as they ate their cafeteria lunch of boiled potatoes and canned carrots. "What do you have planned for tomorrow?"

Alex shrugged. "The usual," he said. "Checking on the elderly, studying theology, fighting for survival. Same old, same old."

Kevin laughed. "You need something new and exciting in your life," he said. "Wanna go body shopping? It's my latest hobby."

Alex knew immediately that this would be something gruesome and disgusting, and if not illegal, most certainly immoral. "Sounds great," he said. "Where and when?"

"First thing tomorrow," Kevin said. "I'll meet you in front of your building around seven o'clock, so we can both visit our old folks first and get to school on time. I know how you hate to be late for classes."

"It's Father Mulrooney," Alex replied. "He makes St. Augustine come alive."

"Which is more than he can do for himself," Kevin said. "Speak of the devil . . ."

Father Mulrooney walked up to the two boys and gestured for them to stay seated. "I looked over your list just now, Mr. Morales," he said. "I noticed there were only seven signatures."

"Yes, Father," Alex said. "Only seven people answered when I knocked on their doors."

Father Mulrooney nodded. "That's to be expected," he said. "I just wanted to confirm. As time goes on, more of the elderly and infirm will die. And, of course, some will move away with their families. Have you any plans to leave New York, Mr. Morales?"

"No, Father," Alex said.

"Very well, then," Father Mulrooney said. "I'll see you later for Latin."

"Yes, Father," Alex said. With the lay staff gone and only three elderly priests left on the faculty, education at St. Vincent de Paul Academy consisted mostly of theology, Latin, and church history. Alex didn't mind that. There was something comforting in those subjects, a connectedness with the past that was soothing when the present was so bad and the future so terrifying.

"Body shopping," he said to Kevin. "Sounds like fun."

"You'll love it," Kevin said. "Bring a face mask and a garbage bag. I'll supply the latex gloves. And when you say your prayers tonight, ask for a fresh crop of corpses."

Alex took a deep breath. "Deal," he said, knowing whatever he'd be doing in the morning, Kevin, at least, thought it would prove worthwhile.

Tuesday, August 9

"Good," Kevin said at seven the next morning. "Face mask and shopping bag. You're set. Here are the latex gloves."

"I put some mentholated gel in this Baggie," Alex said, offering it to Kevin. "Put some under your nose. It helps with the smell."

"Good idea," Kevin said, rubbing it on. "Okay, then. Fifty-fifty, right? Whenever we're together, we split the booty. I'll show you where you can trade it in for food or whatever."

"Fair enough," Alex said.

"Okay, then," Kevin said. "Let's get going. Want to walk across on Eighty-eighth?"

"No," Alex said. "How about Eighty-ninth instead?"

Kevin grinned. "It's taboo, isn't it," he said. "Body shopping on the block where you live. I feel that way, too, even though I don't understand why. Father Mulrooney could probably explain it."

The boys walked up West End Avenue to Eighty-ninth Street. Though there were some bodies on West End Avenue, Kevin walked right past them.

"Nothing worth stopping for," he explained. "You get so you can tell. The glint of a watch is a big help. Watches are always good, but shoes are better, and anything in a wallet:

cash, IDs. Coats are a growth market. The colder it gets, the bigger the demand."

"And we can get food for all that?" Alex asked. The food in the Friday bags was getting sparser, and even though he skipped supper most nights and fasted on Saturdays, there was hardly enough for Julie.

Kevin nodded. "You see what I see?" he asked, pointing to a body lying halfway down the block. "We got a fresh one." He jogged over, Alex following him.

It was a man, fully dressed but no coat. "I bet he's been dumped within the past few minutes," Kevin said. "Hardly stinks at all, but maybe that's the menthol. You get the watch; I'll look through the pockets."

Alex begged God's forgiveness, and unstrapped the watch off the dead man's wrist.

"Nothing," Kevin said with a shrug. "Different families handle it different ways. Some of them think ID'll help some-how, before the bodies get dumped in the crematoriums. Others don't want people to know their address. Guess this one is one of them. Shoes next. Nice ones, too. They were crazy not to keep them for themselves."

Alex pulled the left shoe off the body while Kevin took care of the right one.

"This pair's for you," Kevin said. "Put them in your bag. Is that a body I see over there?"

"Yeah, I think so," Alex said. "A woman."

"Men are better than women," Kevin said. "Bigger de-mand for their shoes. But we should check anyway."

They crossed the street and walked to where the corpse was lying. Alex could smell it half a block down.

"She's a pungent one," Kevin said. "And useless. Look at that: barefoot already."

"How long do you think she's been there?" Alex asked, the bitter taste of bile in his mouth. Most of the woman's flesh had been eaten away, and he could see her partly gnawed bones sticking out from her dress.

"Couple of days probably," Kevin said. "Come on. I see a pile over there. Maybe we'll get lucky."

Alex followed Kevin to the corner of Eighty-ninth and Riverside Drive.

"See how wet Riverside is?" Kevin asked. "That's going to happen all over New York pretty soon. The wetter the city gets, the more people'll need nice dry shoes. Hey, it's a family. Look at that: Daddy, Mommy, and baby."

Alex stared at them. The mother's arms had loosened and the baby had fallen next to her. The father was lying on top of them both.

"I'm going to be sick," Alex said.

"Not on me," Kevin said.

Alex tore the mask off his mouth and turned away from Kevin. He had nothing in his system, but he retched violently. He felt Kevin's hand on his shoulder and turned back to him.

"If we don't take their shoes, someone else will," Kevin said. "See, they were all shot. I bet Daddy shot Mommy and the baby and then himself. Nice of him to do it on the street like this. Or maybe he carried them here and then shot himself. It doesn't matter. I wonder how baby stuff will do. I've traded some kids' things, but never any baby shoes. Booties, that's what they call them, I think."

Alex remembered when Julie was born. I'm doing this for her, he told himself.

"No coats," Kevin said. "But looky here. Daddy's got a brand-new gun."

Alex stared at it. "Are you going to trade it?" he asked.

Kevin shook his head. "It could come in handy someday," he said. "Okay if I keep it?"

"Take it," Alex said.

"Great," Kevin said. "You can have all the shoes, then. I'll keep Daddy's watch and you can have Mommy's."

"Don't call them that," Alex said.

"You don't have to be so touchy," Kevin said. "They're just bodies. Their souls are in heaven or hell or wherever. Probably not Catholics anyway. Come on, take her shoes off. You got to get used to it."

Alex took a deep breath, then pulled off the woman's shoes. Kevin unlaced the man's and took them off. "I'll do the booties," Kevin said.

"Thank you," Alex said.

Kevin shook his head. "You act like you never saw a dead body before," he said. "What are you, a tourist?"

"I don't know," Alex said. "It's different actually touching them."

"It'll be us soon enough," Kevin said. "Tell you what. Let's get our feet wet and walk up a couple more blocks. Then we'll turn this stuff in. When all this turns into loaves and fishes, you'll have a different outlook."

Alex doubted he'd ever feel differently about robbing the dead. But he followed Kevin up Riverside Drive. The water sploshed under his feet, and he could feel his socks getting wet. It was cold out, that weird, unnatural cold he couldn't get accustomed to.

"Do you think we'll ever be warm again?" he asked Kevin.

"We'll be warm enough in hell," Kevin said. "I've got a good feeling about Ninetieth. See? I told you." He ran down the block.

Alex caught up with him. This one wasn't so bad, just an

old dead guy. "He has glasses," he said. "Is there a market for them?"

"Good question," Kevin said. "Let's take them and find out. Nice watch. No coat, but I bet that sweater will be worth a can of Dinty Moore. Come on, help me pull it off."

Alex removed the man's glasses and put them in his garbage bag. He grabbed one arm and Kevin grabbed the other, and they pulled the sweater off the body. Alex took the man's loafers while Kevin searched through his pockets.

"Bad day for wallets," he said. "But on the whole a profitable morning's shopping. You ready to trade in the stuff?"

Alex nodded.

"Then let's get going," Kevin said. "Maybe we'll find some more stuff on the way over."

But the only corpses they saw were old and picked over.

As they turned up Ninety-fifth, Alex spotted a body. "See it?" he asked.

"Sure do," Kevin said.

Alex forced himself to go first. I'm doing this for Julie, he thought. God will forgive me. "He's got his coat on," he said.

"I bet he dropped dead of a heart attack," Kevin said. "Great find, Morales. See if there's a wallet."

Kevin removed the man's coat and Alex searched through his pants pocket for a wallet. "Found it!" Alex said.

"It's yours," Kevin said. "You take the shoes and the watch and I'll take the coat. Fair?"

"Fair," Alex said. "Is that a real Rolex?"

"Looks that way," Kevin said. "The coat's cashmere. Well, I guess death comes to all of us sooner or later. Just sooner for him. We should do pretty well for ourselves today."

"Where next?" Alex asked, relieved the body-shopping part of the event had ended.

"Harvey's," Kevin replied. "Our friendly neighborhood dealer. You'd better learn to love him, because he's got the monopoly around here."

The sign in front of the store said HARVEY'S TAILORING AND ALTERATIONS. Kevin walked in, with Alex following. An older man, bald and none too clean, sat behind the counter. The floor was covered with cartons and bags. It didn't look like a tailor's shop, and Alex doubted the man was the real Harvey.

"Kevin," the man said. "What you got today?"

"Goodies," Kevin replied. "Serious goodies. This is my friend Alex. You be nice to him, Harvey. He may be coming in here on his own, and I don't want to hear you've been cheating him."

"Any friend of yours is a friend of mine," Harvey said. "Show me what you got."

Alex and Kevin pulled everything except the gun from their bags.

"Nice," Harvey said, fingering the coat. "Very nice. Separate checks?"

Kevin nodded.

"Two bottles of vodka for your stuff," Harvey said. "Deal?"

"Three'd be better," Kevin said.

"Sunshine and good times would be better still," Harvey said. "Give me a day of sunshine and you'll get the extra bottle."

"Okay, two," Kevin said. "Now see what you can do for Alex."

"Can you use the glasses?" Alex asked.

"I don't know," Harvey said. "There hasn't been a market for them yet. But I can see how they might come in handy someday. The wallet's usable."

"And a Rolex," Alex said.

Harvey shrugged. "A watch is a watch," he said. "Now that nobody's clocks are running too well." He scratched his chin. "Tell you what," he said. "Seeing as you're new to the game, and a friend of Kevin, I'll give you a half dozen cans of mixed vegetables, plus two cans of tuna and a six-pack of water."

Alex saw Kevin give his head a quick shake.

"Look," Alex said. "I may be new at this, but I'm not stupid. For all I know that water is straight out of the Hudson."

"Like I'd do that to a friend of my buddy Kevin," Harvey protested. "It's imported all the way from Altoona."

"Even if I believe you, and I'm not saying I do, I still want more," Alex said. "I'll take all that for the wallet. Now what are you going to give me for these shoes and watches?"

"I've been saving this for a special occasion," Harvey said, pulling a box of Wheaties out of a carton. "You can tell yourself it's potato chips, only nutritious. Sprinkle it on the tuna and it's dinner fit for a king."

"The king wants more," Alex said.

"Now look," Harvey said. "This ain't the A&P. I gotta stay in business, too, you know."

"Fine," Alex said, pulling the wallet back. "I'll just take all my stuff to an honest businessman."

"What's your hurry?" Harvey said. "Where were we?"

"One useless six-pack of water," Alex said, "a half dozen cans of mixed vegetables, two cans of tuna, and a box of Wheaties. What else do you have in real food?"

"Okay, I'll throw in a couple of cans of salmon," Harvey said. "And this time and this time only, a can of chicken noodle soup."

Kevin gave Alex an almost imperceptible nod.

"Deal," Alex said. He pushed the wallet back and filled his garbage bag with the groceries.

"It's been a pleasure doing business with you," Harvey said. "Kevin, next time could you bring me a sucker? I gotta live, too, you know."

"Oh, admit it, you like the fight," Kevin said. "See you around, Harvey."

"You too, kid," Harvey said.

Kevin and Alex left the shop. "Walk fast but not too fast," Kevin instructed Alex. "People get killed for two bottles of vodka."

"You have a gun," Alex pointed out.

"Hey, yeah," Kevin said. "I wonder if it's loaded."

"How come you didn't trade for food?" Alex asked.

"Dad brings home the bacon," Kevin replied. "Metaphorically speaking, of course. He owns a trucking business. Daley Trucks. 'Rent Weekly. Rent Daley.' That's why we're still here. There's lots of stuff that needs to get moved out of New York these days. We're well taken care of."

"Who's the vodka for?" Alex asked.

Kevin scowled. "My mother," he said. "She prefers it to chicken soup these days. Dad hasn't figured that out yet, so I'm the supplier."

Alex and Kevin walked back to West End, then down the few blocks in silence, lost in thoughts about their families and their needs.

"Well, this is it," Kevin said as they reached Eighty-eighth Street. "Ready to go again tomorrow?"

"Do you think there'll be more bodies?" Alex asked.

Kevin laughed. "We could walk back to Riverside right now and find a couple of new ones," he said. "They're dropping like flies."

Alex thought about how he and Julie wouldn't go to bed hungry. "Same time?" he asked.

"Same time," Kevin replied. "Don't want to be late for theology class."

"Seven o'clock, then," Alex said. "Thank you."

"No problem," Kevin said. "I liked the company. Have a nice supper, Morales."

"We will," Alex said, and for the first time since speaking to Bri, he felt something that approximated happiness.

chapter 10

Monday, August 29

"Oh Alex!" Julie cried, flinging herself into her brother's arms and weeping.

Alex looked down at his little sister. In the three months since everything had happened, he had yet to see, or even hear, his little sister cry. Whine, complain, sulk, scream, and carry on, but never cry. Not when it became obvious neither Mami nor Papi was likely to return. Not when Bri left. Not when she learned Uncle Jimmy had left. Not when she was hungry or lonely or scared. And here she was sobbing for no apparent reason.

"What happened?" he asked as he gently led her away from Holy Angels. "Did someone die?"

Julie shook her head, but she continued to cry, and her tears cut into Alex, more even than Bri's ever had.

"It's the garden," she finally choked out. "We lost everything over the weekend. It's all gone, all the vegetables. All our vegetables. My string beans. I wanted you to eat my string beans, and now they're dead."

Alex pictured row after row of dead string beans lined up in Yankee Stadium. "You're crying over string beans?" he asked. "We got a can of string beans last Friday."

"I hate you!" Julie cried. "You don't understand anything."

"I understand plenty," Alex said. "I understand that you're upset, and I don't blame you. You worked hard all summer in that garden." He stopped for a moment, until the rustle of rats got him moving again. "They'll still feed you lunch, won't they?" he asked. "It's not your fault you can't work." He tried to control his panic as he worked through the options if Julie no longer got lunch.

"I don't know," Julie sniffed. "I don't care. I wish I was dead."

"No you don't," Alex said. "Don't ever say that. Don't even think it."

"You can't tell me what to think," Julie said, but at least she'd stopped crying. "I loved the garden. And it died because it's so cold. It's August, and I'm wearing my winter coat and gloves and my garden froze to death. And I hate corpses! I hate them!"

Alex didn't blame her. They had just passed one that had been decomposing in front of a pizza place for a week now, its flesh eaten away by rats. At first when the bodies started appearing, they got picked up within a day. But now there seemed to be no rhyme or reason to when the sanitation crews removed bodies. With more people dying and fewer trips to the crematorium, the corpses were becoming part of the city landscape. Good for body shopping but nothing else.

"If it's cold like this in August, what's it going to be like in December?" Julie asked.

Alex shook his head. "I don't know," he admitted. "But maybe by then they'll have figured out a way of clearing the ash from the sky. The scientists must be working on that."

"I thought they were working on getting the moon back in place," Julie said.

"First things first," Alex said.

"I hate the scientists," Julie said. "I hate the cold and the volcanoes and the moon. I hate everything."

Alex didn't bother to correct her because at that moment, he hated everything, too.

Tuesday, August 30

Alex walked Julie to Holy Angels that morning, but instead of dropping her off and checking on the five remaining people on his list, he searched out Sister Rita.

Like everyone else, she seemed older than when he'd seen her last. There was sadness in her eyes, and he realized she must be grieving for the loss of the garden as deeply as Julie.

"I'm sorry to bother you, Sister," he said. "But I need to know if Holy Angels will still be feeding the girls lunch every day."

"As far as I know," Sister Rita replied. "At least for the time being."

Alex smiled. "That's good news," he said. "Thank you."

Sister Rita gave Alex a long, hard look. "Your parents never came back, did they?" she said. "Julie doesn't talk about it, but you're responsible for her now."

Alex nodded warily. "We're doing fine," he said. "Briana's at a convent upstate, and Julie and I have enough to eat. I get lunch at Vincent de Paul, and we're okay."

"I'm not interfering," Sister Rita said. "Even if I wanted to, if I thought Julie would be better off, nothing's left. No foster homes, no group homes. At least not in the city. And Julie's doing as well as she possibly could under the circumstances. She's a very bright girl and very hard-working. You must be quite proud of her."

"Thank you, I am," Alex said, startled at the idea that Julie was someone to be proud of. But Sister Rita had a point. Julie was tough, and nowadays that was a virtue.

"For New York to have such a heavy frost in August, that's very bad," Sister Rita said. "I think there's going to be famine throughout the country this winter. Throughout the world. And with famine come epidemics. I think we're in for horrifying times."

Alex thought about his father most likely washed out to sea, his mother most likely drowned in a subway tunnel, his older brother who might or might not have made it to Texas, his uncle and aunt who might or might not have made it to Oklahoma, one sister living with strangers upstate, the other sister surviving on two small meals a day, and decided famine and epidemics were the least of his concerns.

"I'll keep that in mind," he said. "Thank you, Sister."

"Alex," Sister Rita said, and grabbed him by the arm. "Listen to me. What's bad now is nothing compared to what might be coming. Think of Joseph and the seven years of famine. The people survived because he prepared them for what was to come. The archdiocese is providing us with food now, but if the crops all die, there won't be any more coming in. Maybe things will be better down south. Maybe there's someplace safe in the world. But if you're planning to stick it out in New York, you'd better get as many supplies as you can, because food may stop coming and we won't be able to grow our own."

Alex remembered the baby trampled in the food riot. It was an image that haunted him. If things got that bad that fast on a day when at least some people got food, what would it be like if no food at all was available?

"I'll do what I can," he said. "Thank you again."

Wednesday, August 31

Alex dropped Julie off at school, made his rounds, then went to St. Margaret's, arriving there shortly after Mass ended. His wait to see Father Franco was much shorter than it had been earlier in the summer. Fewer people, fewer problems.

He didn't bother asking the priest if there was any more word from Puerto Rico. He'd stopped calling Nana's number even before his phone service had stopped—a couple of weeks before. Papi was gone, the same as Mami, the same as Carlos, the same as the sun.

"I haven't heard anything from my friends at the convent," Father Franco said apologetically. "But I'm sure everything is fine with Briana."

"That's not why I'm here," Alex said. "It's Julie. She's okay; we both are. We still have food and the schools are still serving lunch. But I don't know how much longer that will last, so I wanted to know if there's anyplace outside the city taking girls her age. She'll be thirteen in a few weeks, and she's strong and a good worker."

"You mean someplace like Briana's convent?" Father Franco asked. "That's the only one I know of."

"I mean anyplace," Alex said. "In case things get worse. The church must have someplace for girls to go, an orphanage or something."

Father Franco shook his head.

"There must be something," Alex said. "Can't you call the archdiocese and ask?"

"I'll tell you what I know," Father Franco said. "The past three months, the church has dealt with the dead and the dying. Only two Catholic hospitals are open in the city now. Most of the smaller churches have closed, and I've been told

St. Margaret's will close before New Year's. I just pray it will still be open for Christmas. The social service agencies have all closed. All the children in foster care were sent out of the city in July, and no new children are being accepted. This fall, most of the schools will close. There are federally run evacuee camps inland. The closest one I know of is in Binghamton. You and Julie could go there, but I don't think it would be wise to send her alone, and once you were there, you'd still have to find someplace safe to move to."

"Aren't there any convents taking in girls?" Alex asked. "I know she's too young to be a postulant, but there's got to be a convent somewhere that she could go to."

"The convents have been decimated," Father Franco said. "The ones on the coasts have been flooded out, and the ones inland have had to deal with earthquakes, volcanoes, and disease. No place is safe anymore, Alex. Julie's better off with you than she would be anywhere else. I thank the Blessed Virgin that we found a safe place for Briana. Perhaps in her all-merciful heart, she'll find such a place for Julie, also."

The Blessed Virgin *had* found a place for Julie, Alex thought as he left St. Margaret's. It was with Uncle Jimmy and Aunt Lorraine. Whatever happened to Julie was his fault. She lived in hell because of him, and he would spend eternity in hell for her suffering.

Thursday, September 1

Alex woke up thinking about the thirty-dollar flashlight, not sure why. Of all the decisions he'd made, not buying the flashlight was one he never regretted.

Then he remembered how he'd been told the cost of the flashlight was going to go up to forty bucks, and he figured it out. The value of what he brought in body shopping was going to go down as food became sparser. Today a pair of shoes was worth two cans of beans and a box of pasta. In a month he'd be lucky to get the pasta.

At first he thought he should leave the apartment and search everywhere for new bodies, but then he knew what the flashlight really meant. He had access to four apartments, all filled with things that could be used and bartered. Four treasure chests he'd been ignoring because somewhere in the back of his mind he thought taking things without permission was sinful.

He was damned anyway. He might as well take what he could when he could.

He let Julie sleep while he worked out the system. It had to be done today. He couldn't remember the last time there was electricity over a weekend, so he couldn't wait until then. Friday morning was food line, and Friday afternoon was probably the best time to barter what he could, since he suspected a lot of Harvey's supplies conveniently fell off the food line truck Friday mornings.

As he dressed he thought about asking Kevin to help him unload the apartments, but decided against it. Kevin had been great, but it would be too much temptation.

Still, he felt guilty body shopping with his friend that morning. But guilt was as much a part of his life as cold, hunger, and grief. And if Kevin noticed his mind was elsewhere, he didn't say anything. The two found a fair number of shoes, watches, and coats, which they traded in for soup, mixed vegetables, black beans, and rice for Alex and vodka for Kevin.

Julie was up when he got back. "We're not going to school today," he said, handing her the groceries. "We're spending the day going through the apartments, taking everything we can barter or use and bringing it all down here."

"What about lunch?" Julie asked.

"I don't know," Alex said. "Do we have enough to get us through to Tuesday?"

Julie checked out what Alex had just brought in and what remained in the cabinets. "We can stretch the rice and beans for two meals each," she said. "And we can each have a can of soup for supper tomorrow. We have the can of mixed vegetables and a can of carrots and a can of peas. Won't you get food tomorrow?"

"I hope so," Alex said. "But we can't count on it."

"Then no lunch today," Julie said. She scowled. "I used to like holidays. Now they just mean no lunch."

The refrigerator began its useless whir, and the light that Alex always left on in the living room began to shine. "We've got to use the electricity while we can," he said. "Let's get the shopping carts and garbage bags. We can risk taking the elevator up, but we'd better be careful, because once it goes off, it might stay off until Tuesday."

Julie looked thoughtful. "Maybe we should take all the stuff to one of the upstairs apartments," she said. "If someone looks into our windows, they could see the stuff here."

Alex hadn't thought of that. He looked at the iron grilles on their windows, which prevented people from breaking in. But if someone was desperate enough, he could break the doors down.

"We'll keep the curtains closed," he said. "We're not getting much natural light anyway. And we can cover the windows with blankets, once we have some extra ones. That'll keep some of the cold air out, and no one will be able to look in. I'd rather have the stuff here, where we can control it."

Julie dug out the garbage bags from under the sink. "Okay," she said. "What are we looking for?"

"Anything and everything," Alex replied. "The food's all gone, but I bet there's plenty of coats and sweaters and shoes. Blankets and quilts. Flashlights, candles, batteries, matches. Socks. Liquor. Whatever's in the medicine cabinets. I'll trade what we can't use. We'll need to move fast but be thorough."

"Are things going to get worse?" Julie asked, and Alex could hear the suppressed panic in her voice.

"Yeah, I think so," Alex said. "If you can believe that."

"I don't want to eat rats," Julie said. "Or dead people."

"Me neither," Alex said. "Let's get going so we won't have to."

Monday, September 5

"Julie!" Alex said, unable to keep the irritation out of his voice. "My shirts are filthy. Can't you do a better job with them?" He told himself no one was as clean as they had been, but with school officially starting again the next day, he wanted to look as respectable as possible.

"Why don't you do your own damn laundry," Julie said.

Alex grabbed her arm. "Don't ever talk to me like that again," he said. "Never."

"Or what?" Julie said.

"Or you won't eat," Alex said.

Julie stared at him in horror. "You don't mean that, do you?" she asked. "You'd keep all the food for yourself?"

Alex tried to remember what it felt like not to be hungry. Bri wasn't hungry, he thought. She was fat as a kitten. If he'd let Uncle Jimmy take Julie, maybe she'd be fat as a kitten, too.

"I didn't mean it," he said, releasing Julie from his grasp. "As long as I have food, you'll have food."

"It's hard washing clothes by hand," Julie said. "Maybe I should stay home from school, when the electricity is on. Then I could use the washer and drier."

Alex shook his head. "School is more important," he said. "I'll wash my own clothes. That way if they're not clean enough, I'll have only myself to blame."

"Papi never washed clothes," Julie said.

"Yeah, well, I'm not Papi," Alex said. Papi would never have threatened to starve a child, no matter how dirty his shirts might be.

Tuesday, September 6

Alex was relieved to find that at least some of the guys he'd gone to school with in the spring had returned for fall classes. He did a count at Mass and figured the chapel was about a third full—not bad given that there was no new batch of seventh graders to replace the seniors who'd graduated.

Father Mulrooney welcomed everyone back and said that, once again, attendance at Mass was mandatory. The faculty had increased by two, with a couple of nervous-looking seminarians joining the three elderly priests who'd held the fort during the summertime. Mr. Kim would teach all the science classes, and Mr. Bello all the math classes. There were no more requirements for lunch; if you were at school that day, you would be fed. Alex was relieved. It had grown increasingly more difficult and depressing to check up on the people on his list. He was reluctant to admit it, but physical exertion was getting harder—maybe because he was eating so little or maybe because the air quality was so bad. And although he hated to think about it, the bad air and the lack of food was probably killing off some of the people he'd been checking up on all summer.

He had lunch that day with Kevin, Tony Loretto, and James Flaherty. James had spent the summer in Pennsylvania with his grandparents, and it felt strange to see him back. It was hard to remember that people with money could come and go, and that gone didn't always mean dead.

"What's it like out there?" Alex asked as he devoured in three bites his lunch of red cabbage and baked beans.

"Bad," James replied.

"So's lunch," Kevin said, but Alex noticed he ate everything on his plate as fast as Alex had.

"Bad like how?" Tony asked. "Earthquakes? Floods?"

James shook his head. "It's dead there," he replied. "Here we're still getting food shipments and there's electricity most weekdays. There, nothing. It's a little warmer here, too, if you can believe it. The city traps the bad air and the warm air. Out there, without the skyscrapers, the air stays cleaner but colder. But the crops all died, and a lot of the farmers were talking about how they were going to have to slaughter their animals, since there wouldn't be enough feed for them to get through the winter, even assuming things get better next spring."

"Which they won't," Kevin said.

"I don't think so, either," Tony said. "Not around here, anyway."

"But at least in the country, they don't leave dead bodies lying around everywhere," James said with a shudder. "That's new since I left the city. How do people put up with it, the corpses and the rats?"

"After a while you don't really notice," Tony replied. "You

have to be careful about the rats, in case they're rabid, but for the most part they're okay, too. They eat the bodies and leave everyone else alone."

"I'm surprised you came back," Kevin said. "I thought everyone who left would stay gone."

"My father can't get out yet," James said. "He's a cardiologist. I could have stayed with my grandparents, but there wasn't enough food for all of us. So I'm back until they give Dad the okay to go."

"What's going to become of your grandparents; do you know?" Tony asked.

"We're not sure yet," James replied. "The rules keep shifting about who can get in and who can't."

"I thought the evacuation centers were open to everybody," Alex said.

"Are you crazy?" James said. "Dad would never send his parents to an evac center."

"Don't mind Morales," Kevin said. "He lives under a rock."

"Shut up, Kevin," Alex said. "What's wrong with the evacuation centers?"

"What's *right* with them is more like it," James said. "Half of New York City is crammed into the Binghamton one. The wrong half, at that."

"No one who has a choice goes to an evac center," Tony said. "Not that there aren't a lot of decent people stuck there."

"The decent people don't stand a chance," James said. "Crime, disease, not enough food."

"Sounds like home," Kevin said, but no one laughed.

"How do you know?" Alex demanded. "You ever been to one?"

"My mother has," Tony replied. "A couple of weeks ago

for her job. She was there with two armed bodyguards, and she still said she was never so scared in her life. The one in Binghamton was set up to hold thirty thousand people and it's already at a hundred thousand. The National Guard is supposed to police the place, but they're stretched too thin, and if you wander off looking for food, the townspeople shoot to kill. No showers, no toilets, and now people are freezing to death. You're lucky, James, your father hasn't been assigned to work at one. People are dropping like flies because there aren't nearly enough doctors."

"My father has too many powerful patients," James said. "Wherever they go, we'll go. And trust me, Alex, it won't be to any evac center."

Tony nodded. "Dad won't leave Mom," he said. "And they're not sending my brothers and me off without them, so we're not going anytime soon."

"I'd rather be here," Kevin said. "Corpses and all."

"Me too," James said. "New York, the people may be dead, but at least the city's alive. In the country, everything's dead."

Wednesday, September 7

For supper that night, Alex and Julie shared a can of sauerkraut.

"Sister Rita says vegetarians live longer," Julie said. "She says it's a good thing we eat the way we do."

"I don't need any lectures from sainted Sister Rita about how good we have it," Alex said. "I bet she's eating steak every night while we're starving to death."

"She isn't!" Julie cried. "Are we? Starving to death, I mean?"

"No," Alex said. "I'm sorry. I have things on my mind."

"Can I help?" Julie asked.

Alex shook his head. "Just a problem I have to work out on my own," he said.

Julie carried the dishes and forks to the sink. Alex watched—while trying to come up with a way to keep her alive and safe. When he finally acknowledged there was none, he went into his bedroom, and threw his missal against the wall.

chapter 11

Monday, September 12

Alex could tell as soon as they approached the apartment that something was wrong. The blanket he'd nailed to the inside of the living room window was flapping.

Julie had been right, he thought. Someone broke in. All the food that he'd gotten from Harvey—and he'd pretty much wiped out Harvey's supplies—might be gone. The bottles of booze he'd held in reserve, the blankets and quilts, the two sleeping bags he'd been thrilled to find, the box of cigars, the coffee, the beer, the aspirin and vitamins and sleeping pills and cold medicines and antacids. The electric heater, the heating pad, and the electric blanket. The fur coats, the wool coats, the sweaters, and boots. He'd been an idiot to keep things downstairs. If Papi or Uncle Jimmy, or even Carlos, had suggested keeping the stuff in one of the upstairs apartments, he would have agreed. But it had been Julie, so naturally he'd overruled her.

Julie. What was he going to do about her? He couldn't let her go into the apartment, but it was equally unsafe to have her stand outside.

"Something's the matter," he whispered, pointing to the

flapping blanket. "Go into the lobby and take the stairs to the third floor. Go as fast as you can, but quietly, and don't slam any doors. I'll get you when it's safe. Now move!"

Julie did as she was told. Alex waited five minutes, to make sure she was safely upstairs, then unlocked the outside door to the basement. If it was only one guy in there, the element of surprise might be enough to chase the burglar away. With shaking hands, he unlocked the door to the apartment, and yelled through the door, "Get out now! I have a gun!"

"Alex? Don't shoot. It's me, Bri!"

"Bri?" Alex shouted. "Are you all right?"

"I'm fine," she said. "I'm home. It's just me."

Alex raced into the apartment and hugged his sister hard—until she began coughing.

"Bri, what's happening?" he asked. "Are you okay?"

"I'm okay," she said, gasping. "Really I am. Where's Julie? What happened?"

"Oh God, I hid her," Alex said. "Stay here. Don't go away." He laughed. "Wait till she sees you! Hold on. We'll be back in a couple of minutes." Reluctantly he left Briana, then ran up the stairs to the third floor.

"Everything's okay," he told Julie. "Come on down."

"Maybe you should have nailed the blanket better," Julie said as they went back downstairs.

Alex laughed. "Maybe I should have," he agreed. He couldn't remember ever having been so happy. There was food in the house, supplies left to barter, and his sister back. For once when he thanked Christ for his blessings, he would really mean it.

"Julie!"

"Bri? Bri, is that really you?"

Bri began coughing again. "It's nothing," she choked out. "I'm just so happy."

"How about some tea?" Alex asked. "Julie, boil some water for tea."

Julie ran into the kitchen and put the kettle on.

"I can't believe you're here," Alex said, grasping Bri's hand. "What happened? When did you get here?"

"About an hour ago," Bri whispered. "I was so scared. The blankets on the windows and all those things in Mami's room . . . Is she back? Is Papi?"

Alex shook his head. "Nothing new from Carlos, either," he said.

Julie popped back into the living room. "It's the cold, isn't it," she said. "Your crops froze, too."

Bri nodded.

"So they sent you home?" Alex asked. "They don't want to feed you anymore, so they dumped you?"

"No, Alex, it wasn't like that," Bri said. "The sisters were eating less so we'd have enough. They were wonderful." She began coughing again. "My bag." She gasped.

Alex grabbed her bag and handed it to her. She dug through it and pulled out something. Alex recognized it as an inhaler. He'd gone to school with kids who had asthma. But Bri wasn't asthmatic.

Bri inhaled deeply and stopped coughing. "Some of us got sick," she said. "Me and two other girls. Sister Anne got us to a doctor, and he said we have adult-onset asthma. It's the same as regular asthma, but it starts later. The doctor said we'd be fine except for the air. It's so ashy now, and we were outside all day and it was too much. The sisters couldn't keep any girls who were sick, so they drove us back to New York. Two other girls, too, whose parents wanted them back. They tried to call you, but the phone isn't working."

Alex nodded. "This asthma," he said. "Will it go away now that you're not working outdoors?"

"I don't think so," Bri said. "Not until the air clears up. The doctor said I shouldn't go outside any more than I have to. He said there used to be medicine to prevent asthma attacks, but that's all gone now. He gave us inhalers, but he said we should try to avoid attacks by staying indoors and not exerting ourselves and not getting excited. Only I got so excited seeing you." She smiled. "It was worth it," she said. "Oh, Alex, Julie, I'm so happy to be home!"

Bri would need food, Alex thought, and medications. She wouldn't be able to walk to school, so she couldn't get lunch there. He'd have to take Julie with him on the food line and hope that Kevin kept going. Even with what was in the apartment, and three bags of food rather than two, he'd have to give up supper most nights of the week if Bri and Julie were both to eat twice a day.

His sister wasn't fat as a kitten, he saw. She was pale and as thin as she was when she'd left last spring. Having her gone all summer had worked out well for him and Julie, but perhaps not so well for Bri herself.

But then Bri smiled. "I knew you'd keep your vow," she said. "I knew you'd be here when I got back. I'm never leaving again. Never."

Alex looked at his sister. Things will work out, he thought. The Blessed Virgin returned his sister to him. Through her intercession, they would find the way to survive.

Wednesday, September 14

As Julie and Alex walked home from school, they saw a man leap from a seventh-story window, falling to the sidewalk about twenty feet from them.

Alex grabbed his sister, feeling her thin body shake under her winter coat. "Hurry," he said, pulling her along as he raced to the body. "You get his shoes, and I'll look for his wallet and his watch."

Julie stared in horror at Alex. He pushed her toward the man's feet.

"Alex, I think he's still alive," Julie said. "I think he's still breathing."

"What difference does that make," Alex said. "He'll be dead soon enough. Now take his shoes."

Julie bent over and pulled off the man's shoes. Alex removed the man's watch, then ransacked his pockets, finding nothing.

"Help me with his sweater," he said. "You take the left arm; I'll take the right."

Julie did as she was told, and they pulled off the sweater. Alex took it and the shoes. "No wallet," he told her, "but this stuff should be good for a couple of cans of soup."

"What are you talking about?" Julie cried.

"What do you think I do every morning?" Alex said. "This is how I feed us."

"Does Bri know?" Julie asked.

"No," Alex said. "And you're not going to tell her."

Julie stood absolutely still. "Do you want me to go with you?" she asked. "In the mornings?"

"No," he said. There was no need for this to be on both their consciences.

Friday, September 16

"So much food!" Briana said as Alex unloaded two trash bags onto the kitchen floor. "Three bags this morning, and now all this. Where did it all come from?"

The three bags came from Alex, Julie, and Kevin standing on line for almost five hours in below-freezing weather. Fewer people were waiting on the food line, but fewer people were distributing the food as well. By ten that morning, everyone was coughing, but no one left his place. Kevin took Julie to Holy Angels while Alex took the bags home for Bri to put away. Then he gathered up four bottles of wine found in apartment 11F, one box of cigars from 14J, and a man's coat, watch, and shoes, peeled off a fresh dead man on Alex's walk home. Harvey turned down the watch, saying the market for them had dried up, but he was happy about the wine and cigars, and gave Alex enough food to last a week or more if they were careful. Alex was most excited about the two cans of tuna and one of salmon. The hell with vegetarians living longer.

"Things must be all right if there's so much food," Bri said, putting the groceries away in the cabinets, making them look full and normal again. "Oh, Alex. Powdered eggs! They're almost as good as real eggs."

"Did you have real eggs on the farm?" he asked. The temperature in the apartment was about fifty degrees, which was where he'd set the oil burner thermostat, but Bri made things feel warm and sunny again.

Bri nodded. "Every day at first," she said. "Toward the end, the hens stopped laying. It got harder to milk the cows, too. I pray for the sisters and the girls who stayed on. I think we have it easier."

"That's what I've heard," Alex said.

Bri turned around to face her brother. "Don't stop believing in miracles," she said. "*La madre santisima* is watching over us. I know she is because I prayed to her every night that I would come home and find you and Julie here."

Alex thought about all the prayers he had said in the past four months and how few had been granted. But why should God or even the Blessed Virgin listen to his prayers, he asked himself, when a can of tuna fish was more important to him than the suffering of Christ.

Sunday, September 18

Bri's face glowed as they approached St. Margaret's, and Alex knew he'd made the right decision, letting her go to Mass. Even when Bri slipped off her face mask and used her inhaler because she was starting to cough, Alex felt sure he'd done the right thing. It might be safer to keep Bri indoors, but her life had no meaning without the Church.

His mind wandered as it always did nowadays in church. If crops throughout the U.S., throughout the world for that matter, died from lack of sunlight, how long would New York City continue to get food? If Holy Angels or Vincent de Paul closed, where would the food come from to feed Julie and himself? If Kevin decided he no longer wanted to wait on line on Fridays for food he didn't even eat, would two bags be enough?

And that was the easy stuff. Alex chose not to think about the heating oil running out, or about the Hudson seeping eastward and reaching West End Avenue, or what he was going to do with his sisters when they'd have to leave New York.

Live for the moment, he told himself. Look at Bri. See how happy she is. She's no fool. She knows better than you do how fragile life is. But she rejoices in her faith. Can't you do the same?

The answer was no.

Monday, September 19

That morning Alex had told Julie he'd be late picking her up from school and she was to wait for him. When the school day ended, he went to Father Mulrooney.

"I'd like you to hear my confession," Alex said.

Father Mulrooney's eyebrows did a high jump. "Mr. Morales, it's been many years since I've heard confessions," he said. "Surely you can confess to the priest at St. Margaret's."

Alex shook his head. "He'd be too easy," he said.

"One of the other priests here?" Father Mulrooney suggested.

"No, Father," Alex said, politely but firmly.

Father Mulrooney paused. "Very well, then," he said. "I suppose this office has been used as a confessional before."

"Forgive me, Father, for I have sinned," Alex said. "It's been five months since my last confession."

Father Mulrooney nodded.

"I pushed an old man to the ground," Alex said. "I stepped on him and I probably broke all his fingers. And I didn't save a baby from being trampled. They may both have been killed, for all I know."

"Did you choose not to save the baby?" Father Mulrooney asked. "Did you push the old man to the ground willingly and with malice?"

"There was a riot," Alex said. "I wasn't thinking. If I saved the baby, I might have lost my sister. If I hadn't pushed the old man, I definitely would have. I guess I did it willingly, but I don't know if there was malice. But that's not my only sin, not by a long shot. I steal from the dead. I take everything I can and barter it for food. I made my sister do it, too. I don't even care anymore if they're dead or alive, just as long as I can get food for us. And I don't just do it for my sisters. I eat my share."

"Are you angry at God?" Father Mulrooney asked.

"No," Alex replied. "I almost wish I was. It's like with my parents and my brother. They're all gone. Carlos is probably alive, but I don't even know that for sure. Sometimes when I think about them, the pain and the anger are so strong that I can't bear it. So I turn the feelings off. I just stop feeling. And that's what's happening with me and God. I used to pray and mean the words, but now they're just words. Because if I let myself feel the pain and the anger, I think it might kill me. Or I might kill someone else. I know it's wrong to feel that way about God and I know it's wrong to not feel anything. I hate it. I don't hate God. I hate not loving Him."

"I think it would take a saint to love God under the circumstances," Father Mulrooney said. "And in the forty years I taught at Vincent de Paul, I never once came across a seventeen-year-old saint. If you're guilty of anything, Mr. Morales, it's the sin of pride. Your sufferings are no worse than anyone else's and your guilt is certainly no greater. You're a young man who has set very high goals for himself and has worked hard all his life to achieve those goals. I appreciate that. I wish I had had more students like you. But now your goal must be to stay alive, to keep your sisters alive. Christ understands suffering. His heart is filled with love for you. He asks only that your suffering bring you closer in understanding to His.

If God wanted a world filled with saints, He never would have created adolescence. There now. Have I been too easy?"

Alex wiped away tears. "I don't know," he said, trying to smile. "What's my penance?"

"Go to chapel and pray for humility," Father Mulrooney said. "Pray that you may accept the fact you're only seventeen and cannot understand all that is happening. Offer Christ your gratitude that you and your sisters have lived to see this day. But you must mean the words. God will know it if you don't. He can forgive anger, but He has no love for hypocrisy."

"Yes, Father," Alex said.

"And do something that will make your sisters happy," Father Mulrooney said. "Their joy will be a true gift to God and His gift to you."

Alex nodded. He made his act of contrition and listened as Father Mulrooney gave his sacramental absolution.

There were two boys in chapel silently praying when he got there. Alex genuflected at the cross, then knelt in one of the pews. *Forgive me for the sin of pride,* he prayed. *Forgive me for ever thinking I can do what I must alone, without Your guidance and Your love.*

Tuesday, September 20

"Julie, could you go into Mami's room and redo the list of everything that's there?" Alex asked after school. "The blankets, the coats, the batteries. Make one list for blankets, one for clothing, and one for everything else. Don't leave anything out."

"Why can't Bri do that when we're in school?" Julie asked.

"Because I asked you to," Alex said. "Now, please."

Julie scowled, but she carried her notebook and pen into

Mami's bedroom. Alex gestured to Bri to join him in the kitchen.

"Julie's birthday's coming," he whispered. "How about a surprise party for her?"

"Can we do that?" Bri asked. "A real party? Should we?"

Alex grinned. "We can and we should," he said. "But I can't do it on my own. I know you got cheated out of a birthday party, so I hope you don't mind making one for Julie."

"I'd love to," Bri said. "Oh, Alex! A real party. Can we have boys?"

"Would Julie like that?" Alex asked.

Bri rolled her eyes.

"I'll find the boys, then," Alex said. "Just tell me what you think I should do, and I'll do what I can to make it happen."

Friday, September 30

"Come on," Alex said to Julie. "Let's get going."

"But it's my birthday," Julie whined. "I don't want to have to go to church on my birthday."

"Julie," Alex said. "You know Mami always went to St. Margaret's on all our birthdays to say a special thank-you to Jesus and Mary. We need to light a candle for her and Papi and Carlos. Stop dawdling."

"Is Bri going?" Julie asked.

Briana shook her head. "I'll stay home and prepare a special birthday dinner for you," she replied. "It isn't every day a girl becomes a teenager."

"We'll be back in an hour or so," Alex said. "Come on, Julie. Scarf and gloves."

Julie sighed. "I never had to wear a scarf and gloves on my

birthday before." But she put them on and followed Alex out of the apartment, onto the street.

The two of them walked silently the few blocks to the church, Julie in full sulk mode and Alex with his mind elsewhere. They walked in, took off their gloves, dipped their fingers in the holy water, made the sign of the cross, genuflected to the crucifix, then found a pew and knelt in prayer.

He glanced at Julie, now thirteen. She was still a child, but in some ways she seemed older than Briana. He doubted she'd kept the simple faith that Bri had managed in spite of everything. Julie was always angrier, always less content, and nothing over the past few months had changed that. It was unfair of him to compare his sisters, he knew, and it was especially unfair of him to expect the horrors they were now enduring to make Julie a sweeter, gentler person. Especially since she hadn't been a sweet, gentle person to begin with.

Alex grinned. He wouldn't want to live with two Julies, but it was just as well there was one of them sharing the miseries. He tapped her gently on her shoulder, and gestured for them to get up. They walked to the candles, so few now, and lit one. Alex prayed for all those who were gone, and his prayers were heartfelt.

As they walked back to the apartment, Alex thought of all the things he should be saying to Julie. Lessons about being a woman, lectures on doing well in school and making Mami and Papi proud. But none of the words wanted to come out, and he allowed himself to remain silent.

"Are there more bodies than there used to be?" Julie asked as they reached West End Avenue. "Even more than last week, I mean."

"I don't think more people are dying," Alex replied,

saddened that even on his sister's birthday, death intruded. "I just think they're picking up the bodies less often."

"That's not good," Julie said. "More rats. I hate the rats."

"Don't think of them today," Alex said. "It's your birthday. Think happy thoughts."

"I'll try," Julie said. "I am trying, Alex. I really am. It's just so hard."

"I know," he said. "Come on. Let's see what kind of feast Briana whipped up for you." He unlocked the outside door, and then the door to their apartment.

"SURPRISE!"

"What!" Julie shouted. "Oh, Alex!" She hugged her brother, and then ran to Bri and embraced her as well.

Alex grinned. Everyone was there: Kevin, James, and Tony, Julie's friends Brittany and Lauren, and Father Mulrooney. The soft glow of candlelight illuminated the yellow crepe paper hanging in the doorways, and the big HAPPY BIRTHDAY, JULIE! sign on the blanket covering the living room window.

It was funny, Alex thought, as he shook everyone's hands and thanked them for coming. He'd never invited his classmates over, since he'd always been a little ashamed of where he lived. He wasn't the only scholarship student at Vincent de Paul, but the guys he wanted to impress, the Chris Flynns of his school, all had money and parents with position. But thanks to what was happening, money no longer counted for anything. Position, except in the highest ranks, was a thing of the past. They were all truly equal in the eyes of God and man, and his apartment at least had the advantage of not requiring anyone to walk up ten flights of stairs.

He made a special point of thanking Father Mulrooney. How proud Mami would be to have a priest, the acting head of St. Vincent de Paul Academy, chaperoning her daughter's party.

"I'm glad you invited me, Alex," Father Mulrooney replied. "It's good to see young faces smiling again."

Julie certainly was smiling. Alex couldn't remember the last time she'd been so happy, if she ever had. She'd been born scowling. But now her face was radiant with joy.

"I brought a portable CD player," Tony said. "I thought we might dance."

The four girls giggled. The boys pushed the furniture to the side of the room, creating a dance floor of sorts. The CD that Tony put on was filled with the music of the previous spring, songs that made Alex feel young again. James asked Julie to dance, Kevin asked Bri, Tony asked Brittany, and Alex asked Lauren. None of the boys were particularly good dancers, but the girls didn't seem to mind. Alex had invited James and Tony not merely because they were two of the guys he was most friendly with but because they were two of the better-looking guys left in his school. Not that looks seemed to matter. With four boys and four girls, they all took turns dancing with each other. Even Father Mulrooney got into the act, gamely dancing with Julie.

"I'll have you know I was quite the jitterbug in my youth," Father Mulrooney said. "It's these modern, new-fangled dances like the waltz that take so much out of me."

"But the waltz isn't modern," Lauren said, "is it?"

"No, my dear," Father Mulrooney said. "That was just the excuse of an old man."

Bri had to stop dancing and use her inhaler. Alex worried she'd be self-conscious about it, but Tony said he also had asthma, and the two of them sat on the sofa and talked softly about it. Everyone had gotten so warm from the dancing and the body heat that they'd taken off their coats. Seeing Bri and Tony on the sofa sitting together, dressed as people used to dress, made Alex almost dizzy with nostalgia.

"What we need are refreshments," Kevin said, walking to the kitchen. "Does anyone here want a Coke?"

"Coke?" the girls shrieked.

"I'll get the cups," Bri said, and out of nowhere, it seemed, came paper cups.

"They're my contribution," Tony said. "Paper goods. Kevin gave me my instructions, and I did exactly as I was told."

"I wish you'd do the same in Latin class," Father Mulrooney grumbled, and everybody laughed.

Kevin poured each of them a cupful of Coke. "To Julie," he said. "May she have a life full of love and happiness."

Everyone raised their glasses and said, "To Julie."

Even though the Coke was warm, it was like the songs on Tony's CD, a reminder of how life had been just a few months back.

"And now for something really special," James said. "Well, I hope really special, but I make no guarantees." He went into the kitchen and took a few moments before returning to the living room. When he did, he was carrying a birthday cake, blazing with fourteen birthday candles.

"Happy birthday to you," everyone sang. "Blow out the candles, Julie! Make a wish!"

Julie closed her eyes tightly, then opened them and blew out the candles. It took her two or three attempts. Alex told himself it wasn't because she was no longer strong, but because there were so many candles on her cake.

"It's chocolate cake," Julie said, cutting into it. "Chocolate cake with chocolate icing. Oh, James, where did you find it?"

"I didn't exactly find it," James said. "It's just an old box of cake mix and a package of icing we had lying around. It was pretty exciting, actually. We have an electric oven, so it was just a case of the electricity staying on long enough to bake the cake, which it almost did yesterday. It may be a little soggy on the inside, but it was the best I could do."

"It's the most beautiful birthday cake I ever had," Julie said. "I can't believe your family gave up a real cake."

Alex couldn't believe it, either. He wondered how many pairs of shoes it had cost Kevin to get the cake mix and icing, and he appreciated how his friend had set things up so no one would think of the loss of life that simple, underbaked cake had cost.

But one bite of chocolate cake made him stop thinking about death. It's a miracle, he thought. Chocolate cake and Coke and music and seeing his sisters look young and beautiful were all miracles.

"Tony brought the paper goods, and James brought the cake," Kevin said. "So I brought the birthday present. Happy birthday, Julie. It's not much, but I hope you'll like it." He handed her a small, oddly shaped package, wrapped in leftover Christmas paper.

Julie unwrapped it as though the paper were solid gold. Under the wrapping was a layer of tissues, and lying in the tissues was a lipstick.

"Oh my god!" the girls squealed. "Oh, Julie, it's a perfect color. Oh, Julie, put it on."

Julie turned to Alex. "May I?" she asked.

"Only if you dance one final dance with me," he said.

Julie ran to the bathroom, the girls following in her footsteps. Alex took the opportunity to thank James, Tony, and Kevin for making his sister's birthday so special. They all acted as though it wasn't a big deal, but Alex knew how important it was to Julie, to Bri, and to Julie's friends. No matter what else happened to them, they had gone to a party and danced with real boys.

Julie's lips were a bright pink when she came out of the bathroom, and so were her cheeks. Alex bowed to her and escorted her onto the dance floor. James found a slow song, and Alex and Julie danced for a moment—until Kevin tapped him on the shoulder and cut in.

"We'd better move the furniture back into place," Father Mulrooney said when the song ended. "We don't want to be out after curfew."

It only took a minute or two for the four boys to get things back in order. None of the cake was left, but there were still a couple of cans of Coke, which Kevin told them to keep.

Tony said he'd walk Lauren home, since she lived only a couple of blocks away from him, and Kevin promised the same for Brittany. Both girls giggled some more as they hugged Julie good-bye. James, Tony, and Kevin all gave Julie pecks on the cheek, causing another avalanche of giggles. Everyone put on coats, gloves, and scarves and went out into the icy-cold autumn night.

Julie walked over first to Bri and then to Alex and embraced them. "This is the best birthday I ever had," she told them. "When I say my prayers tonight, I'll thank María, *Madre de Cristo,* for giving me the best brother and the best sister in the world, and for letting me be thirteen."

chapter 12

Monday, October 3

As Alex walked toward his locker, he saw James and Tony standing there. Neither of them looked happy, and Alex worried immediately that something bad had happened because of the party.

"We need to talk to you," James said, which didn't brighten Alex's mood any.

Tony looked almost pained. "We know things are rough for your family right now, and we don't want to make things worse," he said. "But I thought about it all weekend, and James talked to his dad, and at church yesterday we all had a conference, and we need to tell you something."

Alex's mind raced through all the catastrophic possibilities. None made sense, except perhaps that he should be asked to leave Vincent de Paul. But he couldn't think of any reason why. He clenched his fists and waited.

"It's about Briana," Tony said. "Your sister."

"I know who Briana is," Alex said.

"Tony," James said. "Here's the thing, Alex. Bri has asthma, like Tony, and it isn't good for her health to live in a basement apartment. We're not saying you don't keep it clean, because we're sure you do. It's just that basements grow mold, and nowadays with so much water around, that's an even bigger problem."

Alex looked at his well-meaning friends. Tony, with his asthma, probably had never been in a basement before last week. And James, son of a cardiologist, was a model of healthy living.

"My mom says there are still some shelters open," Tony said. "They're under city supervision, and they're still pretty safe."

"We're not moving to a shelter," Alex said. "But I'll see what I can do about getting us out of the basement."

"We apologize for interfering," James said. "If it were just you and Julie, we wouldn't say anything. But we know you're doing everything you can for your family, and Bri really needs to be moved out of the basement."

Alex nodded. Asthma was a whole new world for him, but not for Tony or James's father. If they said Bri needed to get out of the basement, it would be sinful to let pride interfere with good judgment.

Tuesday, October 4

"Julie and I are skipping school tomorrow," Alex announced over supper of elbow macaroni and marinara sauce.

"We are?" Julie asked. "What about lunch?"

"I can skip lunch tomorrow," Bri said. "The two of you can share my meal."

"You eat lunch," Alex said. He was already concerned that Bri wasn't eating when he wasn't around to supervise her. "Julie and I'll manage."

"So why are we skipping school?" Julie asked.

"We're moving," Alex said.

"We can't move!" Bri said. "If we move, Mami and Papi and Carlos won't be able to find us."

"We'll leave a note for them," Alex said. "On the table where they'll be sure to see it. We're not moving far anyway. Just upstairs to apartment twelve B."

"What's wrong with right here?" Julie asked. "All our stuff is here."

"I know," Alex said. He'd spent much of the night trying to work out a system for moving all the things they'd taken from the other apartments up to 12B. Not to mention their clothes and their food. "That's why we're moving tomorrow. Wednesday's usually a good day for electricity, so we'll be able to move the stuff in the elevator. We'll get Bri upstairs first, and then you and I will pack things and take them up. We'll do the unloading, too. Bri can make sure doors stay open, stuff like that."

"I can help with the unloading," Bri said.

"No," Alex said. "No lifting for you. Julie and I can do it without your help."

"How come you made a decision like that without talking to us about it?" Julie asked. "And why twelve B? Fourteen J is a two-bedroom."

"The guys in twelve B said we could use their place," Alex said. "I feel more comfortable with us staying there. You and Bri can share the bedroom, and I'll sleep in the living room. There's probably a sofa bed, and if not, we'll take a mattress from one of the other places and I'll sleep on that. We'll manage fine."

"If you think it's best," Bri said. "I just want to be more helpful."

"You'll help with the unpacking," Alex said. "Getting the food into the cabinets, things like that. Don't worry, Bri. You'll do your share."

"Do you think we're going to be flooded?" Julie persisted. "Is that why we have to move upstairs?"

Alex nodded. "It's going to happen pretty soon," he said. "And we're better off getting all our stuff out of here while we can. Besides, we don't know how much longer the electricity will last, and I don't want to lug all our stuff up by stairs. So tomorrow's moving day."

Bri smiled. "I prayed every night to come home and find you here," she said. "But I guess home isn't this apartment. It's wherever you are."

"We're not going anyplace," Alex said. "Except up twelve flights."

Wednesday, October 5

Alex begged forgiveness from God and Papi as he began hammering the nails needed to hold the doubled-over blankets they used for insulation in place over the windows of apartment 12B.

"It figures," Julie grumbled. "I finally move into a place with a view, and I'll never get to look out again."

Monday, October 10

"Are you going to just stand there, or are you going to help me?" Kevin asked. The jumper had landed funny, his body twisted around, and Kevin was finding it difficult to pull his shoes off.

Alex pulled at one shoe while Kevin worked on the other. "I really hate rigor mortis," Kevin grumbled. "The things I do for Mom."

"You must love her a lot," Alex said. "I have to do this; we need the food. But you're just doing this for vodka."

"You need food; she needs vodka," Kevin said, finally pulling off the shoe. He gave the body a disgusted kick and began walking in search of the next one. "Besides, I figure I owe her."

"How do you mean?" Alex asked.

"She's my mother," Kevin said. "And this isn't something I'd like to get around, but I was a bed wetter. Mom never scolded me or made me feel like I was bad or it was my fault. So now, if I have to go to a little extra effort to give her the one thing she wants, I'm going to do it. You tell anybody what I just said and I'll kill you."

"Don't worry," Alex said. "There's no one around to tell anyway."

"True enough," Kevin said.

Alex remembered a night, shortly after they'd moved to Eighty-eighth Street, when he'd wet the bed. He'd gone to Mami and Papi's room, crying with misery and humiliation.

They'd gone back to his room, Papi helping him change into clean pajamas, while Mami stripped the bed and put on fresh sheets. Carlos had woken up and called Alex a baby, and Papi had told Carlos to shut up, that Carlos had done that and worse in his day. Alex could still remember Papi lifting him onto the top bunk, and his parents kissing him good night.

The power of his loss and his anger punched him in his gut, and he nearly keeled over.

° 197 °

"You okay?" Kevin asked.

Alex wanted to say no, he wasn't okay, he would never be okay again. He felt rage and resentment, and for a moment he included Kevin in his list of things he hated, because Kevin had food and a home and parents.

"Yeah, I'm okay," he said. "It must have been something I ate."

Friday, October 14

By the time Alex picked up Julie at Holy Angels, he was already in a bad mood. There was a pile of a half dozen stripped new deads in front of the apartment building, with no guarantee they'd ever be removed, which meant dodging rats just to get through the door.

He, Kevin, and Julie had stood on line for food for five hours that morning, the temperature well below freezing and a harsh wind blowing the entire time. Kevin had walked Julie to Holy Angels while Alex took the bags, none of which had very much food, up the twelve flights, because the electricity wasn't running. Then he'd taken stuff to Harvey's for barter, and even though he hadn't gotten much in return, he still had to carry it up the twelve flights again. Bri had spent the morning in the apartment without being able to use the electric heater or the electric blanket, stuck in the sleeping bag. He had opened a can of mixed vegetables for her, and then spoon-fed her, so she wouldn't have to take out her arms. Father Mulrooney had given up a full eyebrow look when Alex finally made it to school, and Alex had been worried until lunchtime that he'd be told he wouldn't be allowed in the cafeteria. He had an eyestrain headache from trying to read in dim natural light, and even though the school kept its thermostat at fifty-five degrees, he hadn't been able to shake off the morning chill.

He had a date to go body shopping with Kevin the next morning, but he wasn't optimistic about what they'd get for it, since there was no market for watches anymore, and even shoes and coats weren't bringing in what they used to. But going gave him an excuse to leave the apartment, so he wouldn't have to spend the whole day stuck with his sisters and nothing to do.

Bri still insisted on going to Mass on Sunday, which meant an extra half hour to get down the twelve flights of stairs and then to St. Margaret's and an extra half hour to get back home. They had to stop at every floor for her to catch her breath, and she needed to use her inhaler twice, sometimes three times, before the climb was finished. But that was the only time Bri escaped from the apartment, and Alex couldn't find it in his heart to forbid her. It didn't help that Julie wanted to race ahead, and Alex wouldn't let her. As far as he could tell, they had the building all to themselves, but that didn't mean someone wasn't lurking in the stairwell, and he couldn't risk letting Julie go up by herself. So Julie would spend Sunday afternoon sulking and Bri would spend it gasping and claiming she was fine, and Alex would have to act sympathetic, when all he wanted to do was run.

He could tell right away that the weekend he was already dreading was about to get worse. Julie had that look in her eyes. She hadn't looked that upset since the garden had died.

"What is it?" he asked. "They fed you, didn't they?"

Julie nodded.

Alex prayed for patience and understanding. On Monday, he'd find out who the patron saint of patience was. He could use the extra help.

"I can see something's upsetting you," he said. "Want to tell me about it?"

"You won't like it," Julie said.

Alex snorted.

"Don't!" Julie cried. "You always act like everything's my fault. Bri does everything right and I do everything wrong and I hate it!"

"What?" he shouted. "I said I could see you were upset, and all of a sudden I'm the villain?"

"If you're going to shout at me, I won't tell you," Julie said.

"Fine," Alex said. "Don't. See if I care."

"I wish Carlos was here," she said.

"Me too," Alex said. And Mami and Papi and Uncle Jimmy and Aunt Lorraine, and all the other grown-ups who knew how to handle Julie.

He looked down at his little sister. She'd stood outside with him and Kevin for five hours, not complaining, not whining, hardly saying a word. Something bad had happened at school and Alex, in his bad mood, hadn't given her the chance to tell him in her own way.

"I'm sorry," he said, and he couldn't have even explained what he was sorry about. The list would have been too long. "Tell me when you're ready."

"I wish I was Bri," Julie said. "I mean, I wish I was the one who went away and I was the one who's sick, because I know you like her more than you like me and I'm sorry you're stuck with me when you'd rather do stuff with her."

Alex knew he was supposed to assure Julie that he liked her every bit as much as he liked Bri, but there was no point. Julie knew better. He'd spent thirteen years making sure she did.

"We're stuck with each other," he said. "You wish I was Carlos, after all."

"Holy Angels is closing," Julie blurted.

Alex stood absolutely still, closed his eyes, and prayed he hadn't heard Julie correctly.

"Today was the last day," she said.

"How long have you known?" he asked, as though that would make a difference.

"They told us Monday," Julie replied. "I've been scared to tell you. I knew you wouldn't like it."

"You're right, I don't," Alex said. "If you'd given me some notice, I could have spoken to Sister Rita. Did they tell you where you'd be going now?"

"I'm sorry," Julie said. "It's not my fault. Really."

"Just tell me," Alex said. He hoped it was someplace where they'd feed her lunch.

"Vincent de Paul," she whispered.

"Oh God," Alex said, at the thought of losing his last sanctuary.

"I don't have to go to school," Julie said. "Bri doesn't. I can stay home with her if you want. We can study together. I can skip lunch. It's okay, really."

Alex thought back to that last night when he'd been slicing pizza at Joey's, worrying about the editorship of the paper, dreaming of a full scholarship to Georgetown. To think he was discontented because he was only class vice president. Had he ever been that young, that stupid?

"It'll be fine," he said to his sister, because she deserved to hear it. "It'll be easier. I won't have to drop you off at Holy Angels and pick you up. And you'll like it at Vincent de Paul. Will the sisters be coming along, or will you be taking classes with the boys?"

"Some of the sisters will be coming," Julie said. "There aren't that many girls left at Holy Angels, so some of the sisters are being sent away. But we'll have our own classes. You won't see me, Alex. I promise. We're not going to eat in the cafeteria. We'll have lunch in our classroom. I'm sorry."

"I'm sorry, too," Alex said. "I know how much you like Holy Angels." He thought about how carefully the secret had been kept. Not even Kevin seemed to know girls were coming to Vincent de Paul.

"It doesn't matter," Julie said. "Nothing matters anymore."

Alex didn't have the strength to disagree.

Monday, October 17

Before Mass Father Mulrooney gave the boys a stern lecture about how the Holy Angels students were their guests and any contact between them should be brief and civil. The Holy Angels students would use the third floor of the school, while all Vincent de Paul classes would be held on the first and second. Each school would have separate hours for chapel and library, with the Vincent de Paul morning Mass remaining mandatory.

Alex hadn't gone to school with girls since seventh grade, when he'd begun at Vincent de Paul. Not having girls around helped him focus on what was truly important to him: his grades, his activities, his future. Sure, he would have liked having a girlfriend, and he knew a lot of the boys at Vincent de Paul dated girls from Holy Angels or even from the public high schools. But they had their lives set out for them. They could afford the distraction.

Last spring, he remembered, Chris had asked if he wanted to double-date for the Holy Angels junior prom. Chris's girlfriend had a friend who'd just broken up with her boyfriend and needed a last-minute replacement.

Alex worked Saturday nights at Joey's. Rather than explaining that to Chris, he said instead that his father was away in Puerto Rico for a family funeral, and they weren't sure when he'd be coming back. It was a ridiculous excuse, but Chris accepted it and said how sorry he was.

The prom must have been scheduled for the Saturday Papi didn't come home. Most likely it had been canceled. All the longing and resentment Alex had felt had been for no reason whatsoever.

Friday, October 28

Alex was on his way to the cafeteria when he felt a tap on his shoulder. He turned around and saw Tony.

"I thought you could use this," Tony said, handing him a small brown paper bag.

"What is it?" Alex asked.

"Cartridges for Bri's inhaler," Tony said. "I had a couple of extra ones, so I figured I'd pass them along to you."

"Thanks," Alex said.

"No problem," Tony said, which Alex suspected was also a lie, but was too grateful to question.

Monday, October 31

"Did you give Tony my thank-you note?" Bri asked after Alex and Julie got home from school.

"I sure did," Alex lied. Tony was nowhere to be seen. Alex had taken a rough count at Mass, and another dozen Vincent de Paul students were gone. Maybe some of them would show up later in the week, but he doubted it. Gone was gone. But he'd decided against telling Bri, since it had seemed so important to her to write Tony a thank-you note. It was better to lie than to upset her.

"Tomorrow's All Saints' Day," he said. "I thought the three of us might go to Mass at St. Margaret's."

"Oh, I'd like that," Bri said. "Thank you, Alex."

"Could I skip it?" Julie asked. "You could take me to school first and then go to Mass."

"It's a holy day of obligation," Bri said. "We always went to Mass with Mami on All Saints' Day."

"I know," Julie said. "But I want to go to Mass on Wednesday for All Souls' Day. I want to pray for Mami and Papi's souls."

"But they're not dead," Bri said.

"You're crazy," Julie said. "Isn't she, Alex? Mami and Papi have been dead since that first day. Everyone knows it. You know it, too, Bri. You just won't admit it."

"How can you say that?" Bri cried. "I spoke to Papi. He's stuck in Puerto Rico. And Mami must be alive because she wasn't at Yankee Stadium when Alex looked. Isn't that right, Alex."

"Just because you don't want to believe they're dead doesn't mean they aren't," Julie said. "It's sinful not to pray for their souls, isn't it, Alex."

"What's sinful is to act like your parents are dead when they're alive," Bri said. "Sometimes I think you like it better this way. You get away with more. You should have spent the summer like I did, Julie, and then you'd appreciate home and family."

"You should spend every day like I do!" Julie shouted. "Stuck with a crazy sister who prays all the time instead of doing any work."

"I do work," Bri said. "I do schoolwork when you're at school."

"Yeah, right," Julie said. "I do all the cooking and cleaning."

"I thought you liked doing the cooking," Alex said. "Besides, how much work is it? All our food comes out of cans."

"I wouldn't mind the cooking if I didn't have to do the dishes, too," Julie said. "And the dusting, which you make me do every day, and sweeping and mopping the floor."

"The place has to be really clean for Bri's asthma," Alex said. "And I don't want her standing in the cold kitchen doing the dishes, either. It's bad for her."

"So I do everything!" Julie said. "It's not fair!"

"Oh, grow up," Alex said.

"I hate you!" Julie shouted, storming into the bedroom, slamming the door behind her.

"I can do the dishes," Bri said. "Really I can."

"No," Alex said. "Julie'll get over it."

"What about Mass tomorrow?" Bri asked.

"It's All Saints' Day," Alex said. "Of course we'll go." And the day after, he told himself, he and Julie would go for All Souls' Day to pray for Papi and Mami. And he'd take over the dusting and the mopping.

chapter 13

Wednesday, November 9

Bri was waiting for them when Alex and Julie got home from school. "Today's Papi's birthday," she said. "I thought we'd do something special to celebrate."

Alex and Julie exchanged glances. "Like what?" Alex asked.

Bri smiled. "I don't know," she admitted. "Just something. Maybe go to St. Margaret's and light a candle for him."

"Alex and I did that on the way home," Julie said.

"Did you pray for his safe return?" Bri asked. "I worry a lot that he's trying to get back to New York by boat. That's got to be really dangerous with the tides and the tsunamis."

"I'm sure Papi isn't doing anything dangerous," Alex said. "Let's not worry about him today, okay? That's not how he'd want us to celebrate his birthday."

"I checked our supplies at lunchtime," Bri said. "Do you know we still have a can of clam sauce? And half a box of spaghetti. That would make a wonderful supper."

"I was saving that for Thanksgiving," Julie said. Alex glared at her. "You're right, Bri. Let's have that for supper tonight. For Papi."

"St. Margaret's is going to have a Thanksgiving dinner," Alex said. "They just put up the notice. We'll go to that."

"That would be wonderful," Bri said. "Remember turkey and stuffing?"

"Pumpkin pie," Julie said. "Candied sweet potatoes. We'll probably get rice and beans."

"It doesn't matter," Bri replied. "We have so much to be thankful for. We have this wonderful apartment, and we have food and the church and each other."

"Yeah," Julie said. "But I'd still like some pumpkin pie."

"Remember a couple of years ago when Mami bought Papi all those lottery tickets," Alex said, because he didn't want to think about turkey and stuffing and pumpkin pie and all the things they didn't have to be thankful about.

"One of them won," Bri said. "Fifty dollars."

"And he took us all to the movies," Julie said. "Even Carlos came along."

"Do you think they're still making movies?" Bri asked.

"I don't think so," Alex said. "Not with all the flooding on the West Coast."

Julie looked uncomfortable. "I have some lottery tickets," she said.

"Where did you get lottery tickets?" Alex asked.

"From the bodega," Julie admitted. "Remember when you and Uncle Jimmy left me there alone? I filled up bags of food for us, but I also tore off some instant tickets and put them in my pocket."

"Julie," Bri said. "That's stealing."

"I've confessed and done penance," Julie said. "And even if I wanted to, I can't return the tickets to Uncle Jimmy."

"Have you looked at them?" Alex asked. "Are any of them winning tickets?"

Julie shook her head. "I was saving them for Christmas," she said. "But maybe today would be better, because it's Papi's birthday and he loved lottery tickets."

"Could we do them now?" Bri asked. "Christmas seems so far away."

"Why not," Alex said. "Julie, get the tickets."

Julie ran into the bedroom and returned with the tickets.

"How many are there?" Alex asked.

"Twenty-seven," Julie said.

Alex laughed. "Nine for each of us," he said. "Okay, here's a penny for you, Julie, and one for Bri and one for me. Let's see how rich we are."

Bri squealed almost immediately. "Five dollars!" she cried.

Alex scraped and scraped but came up with nothing.

Julie gasped and made the sign of the cross. "We're rich," she said. "Alex, look at this."

Alex took the ticket from her. Not believing his eyes, he handed the ticket to Bri for confirmation.

"Ten thousand dollars?" she said.

Alex grabbed it back from her and looked more carefully. "Ten thousand dollars."

"That'll get us out of here, won't it, Alex?" Julie asked. "With ten thousand dollars, we can get tickets out of here to someplace, can't we?"

Alex checked the ticket over one more time. He couldn't remember the last time he'd seen money being used, but that didn't mean it wasn't. The government still existed and the government owed the owner of that lottery ticket ten thousand dollars. The question was what good was ten thousand dollars.

"Maybe we should tell Kevin," Julie said.

Alex realized he didn't want to tell Kevin—any more than he had wanted Kevin to know he was bartering liquor and cigars. Some things you kept to yourself. "Harvey might be able to help us," he said. "But we shouldn't get our hopes up."

"Couldn't we use the ticket to get food instead?" Bri asked. "Real food. Lots of it. That way we wouldn't have to leave New York."

"I want to use it to get out," Julie said. "It's my ticket. I'm the one who took it in the first place and it was in my pile and I get to say what we do with it."

"But what will Mami and Papi think if we're not here?" Bri asked. "Or Carlos? How will they find us if we leave?"

"It's been six months!" Julie shouted. "They're dead. And Carlos might as well be. I'm not going to stick around here and die waiting for them to come back. Stay here if you want, but I'm going!"

Bri began to cough.

"Where's the inhaler?" Alex asked, looking around the living room for it.

"Bedroom." Bri gasped.

Alex raced into the bedroom and grabbed the inhaler from Bri's night table. "You're supposed to carry this with you all the time!" he shouted, resisting the temptation to fling it at her.

Bri took a deep puff. Her coughing subsided. "Sorry," she whispered. "Forgot."

"You can't forget," Alex said. "Forgetting can kill you. What if you had an attack and we weren't here?"

Bri began to cry.

"Happy birthday, Papi," Julie muttered.

"That does it!" Alex yelled. "Julie, go to your room, right now."

"Why?" Julie asked. "It isn't my fault Bri's crazy."

"Now," Alex said, trying to keep his rage under control. "Before I pick you up and throw you in there."

"You're too weak to," Julie said, but she took her winning ticket and left, slamming the bedroom door behind her.

Bri kept crying. They'd run out of tissues months ago, and toilet paper was too precious to waste. Alex went to the kitchen and grabbed one of the last three napkins for Bri to blow her nose with.

"Bri, you have to keep your inhaler with you," he said. "You can't just leave it around."

"I know," Bri said. "I'm sorry. I was in the bedroom and then I heard you come in and I was so excited, I forgot it. I always have it with me. Really, Alex."

"Okay," he said. "I'm sorry I yelled at you."

Bri looked up at him, and Alex could see the tears in her eyes. "We can't leave," she said. "This is our home."

"I don't know," he said. "At some point we may have to."

"But not yet," Bri said. "Not until Mami and Papi come back."

"We'll talk about that later," Alex said. "I need to talk to Julie now. Stay where you are, okay?"

"Okay," Bri said.

Alex didn't bother knocking. He found Julie sitting on her end of the bed, staring at the quilt that covered the window of her bedroom.

"I'm using the ticket to get out," she said. "I don't care what you and Bri do. It's my ticket and I hate it here."

"Julie, it's not that simple," Alex said.

"It is," she said. "People leave all the time. All my friends are gone. Most of the sisters are gone. We're the only ones stupid enough to still be here."

"We're not stupid," he said.

"Bri is," Julie said.

"Don't say that," Alex snapped. "Her faith is stronger than yours. Maybe you're the stupid one."

Julie looked Alex straight in the eye. "Tell me Mami and Papi are still alive," she said. "Tell me that's what you really think."

"It doesn't matter what I think," he said. "It doesn't even matter what Bri thinks. What matters is Bri can't walk more than five blocks without having an asthma attack and you're thirteen years old and you can't look out for yourself."

"I could if I had to," Julie said.

Alex shook his head. "You can't," he said. "I can't go off with you and leave Bri behind. And I can't stay behind with Bri and let you go off on your own." He left unsaid the idea of his deserting his sisters while he escaped.

"But maybe with the ticket we could find a way out," Julie said. "Ten thousand dollars, Alex. That's so much money. It could get us to a safe place where Bri could get healthy."

Alex knew Bri would never be healthy again. But he was moved that Julie still had some faith in miracles. "I'll talk to Harvey," he said. "I promise."

"I want to go with you," Julie said. "It's my ticket."

"Okay," Alex said. "We'll go to Harvey's on the way to school tomorrow. Now come on, and start making our supper. Spaghetti and clam sauce. A feast for Papi."

"All right," Julie said, reaching out for Alex's hand. "You won't leave me? You promise?"

"I promise," Alex said. "*Te amo, hermanita,* even if you do drive me crazy."

Julie got up off the bed. "Do you think there's anyplace left in the world with pumpkin pie?" she asked.

"I hope so," Alex said. It didn't seem like too much to ask for.

Thursday, November 10

Julie bounced all the way to Harvey's. "I hope we can go someplace warm and sunny," she said. "Maybe we should go to Texas and find Carlos."

Alex wanted to warn her not to get her hopes up, but there had been so few moments the past six months where Julie had something to hope for that he couldn't find it in him to discourage her. Besides, maybe finding the lottery ticket on Papi's birthday was a miracle. The Morales family was certainly due for one.

Harvey hadn't gotten his weekly food delivery, and the store was almost empty. "This is it?" Julie asked doubtfully as Alex escorted her.

"It's busier on Fridays," he told her.

"Alex," Harvey said. "Pleasure to see you. And who might this be?"

"Harvey, this is my sister Julie," Alex said. "Julie, this is Harvey."

Harvey smiled. Alex noticed he'd lost a tooth since he'd seen him last week. He's rotting away, Alex thought, the same as the city.

"We have something," Julie said. "Something valuable. Don't we, Alex."

"Very valuable," Alex said.

"We want to trade it for a way out of New York," Julie said. "For me and Alex and Bri."

"Who's Bri?" Harvey asked.

"My sister," Julie said. "She has asthma, so it's important we go someplace where the air's better and she can get well. Someplace warm and nice. And she can't walk very much, so it has to be easy to get there."

"That's quite the order," Harvey said. "I know the kind of stuff you usually bring in, Alex. Nice things, don't get me wrong, but nothing worth an all-expense-paid trip to paradise."

"Should I show him?" Julie asked, but before Alex had a chance to say yes or no, she pulled the lottery ticket out of her pocket and waved it around. "It's an instant lottery ticket worth ten thousand dollars!" she cried. "Is that valuable enough?"

Harvey took the ticket from Julie's hand. He looked it over carefully, then put it on the counter.

"It must be worth something," Alex said. "What do you think you could get for it?"

Harvey laughed. "Six months ago, it would have been worth ten thousand," he said. "Maybe even five months ago. But now, it's not worth the paper it's printed on."

"Why?" Julie said. "It's a winning lottery ticket. New York has to pay."

"Sweetheart, New York don't care," Harvey said. "You understand, Alex. No one's using money anymore. It's all food and gas and connections."

"Someone must want it," Julie pleaded. "We don't want real money for it. Just a safe way out of New York."

"You can still get out of the city," Harvey said. "They're still evacuating."

"It isn't the getting out that's the problem," Alex said, although he knew that was only partly true. "It's going someplace safe, where Bri can get medical help."

Harvey shook his head. "That'd take a lot more than a lottery ticket," he said. "There are places like that, but you have to know someone to get in. You have to have the connections."

"Can we get anything for the ticket?" Alex asked. He didn't want to deal with Julie if they left empty-handed.

Harvey looked at the ticket. "You know I like you, Alex. You drive a hard bargain, and I respect that. I don't cheat you. For you, a couple of cans of chicken noodle soup."

"No," Julie said, grabbing the ticket from him. "We'll take the ticket to someone else. Someone who can help."

"Sweetie, there is no one else," Harvey said. "I'm the last of a dying breed. Look, I'll throw in a can of pineapple. That should be a real treat."

Alex thought about the can of pineapple. Bri loved pineapple. "Julie," he said. "Pineapple. It's almost as good as pumpkin pie."

"I hate you!" Julie cried, and ran out of the store.

"Julie," Alex said. "Harvey, I'm sorry. You know girls that age. Everything's a crisis."

"How old is she?" Harvey asked.

"Thirteen," Alex said.

Harvey nodded. "Teenagers," he said. "Look, take the pineapple. It's crazy for me to give anything away nowadays, but if it'll make her feel better, it's worth it."

"Thank you," Alex said, taking the can. "I really appreciate this, Harvey."

"No problem," Harvey said. "See you tomorrow? I'm expecting some good stuff."

Alex thought of the diminishing stock of liquor and sweaters and nodded. "Late morning," he said. "After the food line."

"Best time," Harvey said. "I'll hold something for you."

"I appreciate it," Alex said. "Thanks for the pineapple. And I apologize again for Julie. She had her hopes up."

"Things are tough all over," Harvey said. "Must be real rough having a sick little sister."

"Yeah," Alex said. "Real rough. Thanks again. See you tomorrow." He walked out of the store, but Julie was nowhere to be seen.

Idiota, Alex thought. Storming off. Things didn't go just the way she wanted, and she had to make a big dramatic gesture. He was tempted to go to school and leave her to her own devices. Let her go home and slam the damn bedroom door. Bri could deal with her. Even better, he and Bri could share the pineapple and let Julie miss out. That would show her.

Alex shook his head. Living with a thirteen-year-old was making him think like one. He needed to find Julie. Whether she'd gone to school or home, it was downtown from Harvey's. He'd catch up with her and give her a lecture about running off. Tonight they'd have the pineapple. That would make all of them feel better.

He was so used to the quiet on the streets that at first he didn't recognize the sound when he heard it. The words were muffled, but it was a girl's voice, and it was full of fear.

His first thought was to run, to catch up with the sound,

because he knew it was Julie and someone had grabbed her. But what good would it do if he just ran up to them? Whoever had Julie might be armed, and even if he wasn't, Alex wasn't in condition for a street fight. There were no cops around. Hell, there was no one around, just rats and corpses. And someone who'd grabbed his sister.

Alex took off his shoes, so he wouldn't be heard, and began running toward the sounds. He spotted a large man on Ninety-first Street, dragging Julie toward the park while she struggled to break free.

"Let me go!" she yelled.

The man laughed. "Nobody's here," he said. "Stop fighting."

"Alex!" she screamed. "Alex!"

The man laughed even louder.

Alex had crept as close as he dared behind the man.

Julie tried to kick him. "Help!" she cried. "Someone help me!"

"You're pissing me off," the man said. "You're going to pay for that."

Alex figured he had gotten as close as he could without being noticed. He had one shot and he knew his aim had to be perfect, since the man was wearing a heavy winter coat and wouldn't feel a thing from his neck to his feet. David and Goliath, he said to himself, then threw the can of pineapple directly at the back of the man's head. Bull's-eye. The man let go of Julie as he howled in pain.

"Julie, run!" Alex yelled.

Julie turned around and saw him. She began running as fast as she could. The man bent over and grabbed the can of pineapple.

"Next time," he said.

Alex gathered Julie in his arms, and pulled her back to Broadway. The man didn't follow them, but they kept running anyway. By the time they entered their building, they were coughing so hard they had to sit for a few minutes before they could move.

Once they could breathe, Alex grabbed Julie by her shoulders and shook her. "Don't ever do that!" he yelled. "Don't ever go off by yourself!"

"I know. I'm sorry." She sobbed. "Alex, I was so scared. I'll never do it again, I swear. Never."

Alex let her go. His throbbing toes were half frozen. To distract himself from thinking about the agony of walking up twelve flights of stairs, he concentrated on what might have happened to his sister. She was worth the pineapple. She was worth the pain.

"Do me a favor," he said. "Go upstairs and get my other shoes. They're in the hall closet. If Bri's up, tell her . . ." He tried to come up with a reason why he'd need a different pair of shoes. "Tell her I got dead rat all over my shoes."

"No!" Julie said. "I'm not going into the stairwell alone. I won't."

"No one's in the stairwell," Alex said. "Now, do it."

Julie shook her head. "I won't go in there alone," she said.

Alex's feet throbbed. He told himself to calm down. It would be a mistake to send Julie upstairs anyway. She'd tell Bri everything, and that would bring on an attack, and Julie would run down to get him and he'd still have to climb the twelve flights. He didn't want to think about what might happen if the attack was really bad.

"All right, I'll go," he said. "You wait here."

"No," Julie said. "I'll go upstairs with you. In case he comes back."

"Whatever," Alex said. "I don't care. Just keep quiet, and don't ever tell Bri what happened."

Julie nodded. "I won't tell Bri," she promised. "Just don't ever leave me, Alex."

chapter 14

Veterans Day. Alex had forgotten all about it. He and Kevin had gone to the food line only to find out it had been canceled. All he'd been able to get from Harvey was one of the cans of chicken soup and a badly dented can of string beans. And he was down one pair of shoes.

It was impossible to sleep. Alex grabbed the flashlight, got off the sofa bed, and stumbled into the kitchen. They kept everything there, the food and whatever little they still had for bartering. Maybe if he made a list, he'd feel better. Maybe if he searched through every kitchen cabinet, he'd find an unexpected box of something or a can or a five-course dinner tucked away under a spare blanket.

He couldn't even find the spare blanket. Having Bri home meant they'd had to barter almost everything they'd gotten from the other apartments.

Alex thought, not for the first time, how ironic it was that they were living in a sixteen-story building and could only get into four apartments. Five, if you counted their old one. New York City apartments had steel doors and multiple locks, and even though as best he could tell from the lack of sound and the stench of death, everyone was gone and he and his sisters were the only ones living there, they still couldn't get into the deserted apartments.

In spite of himself, he found a piece of paper and a pen and began making a list. Lists no longer comforted him, but he made them anyway when he couldn't sleep. There was no point making a list of what they had, since they didn't have anything. There was no point in making a list of what they would need, since they needed everything. There was no point, but he still made a list.

GONE, he wrote on the top of the paper.

Papi
Mami
Carlos
Uncle Jimmy and Aunt Lorraine and their girls
Chris Flynn
Tony

Alex stared at the list and realized he'd barely scratched the surface. There were Uncle Carlos and Aunt María, Uncle Jose and Aunt Irene, who'd been with Papi in Milagro del Mar for Nana's funeral. All his cousins were gone. So were the priests from Vincent de Paul, the lay teachers, and the rest of the school staff. His onetime friend Danny O'Brien, plus practically everybody else he'd gone to school with. Mr. Dunlap. Bob, who he never had the chance to swap stories with. Joey from the pizza parlor and the guys he worked with there and the customers who made small talk and left small tips. The New York Yankees. He'd been to their stadium more recently than they had, he guessed. St. John of God Hospital, where

Mami was so excited to get her first job as an operating room technician. Gone. All gone. There wasn't enough paper left in the world to write down everybody and everything that was gone.

What difference did it make, he asked himself. All that mattered was that there was enough food for his sisters to make it until Monday. How long could a can of chicken soup and a dented can of string beans last? Why didn't he throw his shoes at that guy, and keep the pineapple for himself.

Saturday, November 12

"Where's the radio?" Alex asked, after searching the living room for it. If he'd been listening to the radio more regularly, he would have realized Friday was a national holiday and prepared for the possibility of no food line. His sisters' survival depended on his knowing as much as possible.

Julie and Bri exchanged glances.

"What?" he said to Julie. "You got rid of it? You traded it for lipstick? It's my radio and I need it, and you had no business even touching it."

"You always blame me for everything!" Julie cried. "I hate you!" She raced into the bedroom, slamming the door behind her.

"I'm sick and tired of her doing that," Alex said. "Now what the hell did she do to my radio?"

"She didn't do anything," Bri said. "I did. It's all my fault."

"Don't take the blame for her," Alex said. "That won't help Julie any."

"But it *is* my fault," Bri said. "When you go to school, it gets so lonely in here. So I turn on the radio. I don't even care what they say. I just want to hear voices. And sometimes I fall asleep and I forget to turn the radio off. The batteries died last week. I've been scared to tell you."

Alex tried to remember if there were any more C batteries lying around. He was pretty sure he'd bartered them all.

"I'm sorry," Bri said. "Is there anything I can do to make it up to you?"

Get healthy, he thought. Get strong enough so we can leave this hellhole.

"You do enough every day just being here," he said. "I'll go apologize to Julie now."

Monday, November 14

Alex met Kevin outside the building at seven in the morning, the way they always did on Mondays to go body shopping. It was getting harder to find good ones, but Alex needed whatever he could get.

"I guess you'll be going soon," Alex said. "Someplace safe."

Kevin shrugged. "I'm in no hurry," he said.

"You're crazy, you know that?" Alex said. "Where will you go?"

"I'm not sure," he said. "Mom won't leave without Dad, and there's still a lot of stuff to truck out of the city. It'll be awhile."

"But when you leave, it won't be for an evacuation center," Alex said. "You'll go someplace good."

Kevin looked as uncomfortable as Alex had ever seen him. "I asked Dad about you," he said. "And your sisters. Right after Julie's party. He said the evac centers weren't that bad, that you'd be okay there."

"Thanks anyway," Alex said. "I wasn't expecting you to rescue us."

"He doesn't care," Kevin said. "Not about Mom. Not about me. If he did, he would have made us leave months ago. That's how you know if people really love you. The ones who do let you go."

Friday, November 18

Alex, Kevin, and Julie spent five hours on the food line and ended up with enough food for the weekend, maybe Monday. Alex carried the food upstairs, then took three of Papi's cans of beer and the last bottle of scotch. He'd been holding off trading Papi's beer for as long as he could, but times were getting desperate. He was used to not eating supper, and Julie could get used to it if she had to, but there had to be some food for Bri.

He looked in on Bri, lying in the sleeping bag, covered with blankets. She smiled at him.

"I can't wave," she said. "It's too hard to get my arms out of here."

"Don't bother," he said. "Stay warm. I'll be back in a little while with more food."

"Take care," she said. "I love you, Alex."

"Love you, too," he said.

Alex put the liquor in his backpack, then put on the heavy wool coat Greg or Bob had left behind in June when nobody thought about constant cold. He was glad he'd held on to it. All the other coats were gone.

He was more nervous than usual walking toward Harvey's, and he tried to make himself laugh by thinking of the beer cans as weapons. There'd been no sight of the guy who'd tried to take Julie, but that didn't mean he wasn't still around.

But he made it without incident to Harvey's, and he was pleased to see Harvey hadn't lost any more teeth during the week.

"I brought you my best stuff," Alex said, unloading the backpack.

Harvey nodded thoughtfully. "I can always count on you, Alex," he said. "I got a half dozen cans of mixed vegetables, and look at this, four juice boxes—remember those?—and a nice bag of rice."

"That's a start," Alex said, falling into the now-comfortable ritual. "I might trade the scotch for that. What'll you give me for the beer?"

Harvey laughed. "I love ya, kid," he said. "Okay, I'll throw in two of my best cans of spinach, and just because I like you, a can of lima beans."

"I hate lima beans," Alex said, remembering a time when he wouldn't even eat them.

"Sorry," Harvey said. "Want some mushrooms instead?"

Lima beans were more filling. "I'll stick with the lima beans," Alex said. "What else?"

"You're killing me," Harvey said. "Okay, for you, the last known box of Cheerios."

"Deal," Alex said. Between the Cheerios and the rice, they'd all be able to make it for a week or more.

"Hold on, hold on." Harvey said. "I got another proposition for you."

"Sure, what?" Alex said, not that anything was going to be better than Cheerios.

"I didn't want to say anything last Friday, till I asked

around," Harvey said. "See what I could find for you and your sick sister. Someplace safe and easy to get to, right?"

"Right," Alex said. "Harvey, did you find someplace?"

"It wasn't easy," Harvey said. "But the arrangements are all made. A van'll pick you up and take you direct to this place outside Gainesville, Florida. It's one of those safe towns for important people's families. Plenty of food. Electricity. Schools. Even a hospital. Wish I could get into a joint like that." He spit contemptuously. "I'd rather die here than in one of those evac centers," he said. "Glad you won't have that problem anymore."

"Harvey, thank you," Alex said. "How soon can we go?"

Harvey smiled. "How soon can you bring your sister to me? The cute little spitfire?" he asked.

"Could the van pick us up at our apartment instead?" Alex asked. "I don't think Bri can walk this far."

"No problem," Harvey said. "Let me know when you can get the spitfire up here, and the van'll be waiting to take you back to your place for the other one. This'll work out great for you, Alex. You and that sick sister of yours will be just fine, and you won't ever have to worry about the spitfire. I can't name names, but the man who's taking her is very well connected."

Alex stared at Harvey. "You expect me to trade Julie?" he asked. "She's my sister."

"So what?" Harvey said. "You have another."

Alex wanted to strangle Harvey, choke him so hard his rotting teeth would fly out. But without Harvey there wouldn't be enough food for any of them to live.

He pulled his lips apart in what he hoped resembled a smile. "I don't think so," he said. "Thanks anyway, Harvey. I appreciate the offer, but I can't accept."

Harvey shrugged. "It was the best I could do," he said. "There'll always be a market for her, but I can't guarantee door-to-door service to Florida."

"I understand," Alex said. He put his hand out to shake Harvey's. "No hard feelings?"

"No hard feelings," Harvey said.

Alex put the vegetables and the juice boxes and the spinach and the lima beans and the rice and the Cheerios into his backpack. "See you next week," he said, trying not to tremble as he put his coat back on.

Harvey nodded.

Alex walked out of the store and went around the corner. There was no food in his body, but that didn't stop him from heaving until he collapsed from horror and exhaustion.

Monday, November 21

Alex confessed his sins, including homicidal thoughts, to Father Franco on Saturday and spent the rest of the day in silent prayer and fasting. He didn't eat again until after Mass on Sunday, and he used the twelve flights of stairs he climbed by Bri's side to meditate on the twelve stations of the cross.

By Sunday night he'd made his plan. The only thing that had held him back for so long, he acknowledged, was his false pride. And nowadays, pride could kill.

He didn't think twice about the easy deceptions of Monday morning. Body shopping with Kevin, neither one of them doing much talking. Going back to the apartment with the little he'd garnered. Saying hi to Bri, awake but still in bed. Urging Julie to get ready for school, since they always ran late on Mondays. Going into Vincent de Paul, placing his backpack in his locker, and leaving without a word to Father Mulrooney or any of his other teachers. Boys came in and out now, and no one seemed to care.

He took out the card Chris Flynn had handed him so long ago, and checked the address, even though he'd committed it to memory. West Fifty-second Street, farther south than Alex had been since he'd gone to the Port Authority back in May.

It felt weird to see the skyscrapers once brimming with life and now half dead. But even half dead was busier than his neighborhood, and the people he saw walked with purpose. They were the important people, he realized, the ones with connections, the ones whose families were safe. Everything about them was cleaner, even their face masks. And they still had flesh on their bodies; not a single one was a walking skeleton. Alex wondered what it must be like, not to be hungry and dirty and scared. Although if they were sane, they were scared.

He hoped the people wouldn't notice he didn't belong and force him back uptown before he saw Mr. Flynn. All his life he'd had moments of feeling like an outsider—in his family because he loved school so much, at school because his family had so little money. But he'd never felt like an outsider in New York before. Now he did and it frightened him.

As he walked south of Central Park, he found there were no corpses and no rats. Either people were healthier midtown or the body collecting was more efficient. Either way, it showed that there was more than one New York, and this was the one that counted.

He fingered Mr. Flynn's business card like rosary beads. He couldn't even be sure Chris's father was still in New York.

But there was no one left Alex could turn to who might possibly help. Bri's and Julie's lives depended on it. He paused for a moment outside the office building, prayed to Christ for strength and mercy, then straightened his tie and walked in.

There was a sole security guard in the otherwise empty lobby. "Yeah?" he said.

"I'm here to see Robert Flynn," Alex said. "Danforth Global Insurance. He's a vice president."

"He expecting you?" the guard asked, his hand starting for the gun in his holster.

"He knows who I am," Alex said. "I'm a friend of his son's. I have his business card."

"Well, that means a lot," the guard said. "Let me frisk you."

Alex walked over and stood absolutely still as the guard ran his hands over him. At least he wasn't armed with a can of pineapple.

"Okay, I guess you won't kill him," the guard said. "Let me check. Yeah, Flynn's a level six. You'll find him on the sixth floor somewhere. Stairs are over there."

"Are the elevators running?" Alex asked.

"Don't matter," the guard said. "Elevators are only for executives. You take the stairs."

"All right," Alex said. He walked over to where the guard had pointed and began the climb. So far so good.

He opened the fire door to the sixth floor, then checked all the doors until he found one with a handwritten sign saying, DGI, ROBERT FLYNN. He knocked on the door.

"Come in."

Alex opened the door. He didn't know what to expect, but he'd thought there'd be some people, maybe a receptionist, waiting behind the door. Instead there was that same look of desertion he'd become accustomed to: no people, but boxes filled with papers covering the furniture and the floor. But the room was warm, maybe as warm as sixty-five. One office door was open and Alex walked over to it.

"Mr. Flynn?" he asked, but there was no need. The man behind the desk looked like an older, much wearier version of Chris. It shook Alex up to see him, as though he'd caught a glimpse of what Chris was going to look like in thirty years. Assuming Chris was alive in thirty years.

"Yes?"

"My name is Alex Morales. I don't know if you remember, but I was in school with Chris. St. Vincent de Paul Academy?"

Mr. Flynn stared at Alex. "Oh yes," he said. "Alex. Chris's friend. Chris spoke of you often."

"How is Chris?" Alex asked. "Does he like South Carolina?"

"Does anyone like anything these days?" Mr. Flynn replied. "He's fine, I suppose. I haven't heard anything in a while, but the last I knew he was in school. How are things at Vincent de Paul? Is it still open?"

"Yes sir," Alex said. "There aren't a lot of teachers left, but we're still learning."

"Good, good," Mr. Flynn said. "Sit down, Alex. I'll be sure to tell Chris I saw you."

"Please do," Alex said. "I apologize for bothering you, sir, but Chris told me if I ever had a problem, a really big one, I could turn to you for help. That was right before he left."

"I hope it's a problem I can solve," Mr. Flynn said. "It feels like a long time since I've been able to solve a problem."

"It's my sisters," Alex said. "Briana and Julie. Bri's fifteen and she has asthma. It began this summer and it's left her very weak. Julie's thirteen and she's tough, but she's a girl, if you know what I mean, sir."

"Where are your parents?" Mr. Flynn asked. "Can't they help?"

"They're gone," Alex said, surprised at how much it still hurt to say it. "They've been gone since the beginning. We have a brother, but he's in the Marines. I'm the head of the family now."

"You're just a kid yourself," Mr. Flynn said. "How old are you, eighteen?"

"Next month," Alex replied. "We've been managing all right, up until now. Do you remember Chris's friend Kevin Daley? He's been a big help."

"The weaselly one?" Mr. Flynn asked with a laugh. "I haven't thought about him in months. Is that it? Kevin's all you have?"

"The church, too," Alex said. "But it's done all it can for us. I know there are evacuation centers, but Bri wouldn't survive in one, and Julie has to be protected. That's why I've come to you. I don't know where else to turn."

Mr. Flynn nodded. "We have to move fast," he said. "For your sisters' sake and for your own."

"I can stay on," Alex said. "I can manage on my own, especially if I know Bri and Julie are safe."

"You might be all right now, but not for much longer," Mr. Flynn said. "Listen to me, Alex, as if I were your father. New York City is on life support. It's being kept alive for as long as it takes to get everything out of it that must be removed. Do you have any idea how complicated it is to transport things? Papers, computers, people? Scores of embassies, all of the United Nations? Every piece of art from the Metropolitan Museum and all the other museums we used to take for granted? Gutenberg Bibles. First Shakespeare folios. Cleopatra's Needle, for God's sake. You can't just carry a Rembrandt out of town. Everything has to be labeled and cataloged and shipped to a safe location. Originally the plan was to move New York City out to Nevada. The rich and the mighty, not people like you and your sisters. The president, the mayor, the heads of the Fortune 500: All those people debated where we should go and when and how. For better or worse, our president is an optimistic person. He didn't listen when the scientists said Nevada wasn't such a good idea. Then the volcanoes started to erupt and Nevada no longer worked, and then the cold set in, and no place seemed to work, but the rich and the mighty still had to go someplace, and so did the Rembrandts. So they're keeping New York alive a little longer. But as soon as they can, they'll pull the plug and let the city die. It will anyway. It's an island, Alex, and islands can't survive in this world, not anymore. Get out while you can."

"Thank you," Alex said. "If you can get Bri and Julie to a safe place, I'll leave New York. I can manage in an evac center, until I can figure out a way of getting us all back together."

"That won't be necessary," Mr. Flynn said. "I can get all of you out if we move fast enough." He got up and walked over to the wall and removed a painting, revealing a wall safe. He spun the lock a few times, pulled out some envelopes, and then, finding the one he was looking for, put everything back in the safe, and hid it once again.

Just like in the movies, Alex thought. A perfect place for a winning lottery ticket.

"Here are three passes," Mr. Flynn said, handing Alex three cards. "They're guaranteed passage and housing for my three family members. I applied for them when this all happened, but I was able to get my wife and children out before the passes arrived. I've held on to them ever since, figuring they'd be valuable someday, and now they are."

Alex stared at the three cards that would carry his sisters and himself to a place of safety.

Mr. Flynn rifled through a sheet of papers. "People leave in convoys," he said. "I haven't kept track of where they're sending families now, because mine is safe and sound in South Carolina. But I know the safe towns are in the south, inland, and they have police and medical facilities and food and schools. That I can guarantee you. The next convoy leaves on November twenty-eighth, but reservations have to be made two weeks in advance, so that doesn't do us any good. Okay, the one after that is December twelfth. When's your birthday?"

"December twenty-second," Alex said.

"You'll just make it, then," Mr. Flynn said. "Dependents have to be under the age of eighteen. You'll need to bring your birth certificates and proof of residency." He pulled out a piece of business stationery from under a pile. "Is Julie a nickname?" he asked. "What about Alex?"

"Julie is Julie," Alex replied. "Legally I'm Alejandro."

"All right," Mr. Flynn said, writing furiously. "Alejandro, Briana, and Julie Morales are now my legal wards. If they give you any grief about the passes, give them this letter. I'll be making the reservations, so it shouldn't be a problem. And here's the list of what you can take with you. Not much, as you can see, but the town they'll take you to should be fully supplied."

"Thank you," Alex said, taking the papers from him.

"The convoy leaves out of Port Authority at two PM on Monday, December twelfth," Mr. Flynn said. "Get there by eleven. Maybe Kevin Daley's father could drive you down. He's in trucking." He paused. "No, on second thought, don't ask him. Don't tell anyone about the passes; they're too valuable. Don't tell anyone you're leaving New York until the day you go."

Alex nodded. "Thank you, Mr. Flynn," he said. "You're saving my sisters' lives."

"Yours, too," Mr. Flynn said. "I couldn't look Chris in the eye and tell him I let you die along with the city. I always appreciated what you did for Chris. Until he had you to compete against, he assumed winning came automatically. You gave him valuable lessons in losing. My guess is those lessons are helping him survive today."

"The lessons he taught me have helped me survive, too," Alex said. "Thank you, Mr. Flynn, for everything. I'll be in your debt forever."

"Stay alive," Mr. Flynn said. "That will be payment enough."

Thursday, November 24

There wasn't pumpkin pie at St. Margaret's Thanksgiving dinner, but there was pumpkin pudding in meringue shells. The string beans obviously came from a can but someone had thrown in some slivered almonds; the sweet potatoes had marshmallows mixed in, and there was enough stuffing for everybody. There was punch and even some apple juice. So what if there was no turkey.

Only eighteen more days until they were safely out of New York. Of all the secrets Alex had kept in the past six months, this was the only one that made him smile. He didn't care that he had no idea where he and his sisters would end up. Maybe it would be Florida or maybe Oklahoma or Texas or someplace altogether different. It wouldn't be the paradise Julie had fantasized about, with sunlight and clean air. But it would be safe and there'd be food and medicine, and from there they could make a fresh start.

For the first time in months, Alex allowed himself to think about the future. If he was too old to go to school, he could get a job. Towns couldn't exist without workers. If he could leave and come back, he thought he might try to find Carlos or Uncle Jimmy. If not, he would stay on as a laborer until Bri and Julie were taken care of. It wouldn't surprise him if, after high school, Bri entered a convent. Julie would probably find a guy while she was in high school and get pregnant, the way Mami had.

Alex finished his pumpkin pudding and grinned. If anyone had told him seven months ago that he'd be looking forward to a future where his kid sister had a baby before she turned eighteen and he would be a laborer instead of a college grad, he would have been furious. But now it sounded like heaven on earth.

It seemed like everyone left on the Upper West Side was at St. Margaret's that afternoon. What remained of the Vincent de Paul and Holy Angels faculties sat at one table, laughing together. Harvey sat at another, gumming away at his food. Alex couldn't even hate him anymore. Life, for once, was too good for him to feel angry.

As he and his sisters walked home, they heard some noise on Ninetieth Street.

"What is that?" Julie asked, and Alex could see her tense up.

Bri looked puzzled. "It sounds like people having fun," she said. "Hear? I think they're laughing."

The idea of people actually enjoying themselves was so implausible, they lost all fear and went to look. There, on Ninetieth and Columbus, were a dozen men playing touch football.

One of them spotted Alex and his sisters. "Come on," he yelled. "We could use more players."

Alex gestured to his sisters. "What about them?" he asked.

"Cheerleaders!" the guy called back.

"Can we?" Julie asked. "Oh, Alex, please."

Alex looked at Julie and Bri. Half the football players were coughing from the polluted air. Bri couldn't possibly stay out long. But none of them had had any fun since Julie's birthday. "Just for a few minutes," he said. "Bri, you watch."

"All right," Bri said, but she was bursting with excitement also. They crossed the street and joined the crowd.

"It's not Thanksgiving without football," one of the guys said.

"Touch football," another said. "No helmets, no hits."

"No Cowboys, either," the first man said. "Jets versus Giants."

"We need another guy on our team!" another man yelled. "Come on, kid. You're a Giant."

And for one glorious moment, that was just how Alex felt.

Tuesday, November 29

There had been eighteen seniors in St. Vincent de Paul Academy before the Thanksgiving break. Now there were five. Alex figured most of them had gone on the convoy the day before.

James Flaherty was one of the newly missing. It worried Alex to see him gone. His father was a doctor, and Alex had counted on him to get more cartridges for Bri's inhaler when she ran out.

It didn't matter, he told himself. Bri had enough until they made it to the safe town, a place with doctors and hospitals and real medicine.

Two weeks. They'd made it this long. They could certainly make it for another two weeks.

Thursday, December 1

He had no idea what time it was when he woke up, but he knew he was cold. He was used to being cold by now, but this was different.

He fumbled around the end table, searching for the flashlight, and knocked over the half-filled glass of water he always kept by his side. But there was no sound of water spilling.

He flashed the light onto the glass and saw why no water had come out. It was more ice than water. The furnace must have run out of heating oil.

He'd known that would happen eventually, but he'd devoted a fair amount of prayer that it might last until they moved out.

"You couldn't wait two more weeks?" he asked.

Apparently it couldn't. The question became if his sisters, Bri in particular, could make it until then.

He allowed the familiar feeling of panic to wash over him, and then he began to think. It was only for twelve days, and for some of them at least, there would be electricity during the day. With electricity, Bri could keep the electric blanket and electric heater on. He and Julie would be at school, and there was no reason to assume the oil would run out there.

For the rest of the day, or what passed for day, they should all be okay if they kept on sweaters, coats, scarves, gloves, and multiple pairs of socks. The building provided some insulation from the cold. It was hard to tell, but Alex didn't think the temperature got much below twenty degrees in the daytime outside, so it would probably be about that, maybe a bit warmer, inside.

Nighttime would be harder, but they still had a couple of unused blankets. The girls slept in the sleeping bags. They were both so thin they could share one bag, which would help both of them since they'd share body warmth that way. It would help him as well, because he'd be warmer in a sleeping bag. Julie wouldn't like giving up her bag, but tough. Asthma wasn't contagious.

With both girls in one bag, sleeping in coats and scarves and with extra blankets piled on them, they should be okay. He'd wrap himself in a blanket inside the sleeping bag, and that would have to do.

They'd all need to sleep with as much of their heads covered as possible. But 11F had had a couple of ski masks, so the girls could wear those day and night. He'd wrap his head in a sweater, and that should help.

It was for less than two weeks, he reminded himself. After that they'd be living in a building with heat and hot water. He just had to keep them alive for eleven more days, and then things would be all right.

He brought the two extra blankets into the bedroom and put them over his sisters' sleeping bodies. In the morning he'd explain the new rules to them.

With the flashlight glowing onto his watch, he could tell

it was just after five o'clock. No point going back to sleep. Instead, shaking with the cold, he dressed, then knelt in front of the crucifix they'd taken from home and prayed for the strength he and his sisters would need in the days to come.

Friday, December 2

There was hardly anyone on the food line, but that didn't make things move any faster. Julie stuck by Alex's side, the way she did now when they went to school and church. Kevin told her jokes and really seemed to listen to her. Alex could see how much she liked that.

Every night, when Alex said his prayers, he thanked Christ for the gift of Kevin's friendship. He would have told Kevin that, but he didn't think Kevin would want to know.

"How are you doing?" he asked Kevin instead, at lunch. "How's your family?"

"Fine," Kevin said. "Or as fine as we can be under the circumstances."

"Good," Alex said. "Are you warm enough?"

"Right now, this very minute, no," Kevin said.

Alex laughed. "I mean at home," he said. "Does your building still have heat?"

"Yeah, sure," Kevin said. "They moved us to a DRU before Thanksgiving, so we're okay. Mom complains because they keep the thermostat at sixty-five. But no one ever froze to death at sixty-five."

"What's a DRU?" Alex asked.

Kevin looked uncomfortable. "Designated Residential Unit," he said. "They're for the families of essential personnel, to make things bearable until we get out."

"I guess you have to be a level six for something like that," Alex said.

Kevin laughed. "A level six?" he said. "That just means you can walk up six flights of stairs without risking a heart attack. Where'd you pick that up?"

"I heard it somewhere," Alex said. "I guess I misunderstood."

"I guess so," Kevin said. "You okay? Do you still have heat?"

"Oh yeah, we're fine," Alex said. "I was just wondering how your mother is doing."

"She misses our old apartment," Kevin said. "When she's sober enough to remember."

"What do you miss?" Alex said. "What's the one thing you miss the most?"

Kevin shrugged. "TV maybe," he said. "Decent food. The Internet. I don't miss the sun that much. At least I'm not freckling anymore. What about you?"

Alex tried to come up with an answer that was short yet honest. "Family," he finally said.

"Stupid of me to ask," Kevin replied. "I miss knowing I'm smart. That used to compensate for a lot in my life."

"Mine, too," Alex said.

"You ever think this is just a nightmare and someday you'll wake up and things'll be the way they were before?" Kevin asked.

Alex shook his head.

"Me neither," Kevin said. "My mother does, though. That's why she stays drunk. When she's sober, she has to remember all this is real. Harvey'd better not run out of booze anytime soon. I think Mom'll kill herself if she has to stay sober."

"I'm sorry," Alex said. "That must be really hard."

"It's okay," Kevin replied. "I'd be drunk all the time too if I didn't have to look out for her."

The line began to move. A woman standing a few feet ahead of them fainted. Alex and Kevin stepped around her.

Kevin handed his bag to Alex when they finally got them. "Not much this time," he said.

Alex looked. Each bag had a box of rice, a can of red beans, a can of mixed vegetables, and two cans of tomato soup.

"Maybe Harvey'll have some stuff," he said. "Are we still on for Monday morning?"

"Wouldn't miss it," Kevin said. "Seven o'clock, in front of your building."

"Good," Alex said. "Well, I'd better go home. See you at school."

"Sure thing," Kevin said.

"Oh, and Kevin," Alex said.

Kevin paused.

"Nothing," Alex said. "Just thanks for doing this with me."

"Any time," Kevin said. "See you in school."

Saturday, December 3

"What's that sound?" Bri asked that morning. "It sounds like broken glass is falling from the sky."

"Great," Alex said. "That's just what we need."

Bri giggled. "You sound like Julie," she said.

"What's wrong with that?" Julie asked. "Alex, can we look out the window and see what's happening?"

Alex could think of two good reasons why they shouldn't. The first was it would involve pulling nails out of a wall so they could fold back a section of the blanket that covered the window. The second reason was because he knew he didn't want to see what was happening. Ostriches definitely have the right idea, he thought, as he freed himself from the blankets he'd wrapped around his body and went to the kitchen to get a hammer. He could see his breath. Nine more days, he reminded himself. We only have to survive here for nine more days.

Julie and Bri crowded around the window as Alex lifted the blanket.

Bri gasped. "Everything's white."

"More like gray," Julie said. "I never saw gray snow before."

Alex knew it was a mistake to look. West Eighty-eighth Street was covered with snow. It was hard to estimate how much had fallen, but he guessed at least six inches, maybe more. And now it was sleeting, the snow already glistening with ice.

"It must have started after we got home from school," Julie said. "Do you think school will be open on Monday?"

"I don't see why not," Alex said, quickly calculating how much food they had in the house and how long it could last if he and Julie didn't eat lunch at school. "It's not like we take a bus to get there."

"I used to love snow," Bri said. "I guess now it just makes things harder."

Bri's right, Alex thought, staring down the street. It was going to be hard enough to get Bri to Port Authority by foot. But now there was snow and ice on the streets, and no one would plow this far uptown.

He looked at Bri, or more accurately, at Bri's eyes, since the rest of her face and body was covered. How much could she weigh? He'd foolishly weighed himself the week before and found he was down to 112. Bri probably weighed about ninety pounds. He'd never be able to carry her over two miles.

What if he rigged up some kind of stretcher and he and Julie lifted together. He looked at his baby sister, who was staring out the window, transfixed by the sight of snow. He doubted she weighed eighty pounds. She seemed healthy enough and she had less trouble climbing stairs than he did lately. But it was dangerous to assume she'd be able to share the burden for such a long distance.

Could they drag Bri on a mattress? Even if they could, the mattress would get wet, and it wouldn't be good for Bri to be lying on a wet mattress in below-freezing weather for the three hours or more it might take. Besides, as the mattress took on moisture, it would get heavier and harder to pull.

How could God do this to them? What had they done that deserved such punishment?

"I don't care if it is gray," Bri said. "It's still beautiful. And look how it covers the corpses."

"Great," Julie said. "Now the rats'll be pissed off."

"Don't use language like that," Alex said automatically, and in spite of himself, he laughed.

Humility, he reminded himself. God wasn't singling him out. If he placed his faith in Christ and used whatever brain cells he had left, the solution would come to him. Because somewhere there was a solution. There had to be. There had to.

Sunday, December 4

"Come on," Bri said, going into the living room and shaking Alex awake. "It's Sunday. We don't want to miss Mass."

"Go back to bed," Alex said. "You'll freeze standing there."

"I'm not so cold," Bri said. "Besides, there's heat at St. Margaret's. Please, Alex. Get ready, and then I'll wake Julie."

Alex reluctantly climbed out of the sleeping bag and walked to the window. He pulled the blanket away and gestured for Bri to join him.

"Look out there," he said. "There's snow and sleet and snow on top of the sleet. How the hell do you think we're going to get to church?"

"We can manage," Bri said. "I won't hold you back, I promise."

"No," Alex said. "Maybe next Sunday if the snow disappears. But not today."

Bri began to cry.

"What?" Alex said, trying to keep the irritation out of his voice. "It's just one Sunday. God will understand."

Bri shook her head. "It's not that," she said. "I know Christ will forgive us for not going to church today." She took a deep breath. "I'm sorry," she said. "I know everyone is suffering. It's just I feel so trapped. Sunday is the only day I'm outside. I guess God could tell my motives were impure. I'll pray for His forgiveness."

"Tell you what," Alex said. "Go back to bed and sleep a while longer. We'll all pray this afternoon for God's forgiveness."

Bri giggled. "Julie'll love that," she said. "But thanks, Alex, for understanding."

"I try," Alex said. "Now go. You may not be cold, but I'm freezing."

Bri gave her brother a quick kiss. "See you later," she said, going back to her room.

Alex continued to stare outside. A foot of snow, he estimated, with an inch or more of ice sandwiched in there. Bri was right to feel trapped.

He dressed quickly, wrote a note for his sisters saying he was going out to see how conditions were, then walked down the twelve flights of stairs. Down was easier than up, but he was still short of breath by the time he reached the building's lobby.

The front door opened inward, so it was no problem getting it open. But the snow was even deeper than he'd guessed.

He cursed himself as he walked down to Papi's office in search of a shovel and rock salt. He should have eaten something. It was going to be hard enough to shovel the snow just so they could get out of the building. It would be that much harder with his not having eaten in twenty hours.

But the thought of climbing the twelve flights just to ram cold rice and beans into his mouth was even worse. He'd manage. He had no choice.

The shovel and bag of rock salt were right where he remembered. Of all Papi's janitorial obligations, this was the one he liked the least, so Carlos and Alex had done the brunt of the shoveling. It had snowed a lot the previous winter; Alex could remember a half dozen mornings when Papi woke him before dawn so he could get the shoveling done before the people in the building got up. Papi gave him hell if he left any snow on the sidewalk, even though scores of people would walk over it and it would melt before noon.

He tried carrying both the shovel and the twenty-pound bag of rock salt, but couldn't manage it. So he left the bag of rock salt in the stairwell, and took the shovel upstairs. He could hear Papi laughing at him for his weakness, and he used his anger and resentment to give him the energy he needed to clear the snow from in front of the door.

The work was brutal. It was a heavy snow, and with the ice intermixed, every shovelful took all his strength to lift and carry. It didn't help that twice as he flung the snow onto a pile of decomposing bodies, he found he was also tossing rats that had frozen in the snowfall. After a few minutes he realized he needed to stop just to catch his breath every single time he shoveled. He really was *blanducho,* the way Papi always said.

After half an hour he'd cleared enough space in front of the door that he could stand outside and survey what remained to be done. Not that much really, he decided. Just shovel from the building to the street, then shovel West Eighty-eighth down to West End, then West End to Columbus Circle, and over to Eighth Avenue, and then down Eighth to Forty-second Street and Port Authority. Probably not even that much. If the powerful people had had the good sense to leave some other people around to do the cleaning for them, from Columbus Circle down was probably clear of snow. He'd only have to shovel for a mile and a half. Piece of cake for a level twelve.

He still had no idea how he could get Bri from Eighty-eighth Street downtown. He doubted she'd have the strength to walk as far as Broadway.

Alex began shoveling from the building to the street, not knowing what else to do. He was accustomed to the silence now, but except for the wind whipping around, things seemed even quieter than they had been just two days before. The whole block was deserted, he realized. He, Bri, and Julie seemed to be the only people still alive on West Eighty-eighth. When they left, there'd be nobody.

He stood for a moment, resting against the shovel. He never should have let Bri go to the convent. That was the first mistake. If he hadn't sent her away, she would have gone with Uncle Jimmy and Aunt Lorraine, and for all he knew, she never would have become asthmatic. If he'd known Bri was someplace safe, he could have looked for a place for Julie to go. It might not have been with *la familia,* but things hadn't been that desperate in June, and there would have been somebody trustworthy who'd have agreed to take her and protect her.

And if he hadn't had his sisters tying him down, he could have left New York and tried his luck elsewhere. Maybe he could have tracked down Carlos and joined the Marines. Carlos was probably someplace warm, eating three meals a day and sleeping in a real bed. That was the life.

He felt like screaming. Every single thing he'd done had been wrong, and his sisters' lives were at risk because of him.

He got on his knees, not caring that the icy wetness seeped through his pants legs, and begged for God's mercy for his sisters.

"Alex?"

He looked up and saw Julie standing in the doorway.

"What?" he said.

"Bri told me to get you," she said. "She was worried."

He stood up, feeling like a fool. "Tell her I'm fine," he said. "I'll be upstairs in a few minutes. I have to finish shoveling the sidewalk."

"You don't have to," Julie asked. "There's no one here except us."

"I know," Alex said. "But Papi would expect me to."

chapter 16

Monday, December 5

Alex decided he'd give Kevin fifteen minutes to show before going back inside. If the apartment had any kind of heat, he would have stood by the front door of his building for five, but since it was just marginally warmer indoors, he opted for fifteen.

He would have needed only the five-minute deadline. Kevin showed up at 7:03.

"You're crazy, you know that," Alex said. "How'd you even manage to get here?"

"It wasn't that bad," Kevin replied. "They've done some shoveling and plowing in my neighborhood." He looked at the sidewalk in front of Alex's building. "Nice job," he said. "You pay a kid to do it?"

"I wish," Alex said. "You really think we're going to find anything?"

"I wouldn't be here if I didn't," Kevin said. "The pickings should be really good. Lots of new bodies by the park. Some suicides; the storm was just too much for them, I guess. And people are dropping like flies. One of the doctors in our DRU says there's a mean flu bug going around."

"Great," Alex said. "Just what we need."

Kevin laughed. "We're lucky it's not plague," he said. "Harvey says there's an uptick in the market for jewelry. So we need to start taking wedding rings and engagement rings and earrings and anything else we can find. I guess they realized nobody's going to be mining for a while."

Alex hated taking wedding rings off bodies, but they needed food for one more week. He'd leave a note for Kevin when they left so he wouldn't worry. He'd be gone soon enough himself, maybe even to the same town as Alex.

Alex followed the footsteps Kevin had made going to his apartment. They were the only footprints in the snow. If there were still people living on the Upper West Side, they hadn't left their apartments since Saturday.

It was hard walking and the boys kept mostly to themselves as they walked east. The city would have been beautiful if the snow were white. But everything was corpse gray. No matter where Alex ended up, he wasn't going to miss New York. He'd be sorry to leave Kevin and Vincent de Paul and St. Margaret's and even Father Mulrooney, but that was it. Anyplace would be better than this.

He thought about Chris Flynn in South Carolina. Maybe it was warm there, or at least warmer. If there were still colleges, Chris would be sure to find one. A year ago, it would have driven him crazy to think of Chris getting into a good school somewhere while he didn't even know if he'd be going to college. Now, what difference did it make.

"Do you ever think about Chris Flynn?" he asked Kevin.

"Muhuhmhm," Kevin said. He'd wrapped his scarf around his mouth, and between that and the wind howling down Central Park West, it was impossible to understand what he was saying.

Not that it mattered. Chris had his life and Kevin had his.

The only important thing was getting Alex's sisters and himself to a place of safety.

He looked ahead and thought he saw the glint of a diamond about a block away. Maybe a fluicide, he thought, and he began to laugh. He trudged ahead, trying to maintain traction on the ice-crusted snow. If a ten-thousand-dollar lottery ticket could buy a can of pineapple, who knew what a diamond ring was worth.

Alex wasn't sure what caught his attention first, the odd crackling noise or the funny sound Kevin made or even the silence that followed. But something made him stop and turn around.

He wished he hadn't. He wished he'd kept on trudging toward the diamond ring that might have brought his family a can of sliced peaches. He wished he'd kept on walking until he'd walked out of New York City altogether to someplace warm and safe.

Instead he turned around and saw Kevin lying on the sidewalk, an ice-laden tree limb across his neck, pinning him down.

Alex retraced his steps in the snow. Kevin was lying facedown, and Alex's first thought was that he would suffocate in the snow. He tried lifting the branch off him, but it was too large and too heavy with snow and ice. Alex looked up and could see the fresh torn gap in the tree where the limb had fallen from.

"Help!" Alex screamed. "Someone help me!"

But of course no one did. No one had helped Julie when she'd cried out a few weeks before. New York was more dead than alive, and those people who were still around didn't help anyone but themselves.

Kevin's head was twisted and Alex could see his right eye,

looking more startled than scared or dead. He pulled off his gloves and tried to find Kevin's pulse. Then he decided that was a waste of time; what he needed to do was get Kevin out from under the branch. If he couldn't lift it, he'd tunnel Kevin out. Without even bothering to put his glove back on, he began digging the icy snow under Kevin's head and under the tree branch, so he could pull Kevin out. Kevin wasn't breathing, and Alex realized he needed to unwrap the scarf around Kevin's mouth. It was caught in the branch, and Alex had to yank at it, making Kevin's head jerk. Alex screamed in horror, and that was when he knew the only friend he'd ever really had was dead. If Kevin had been alive, even if his life were just a flicker, he would have laughed at scaring Alex so effectively.

But Alex kept digging. Eventually he created a pocket big enough to wiggle Kevin out from under the limb. He grabbed under Kevin's arms and pulled. It took more strength than he knew he had, but Kevin was finally freed.

Alex's heart was racing, but he didn't know if it was from the exertion or from seeing Kevin lying there. It didn't matter. He turned Kevin over so he was lying flat on his back.

He felt for a pulse again. He put his ear next to Kevin's mouth. He pounded on Kevin's chest in some vague imitation of CPR.

"Wake up!" he screamed at Kevin. "Make him wake up!" he screamed at God.

Kevin's eyes stared at the sky. His mouth was half twisted, almost smiling—the red of the blood that had dripped out of his nose and mouth the only color left in New York.

Please, God, Alex prayed. *Cherish this soul. He didn't mean half the things he said.*

With Kevin staring heavenward, Alex pulled off his watch so he could give it to Kevin's parents. Then Alex realized he had no idea where Kevin's parents were. He didn't know the address of their DRU, and he didn't know where Daley Trucking was located.

It seemed unlikely that Kevin would have carried ID on him, let alone up-to-the-minute ID, but Alex had to make sure. Almost apologetically, he went through Kevin's pockets. All he found was the gun.

Alex pulled it out. He recognized it right away, from that first day they'd gone body shopping. Funny to think Kevin carried it around and Alex hadn't known. He knew more about Kevin than about almost anyone else in his life, but apparently he hadn't known nearly as much as he thought he had.

Alex took off his other glove, then fumbled around trying to unclasp the cross he always wore around his neck. He was shaking so hard it took a minute or more before he could undo it, but when he did, he kissed it, then put it over Kevin's heart. Then he closed his friend's eyes.

At some point Kevin's parents would worry about him, he realized, as he walked toward the diamond ring and the body wearing it. Maybe they knew where Alex lived and maybe they didn't, but it was unlikely they knew which apartment the Morales family had taken over. Most likely they'd check at Vincent de Paul to see if Kevin had shown up for school.

Alex twisted the diamond ring off the dead woman's finger. He'd take Kevin's watch to school and give it to Father Mulrooney, he decided. It was a priest's job to comfort a family. Alex's job was to keep his sisters alive and safe.

With the ring and the gun and the watch in his pocket, Alex began the long journey back uptown. Maybe, he thought, the diamond ring and the gun could buy Bri a safe way to get to the convoy. Kevin would like that.

Tuesday, December 6

"I have some very sad news to convey," Father Mulrooney informed the handful of boys that made up the student body of St. Vincent de Paul Academy.

Alex waited for the announcement of Kevin's death. When he'd told the priest about Kevin the day before, Father Mulrooney had seemed genuinely saddened.

"Mr. Kim has died," Father Mulrooney said instead. "Most unexpectedly. His death will be profoundly felt in our community."

Mr. Kim had taught science with enthusiasm if not much scholarship. Alex had liked him well enough, but he wouldn't have been someone he'd miss once he and his sisters were gone.

Still, it was odd to hear he'd died. Another fluicide, he guessed.

Wednesday, December 7

"I need something from you," Alex said to Harvey. "I'm willing to barter."

"Anything for a friend of Kevin's," Harvey replied. "Funny, I haven't seen him the past couple of days."

Alex shrugged. "I need a sled," he said.

Harvey laughed. "Want a dog team to go along with that?" he asked.

"Just a regular sled," Alex said. "But I've got to be able to pull it. Good-sized, too, not a little kiddie one."

Harvey looked thoughtful. "I might be able to do that," he said. "When do you need it?"

"As soon as possible," Alex said. He only wished he'd

thought of a sled earlier in the week. But Kevin's death had made it hard for him to think about much of anything. Or maybe he was just too hungry these days to think and Kevin's death was merely an excuse. It didn't matter. Nothing mattered except figuring out a way of getting Bri downtown, and a sled seemed to make the most sense.

"You said you had something to barter," Harvey said. "A sled's a big-ticket item. It ain't no can of green peas. Whatcha got?"

Alex pulled out the diamond ring and Kevin's gun. "How's this?" he asked.

"Pretty impressive," Harvey said. "I like the gun. Always a market for those. You been holdin' out on me, kid? You got any more merchandise like that?"

Alex thought about the last four cans of Papi's beer that he'd been saving for an emergency. "Nothing this good," he said. "I really need that sled, Harvey."

"Tell you what," Harvey said. "You come by tomorrow morning. Either I'll have the sled or I won't, but I'll know by then. You got anything else for me today?"

Alex looked at the cans of spinach on the shelf behind the counter.

"I don't suppose I could have some spinach on account," he said.

"On accounta what?" Harvey asked, then burst out laughing. "Sorry, kid. Cash and carry. No more handouts just because I like someone."

Alex nodded. "Just thought I'd ask," he said.

"Never hurts to ask," Harvey said. "See you in the morning. Maybe I'll have that sled for you. And who knows. Maybe I'll throw in a can of that spinach while I'm at it."

Thursday, December 8

Harvey had outdone himself, Alex thought as he carried the sled into his old basement apartment. The sled was close to perfect. It was large enough for Bri to sit on comfortably and it had footrests so she could shift her weight around during the long trip to Port Authority. It was heavy plastic, with runners high enough that he wouldn't have to worry about Bri getting wet from the snow. Its only drawback was its single pull rope, which meant he'd have to do the dragging by himself. But he and Julie probably wouldn't have been able to pull in unison anyway.

It felt strange unlocking the door to the basement apartment. Alex hadn't been there since the move to 12B, but it made no sense to carry the sled upstairs when they'd be using it in just a few days. There'd been no electricity, not even on weekdays, since the snowstorm. Alex couldn't wait to get out.

Everything smelled damp and musty. It was hard to believe they'd all lived there and never noticed that. We were mole people, he thought. In a few days, though, they'd be the elite.

He went to Mami's bedroom and pulled down the boxes from her closet shelf. It was hard to see anything, since so little natural light came in and he hadn't thought to bring a flashlight or candles with him. But eventually he found their birth certificates and baptismal certificates.

Alex looked through the rest of the apartment, in case there was anything there they needed to take with them. On the kitchen counter by the phone was the note he'd left saying they'd moved to 12B. He wasn't sure what to do about it. There seemed to be no point in writing a new note, since he didn't know where they'd be going.

Once Bri and Julie were settled and safe, he'd somehow locate Carlos and tell him where the girls were. Mami or Papi could find him also, if they ever came back. In case anyone showed up before Monday, Alex left the note. He gave his home one more look. He still remembered moving there when he was five. He'd gone outside to play with some kids and he'd said something in Spanish. The kids had all laughed at him and he'd run back to Mami, crying.

"Here you speak English," she said to him. "No more Spanish."

That had been easy enough; he'd grown up hearing both. But he never tried to play with the neighborhood kids after that. Carlos had, no problem. But Alex always felt the kids looked down on him. They were all Danny O'Briens.

But in five days he'd become a Danny O'Brien. It was like something out of a Dickens novel, he thought. Foundling discovers he's really a long-lost millionaire. Of course he wasn't a foundling or a millionaire, but it was the same basic concept. And he'd earned this trip up the social ladder through his hard work at Vincent de Paul. Mr. Flynn wouldn't have given the passes to just anybody. It wasn't an act of charity. It was an act of respect.

Papi would be proud of me, he thought. I've taken care of my sisters. I've been a man.

Friday, December 9

He'd woken Julie and made her go on the food line with him. He wished he didn't have to, but there was no food in the house and if they were going to make it through the weekend, they needed every can they could get.

The line seemed safe enough, though; there were so few

people on it. Alex made sure Julie stood by his side for the couple of hours they waited. He guessed the temperature had fallen below zero. Hell won't be hot, he thought. It'll be cold like this.

"Where's Kevin?" Julie finally asked.

He knew she would ask, but that didn't make it easier. "He's dead," he replied.

"Are you sure?" Julie asked. "Maybe he's just gone."

"I was there," Alex said. "He's dead all right."

"Oh," Julie said. "Three of the sisters died, too. Well, Sister Joanne was just a postulant."

"How'd they die?" Alex asked, not wanting to talk about Kevin.

Julie shrugged. "They got sick," she said. "Sister Rita didn't tell us of what or anything. She was crying, only she was pretending not to. But we could all tell. Not that there are that many of us left. Maybe some of the girls have died, too."

"They've probably just moved on," Alex said. "Most people have."

"I don't want to die," Julie said. "Sister Rita said Sister Dolores and Sister Claire and Sister Joanne are in heaven with the Holy Virgin, but I'd still rather be alive."

"Me too," Alex said.

They stood silently for a while. Then Julie took his hand.

"I'm sorry Kevin died," she said. "He was a good friend."

"Yes," Alex said. "He was."

Sunday, December 11

"Julie, I need you to go to eleven F," Alex said after lunch. "I want you to see if there's anything left we can use."

"Why do I have to go?" Julie said. "There's nothing there."

"You have to go because I told you to," Alex said. "Julie, just do it. Don't give me a hard time."

"What if there's someone in the stairwell?" she asked.

"There isn't," Alex said. "No one's left here but us. Please. It's just one floor. You'll be fine."

Julie grabbed the flashlight. "You'd better hope no one's there," she said. "God'll never forgive you if there is."

"I'll take my chances," Alex said. "Now go." He watched as Julie left the apartment. When he heard her walk down the hallway, he went into the bedroom. Bri was huddled in the sleeping bag, but even though she had on two coats and several blankets, she was still shaking from cold. Just one more day, Alex told himself. In one more day they'd be on their way to safety.

Bri looked up at him and smiled. "I thought Julie would come in to get my plate," she said. "Are you doing the housework now?"

Alex grinned. "Not a chance," he said. "No, I need to talk to you, Bri. Alone. I sent Julie off on an errand so we can talk."

Bri struggled to sit up. The exertion made her cough. She grabbed her inhaler and took a deep breath.

One more day, Alex thought. He sat on the bed next to his sister. "Bri, I'm going to tell you something and I don't want you to get upset," he began. "I'm going to ask you to make a big sacrifice for Julie."

"I'd do anything for Julie," Bri said. "You know that."

Alex nodded. He was counting on it. "Bri, it isn't safe for Julie in New York anymore," he said. "I'm not talking about the cold or being hungry. I mean safe for a girl."

Bri's eyes opened wide. "Nothing's happened, has it?" she asked.

"Nothing's happened," Alex said. "But Papi taught me the

most important thing a man can do is to protect the women he loves. I have to protect you and Julie, and I've been trying the best I can up until now. But conditions are getting worse, so I've made arrangements for all of us. We're leaving New York tomorrow. Remember Chris Flynn? His father gave me passes for the three of us to take us to a safe place, a place where the families of the really important people go."

"No," Bri said, half choking. "You go. You and Julie. I'll stay here for Mami and Papi."

Alex stroked Bri's hair. "Julie won't go without you and neither will I. For our sake, you have to come with us."

"But what about Mami and Papi?" Bri cried. "How will they find us?"

"I figured that out," Alex said. "After we've moved I'll find Carlos and tell him where we are. He can tell Mami and Papi. But we have to leave, Bri. If Julie's life means anything to you, we all have to leave tomorrow."

"I'm scared," Bri said. "Alex, it scares me. I know I'm holding you back." She began to cry. "I'm sorry I ever came home. I should have stayed at the convent and died there."

"*Idiota,*" Alex said, kissing Bri on her forehead. "I need you alive and so does Julie. Now don't be a *dramatica* like Aunt Lorraine. Think about how wonderful it's going to be living someplace with heat and electricity and three meals a day."

Bri took another puff from her inhaler. "Do you think I'll get better?" she asked.

"It's what I pray for," Alex said.

Bri took a deep breath. "I'm sorry," she said. "I don't make things any easier for you. But I'm sure I'm strong enough to walk to Port Authority."

"You won't have to," Alex replied. "You should see the sled I got you. Well, you will see it tomorrow. You'll ride in luxury all the way there. After that the bus will take us to our new home. That may take a couple of days, but the bus will have heat. Can you believe that? Heat." He laughed. "We'll be living like royalty starting tomorrow."

"Julie must be so happy," Bri said.

"She will be," Alex said. "I haven't told her yet. You're the next oldest, so you deserved to be told first."

"When she gets back, can you tell her in here?" Bri asked. "I want to see her face when she finds out."

Alex nodded. "That's a good idea," he said. "Now rest up, and I'll come back when Julie gets home. Tomorrow's going to be a big day for all of us, and I want you to be as strong and ready for it as possible."

"I have my rosary beads in the sleeping bag with me," Bri said. "I'll pray now. And I'll thank God for you and for Mr. Flynn and for everyone else who's been so kind."

chapter 17

Monday, December 12

Only five more blocks, Alex told himself. They'd made it this far; five more blocks was nothing.

The trip downtown had been far more difficult than he'd imagined, in spite of how well it had started. He'd been pleased with how he'd handled things, from breaking the news to Bri and then to Julie (who'd kept her rejoicing to a quiet roar, which he appreciated), slipping a note under the door at Vincent de Paul so Father Mulrooney and Sister Rita wouldn't worry about them, then returning back to 12B and helping Bri and Julie pack. Then he and Julie tidied and cleaned the apartment until it was as close to immaculate as could be managed under the circumstances. They'd all eaten supper, leaving enough food so they could have breakfast the next day.

He hadn't slept well, but that was excitement, and he figured he'd have plenty of time to sleep on the bus. He finally stopped trying around four-thirty, finished up whatever he needed to do, then woke his sisters. It felt strange and wonderful to eat breakfast; he couldn't remember the last time he'd started the day not hungry.

He made sure Bri and Julie had packed what they intended, a couple of changes of clothes, and a personal item or two, nothing too heavy and certainly nothing bulky, since they were limited to what fit in their backpacks. They each wore several layers of clothing, more than usual, both as a packing trick and because they were going to be outside for several hours.

Finally they were ready to go. It was a slow walk down the twelve flights of stairs, since they had to stop at almost every floor so Bri could catch her breath. She wouldn't have been able to survive much longer under these conditions, Alex thought. He was sure her inhaler cartridges were running low, and he had no idea how to replace them. But in a matter of days they'd be in the safe place and that would be no problem.

Alex left Bri and Julie in the lobby while he walked down the final flight of stairs to their old apartment. Everything was as he'd left it. He carried up the sled, and was rewarded by squeals of admiration and excitement. He put the sled out onto the street, then went into the building and carried out Bri, placing her carefully on the sled so she never got wet. It was funny to think they'd never be back, never see West Eighty-eighth Street again, or even New York City.

He suggested that before they go they pray silently, and he could see the gratitude in Bri's eyes at his suggestion. Then when the time had come, he began pulling Bri while Julie walked along.

It was never easy, since he and Julie both had to trudge through unshoveled snow, and before long his arms and back began to ache from the burden of pulling the sled with Bri and the backpacks on it. Julie volunteered to help with the backpacks, so she ended up wearing one on her back and one on her chest. It didn't make that much of a difference, but Alex was grateful that Julie made the effort.

It took an hour just to get to Seventieth Street, and by then Bri was having difficulty breathing. Julie fell on Sixty-eighth Street, and Alex had to pull her up, which took more energy than he cared to spare at that point. Some of the snow got into Julie's boots, and she began shivering uncontrollably. Alex didn't know whether to shake her, slap her, or hug her.

"Come on," he said, at least as much to himself as to his sisters. "It's not that much farther. We can do it."

But by Sixty-second Street, he wasn't so sure. They still had to navigate Columbus Circle and walk a mile's worth of city streets. Did they have the strength? Bri was coughing and Julie's steps were more and more labored.

This is ridiculous, he told himself. In two hours, less if everything went well, they'd be inside Port Authority, finding where they needed to go and getting ready for the bus ride to salvation. They just had to make it until then.

The wind picked up, and Alex could taste salt breeze intermixed with the familiar ash. His eyes smarted and teared until he could hardly see two feet ahead of him. He thought of Harvey's offer, a ride from their apartment to a safe place for Bri and himself in exchange for Julie. Bri could die on the sled, he realized. Had that been another wrong decision on his part? Could he be that sure Julie would be better protected by him than by some stranger?

The wind began to sound like mocking laughter: Papi calling him a *debilucho,* Carlos calling him a sissy. They were real men. They never would have let things get this bad.

Julie fell again. The backpack on her chest got soaked in snow, and it was obviously too heavy for her to manage. Alex took it off her and put it on the sled.

"I can manage the other one," Julie said. "Put that one on me."

Alex shook his head. "We're fine this way," he said. "Let's get a move on."

But things got even worse at Fifty-seventh Street, because there civilization began again. Eighth Avenue had been plowed and the sidewalks shoveled, which meant the sled could no longer be used.

A truck drove by, its driver honking furiously and screaming curses at them.

"We have to get on the sidewalk," Alex said.

"We won't be able to pull the sled," Julie said.

Alex nodded. "We'll figure something out," he said, pulling the sled to the curb.

He grabbed Bri and lifted her over his shoulder, firefighter style. Julie lifted the sled onto the sidewalk. She pulled it from there, while Alex tried to maintain his balance on the icy sidewalk.

Twice he fell. The first time Julie managed to position herself to break his fall, and the three of them tumbled onto the sidewalk together. It would have been funny if there'd been any humor left in the world.

The second time Julie had no chance to help, and Alex took a painful fall, his nose hitting the sidewalk so hard he was afraid he'd broken it. The shock jolted Bri and she began desperately gasping for breath.

As Alex wiped away the blood from his face, Julie rifled through Bri's backpack, finally finding Bri's rosary beads, which she handed to her sister. Bri clutched the beads as though they were her lifeline.

"Dios te salve, María. Llena eres de gracia," Julie began. Hearing the familiar words of the Hail Mary in Spanish, as Mami al-

ways said it, helped calm Bri down. When she was able, she recited it along with Julie, while Alex stood there and told himself never to underestimate his little sister again.

The journey got easier as they got closer to Port Authority, and Alex regained his faith that they would actually make it. They saw a handful of people as they walked down Eighth Avenue, and while no one offered to help, no one cursed them out, either. There were a lot of bodies, and Alex could see, from the height of the piles, that many of them were new dead. Fluicide, he decided. There'd be no need for that word where they were going.

The last time Alex had been at Port Authority it was May, crowded with hysterical people trying to escape. Now it was deserted. It surprised him not to see anyone there for the convoy, but he thought maybe they used a different entrance or maybe they were all inside already. He couldn't look at his watch without shifting Bri around, so he asked Julie what time it was. She stopped pulling the sled and checked.

"Ten-fifteen," she said.

"I guess we're the first ones here," Alex said. "That's good. We can get seats together."

"I see a cop!" Julie cried, pointing toward the building. "He can tell us where to go."

Alex gently put Bri down and walked over to the cop. "We have passes on the convoy out," he said to the cop. "Do you know which entrance we need?"

"No convoy today," the cop said.

"What do you mean?" Alex asked. "The December twelfth convoy. We have our passes and our reservations." For a moment he panicked that somehow it was December 13 and they'd missed the convoy by a day. "It is the twelfth, isn't it?" he asked, unable to keep the terror out of his voice.

"It don't matter what today's date is," the cop said. "No convoys because of the quarantine."

"What quarantine?" Alex asked. "What are you talking about?"

The cop looked at Alex, then at Bri and Julie and the sled. "No one told you?" he asked, and Alex could hear pity in his voice.

"Told us what?" Alex said, already knowing how much he was going to hate the answer.

"New York City is under quarantine because of the flu," the cop said. "No one allowed in or out of the city."

"Until when?" Alex asked. "For how long?"

The cop shrugged. "Until it runs its course," he said. "Or until everyone in the country gets it so it won't matter anymore. Or until we all die. Take your pick."

"Do you know about the convoys?" Alex asked. "Will they start running again? Will they let us on if they do?"

"I know all about the convoys," the cop said. "I know all about the lucky people who get to go on them. Yeah, there'll be another one. They run every two weeks, and if that one can't go out, then the one after that will take care of you and your family. If you hear the quarantine's been lifted, come back in two weeks. If it hasn't by then, come back in four. For people like you, there's always a way out."

Alex would have laughed, except if he did, he wouldn't have been able to stop. Instead he thought about the next convoy. Two weeks was December 26. Christ was certainly too merciful to have them die before Christmas. Alex would keep his sisters alive for two more weeks and the convoys would be running again. He'd be eighteen and wouldn't be allowed to go with them, but that would be all right. The buses would be filled with women and children, and one of the women would certainly volunteer to look after Bri and Julie until they got settled in. Someone would be kind.

"Thank you," he said to the cop.

"Good luck, kid," the cop said. "Tough break. You have far to go?"

"Yeah," Alex said. "But if we made it here, we can make it back home."

Tuesday, December 13

Alex and Julie walked to Vincent de Paul hardly saying a word. None of them had talked much since the nightmare walk back from Port Authority. All Alex told his sisters was that the city was under a quarantine and once that ended, the convoys would be running again. They'd see how things were in two weeks.

He wouldn't tell them he couldn't go along with them until they were safely on the bus. But what was one more secret.

There was a big, handwritten sign on the front door of the school: CLOSED UNTIL FURTHER NOTICE DUE TO QUARANTINE

"How long do you think 'further notice' is?" Julie asked.

Alex shook his head. "I don't know," he said. "Maybe just a week if we're lucky."

"Do you think Harvey still has food?" Julie asked as they began their walk home.

"Yeah, I'm sure he does," Alex said. "I don't know what I have left I can barter with, though."

"Maybe you could bring him the sled," Julie said. "I bet he'd give you lots of food for that."

"We'll need the sled in two weeks," Alex said. "I can't carry Bri all the way to Port Authority."

"She'll die anyway if we don't get food," Julie said.

"Harvey won't want the sled back," Alex said. "We're the only people who'd want it. Think, Julie. Is there any food left at all?"

Julie nodded. "I left twelve B a can of beans," she said. "It seemed wrong to leave nothing in case they ever came back. And there's a canister of macaroni we never used because it had things in it."

"Things?" Alex said.

"Bugs," Julie replied. "I thought it would be wrong to throw it out, so I never did."

"We can eat that," Alex said. "People eat bugs all the time."

"Yuck," Julie said.

"It's better than starving," Alex said. "Besides, it's only until Friday. We'll get our bags of food then. And maybe Vincent de Paul will open again by Monday. We really just have to get through today, tomorrow, and Thursday and we'll be all right."

"We still have to cook the macaroni," Julie said.

"Oh," Alex said. "How do you do that?"

Julie shook her head. "You're totally useless," she said. "Even Carlos knows how to boil water."

"So you boil water and you cook the macaroni in that?" Alex asked. "That doesn't sound too hard."

"It isn't," Julie replied. "Except the stove hasn't worked in weeks. Bri's done all the cooking in the microwave when there's been electricity. Which there isn't anymore, in case you hadn't noticed."

"It's not my fault there hasn't been electricity since the storm and the stove doesn't work and I don't know how to cook," Alex said. "How long will the can of beans last us?"

"Depends whether we eat it or just look at it," Julie said.

"You boil water in a pot, right?" Alex said. "Over a flame."

"Yeah," Julie said.

"Well, we have the pot," Alex said. "And we still have running water. So the only thing we don't have is the flame."

"We could set fire to the apartment," Julie said. "Then we'd have the flame and we'd be warm for a change."

"Fire," Alex said. "We'll make a fire."

"Inside the apartment?" Julie asked. "Like a campfire?"

Alex shook his head. "We can't expose Bri to the smoke," he said. "We'll build the fire in one of the other apartments. In the sink. And we'll put the pot on top of it and the water'll boil and we'll have macaroni and beans."

"And bugs," Julie said, but Alex could hear the excitement and relief in her voice. "We don't have any firewood, though. What can we burn?"

"Magazines," Alex replied. "There are plenty of those left behind."

"We'd better boil lots of water," Julie said. "We're almost out of the water Bri boiled in the microwave. She boiled lots every afternoon, so we'd have it for an emergency, but we've pretty much used it all."

"You and Bri have taken really good care of me, haven't you," Alex said.

"It wasn't so bad before the snowstorm," Julie replied. "Bri used to thaw our suppers in the microwave when we were in school. Now we keep the cans in our sleeping bag."

Alex thought about how often he'd felt burdened by his sisters. But he'd been as dependent on them for survival as they were on him. "It's only for a couple more weeks," he said. "We'll get on the next convoy. And Friday there'll be food. Until then, we'll eat macaroni and beans."

"And bugs," Julie said. "Oh well. It's better than nothing."

Friday, December 16

Alex would have preferred to keep Julie home on Friday, but they needed the two bags of food. They'd finished the macaroni and beans by lunchtime the day before, and with the minimal amount of food in each bag, there was no way they could survive on what he alone would bring home.

There was nothing in any of the apartments left to barter. Alex had searched carefully at first and then frantically all Wednesday and Thursday. He'd done it by candlelight since all the flashlight batteries had burned out. They still had two candles left and half a box of matches.

Mostly they slept. Alex wasn't sure whether that was good for them or not, but there was nothing else to do, and he figured they probably burned fewer calories that way. He saw to it that Julie prayed during her waking moments. Prayer came naturally to Bri, so that was no problem.

Everything was gone, used over months of bartering for cans of beans and bags of rice. The only things Alex could think of to bring to Harvey were the coat he was wearing and a bottle of aspirin he'd insisted on holding on to.

That wasn't true and he knew it. While he'd traded practically everything he'd found in the medicine cabinets, he'd kept a half dozen prescription sleeping pills, so if he ever had to, he could drug Bri and Julie and smother them while they were sleeping. He was sure they'd be in a state of grace when they died and that was what mattered.

He told himself not to go crazy, that Julie could figure out how to stretch two bags of food for ten days, or maybe the quarantine would be over and Vincent de Paul would reopen. If they could just make it to December 26, they had a chance.

He hated seeing how weak Julie had gotten. He knew she'd been taking less food for herself so that Bri could have a little more. Silently he begged her forgiveness for ever complaining about her.

There was no one on line when they got to the school. They both knew what that meant, but they walked up to the door anyway.

FOOD DELIVERIES SUSPENDED INDEFINITELY

Alex stared at the sign. What did "indefinitely" mean? Was it just until the quarantine ended? Or had the plug been pulled on the city? And if the city had been left to die, did that mean the convoys had stopped altogether? He willed Julie to start crying. Maybe if he had to comfort her, he wouldn't feel so helpless, so terrified, himself.

But Julie never did what he wanted her to, and this time was no exception. "It doesn't matter," she said instead. "It wouldn't have been enough."

"You're probably right," Alex said.

They began the walk home. "I'll try Harvey," he said. "I have my coat and a bottle of aspirin. Maybe he'll give me something for that."

"How can you survive without your coat?" Julie asked.

"I can manage," Alex said. "I'll just walk around wrapped in a blanket. Maybe you and Bri can figure out a way of making it more like a coat for when we go back to Port Authority, so my arms will be free to pull the sled."

Julie stood absolutely still. "I don't think we're going to need the sled," she whispered, as though there was anyone within five blocks to hear her.

"We'll need it for Bri," Alex said.

"She's down to her last cartridge," Julie said softly. "She's been using it for a couple of weeks. Sometimes at night she coughs and she doesn't use it and I think she'll die right then in the sleeping bag."

"Bri isn't going to die," Alex said. "We'll be on the convoy in less than two weeks. We just need enough food to keep us going until then."

"You sound like her," Julie said. "When she goes on about Mami and Papi still being alive."

"It's different," Alex said. "We can't do anything about Mami and Papi. But we can still keep ourselves alive. Including Bri."

"Would it help if you took my coat?" Julie asked. "It's too big for me anyway."

"Keep your coat," Alex said. "Maybe next week we'll bring it to Harvey."

They walked in silence until they got back to their building. "I'm not afraid to die," Julie said. "I figure I'm going to know more people in heaven than I do on earth anyway. Mami and Papi and Kevin. Lots of people. I just don't want to be the last one to die. That's what scares me most, that you and Bri will both die and I'll be all alone."

"That won't happen," Alex said.

Julie stared up at him, with that strange combination of extreme youth and unnatural aging. "Promise?" she said.

"Promise," he said. He hated the thought of climbing the twelve flights of stairs, but he hadn't taken the bottle of aspirin with him and he had to get it. It took them twice as long to get up the stairs as it had the week before. He didn't know how on the twenty-sixth he'd manage to carry Bri down the stairs to the sled.

She was sleeping when they got in and her breathing was

labored. When her cartridge ran out, Alex told himself, that night he'd find the strength to give them the pills. They'd die peacefully and that was the best anyone could hope for.

He found the bottle of aspirin and told Julie that he was going. "Do you want me to go with you?" she asked.

"No, stay here," Alex said. He wasn't sure what he'd do if Harvey made an offer for her while she was with him. He took his time walking down the stairs, and then slowly made his way to Harvey's. He knew it was possible no food had come in during the week and Harvey might not have any to barter. He also knew Harvey might find his coat and a bottle of aspirin worthless. He knew lots of things that he didn't want to know.

But at the store he found the one thing he didn't expect: The door was locked.

Alex banged at it. Maybe Harvey was in the john. But there was no sound. Had Harvey gone? Had he somehow escaped, in spite of the quarantine?

The thought enraged Alex. If Harvey had left, he certainly would have taken his food with him. But Alex was too angry to be rational. He pulled off his shoe, and using what little energy he had left, used it to smash open the storefront window. Shards of glass fell onto the snow.

Alex put his shoe back on, reached in, and unlocked the door. Harvey was lying on the floor, his right arm stretched out, as though he was grabbing for something.

Alex took off his glove, knelt, and felt for a pulse. He couldn't find one, but Harvey was still warm, so he put his ear to Harvey's mouth to try to sense any breathing. Not that he'd know what to do if Harvey was still alive.

It didn't matter. Harvey was fresh dead. Probably no more than ten minutes. The last of a dead breed.

Alex knew he should pray for Harvey's soul, but the only prayer he could utter was "Please God, let me find some food." He stepped around Harvey and began to search.

The storefront was completely empty. Desperate, Alex opened the door to the bathroom. He found a couple of candles on the sink, and two boxes on top of the toilet.

The first box held nothing but clothes, so filthy Alex could barely make himself touch them. He threw the box onto the floor, took a deep breath, and opened the second one. It was half full with food. Two bags of rice, six cans of red beans, two of black beans, four of spinach, two of split pea soup, one of lentil, one of carrots, three of mixed vegetables, and one of sardines.

If they were careful, the food could last until the twenty-sixth. They'd save the sardines for Christmas.

Alex knew he'd have to move fast. He wasn't the only person on the Upper West Side praying for food. He pulled out one of Harvey's shirts, loaded it with the cans and bags and candles, then tied the sleeves together. He unbuttoned his coat, slid the bundle next to his chest, and buttoned the coat back up. It wasn't much of a disguise, but it would have to do, on the off chance he saw another human being between Harvey's and home.

He went back through the storefront, glancing briefly at Harvey. "I'll pray for your soul when I get home," he promised, then unlocked the door, looked around at the empty street, grabbed the sharpest shard of glass for protection, and began the journey back to safety.

chapter 18

Saturday, December 17

"Alex, what are you doing?"

"Taking off my coat," Alex said. "It's awfully hot in here. I think I'll open a window."

"Alex, it's freezing in here. Alex? Alex, answer me. Bri! Bri, come in here now! Alex's collapsed!"

Sunday, December 18

"Alex, drink this. Alex, you have to swallow this."

"Mami?" When did Mami come home? She was at work, at her new job. How could she be home? And why wasn't he at school? It was too hot to be a snow day. It must be a hundred degrees.

"He's kicking the blankets off again. Julie, help me."

"No!" Alex said. "Mami, no. I'm too hot."

"Alex, it's all right," Mami said, but she didn't sound like Mami. She sounded like Bri. Only Bri was coughing. Bri coughed too much. Papi never coughed. A man didn't cough. Alex was going to be a man just like Papi. He would never cough.

"Julie, hold him while I get the soup down."

Alex laughed. How could Julie hold him? Papi could hold him, but not Julie. Where was Papi, anyway? He'd gone away a long time ago, but he should be back by now. Apartment 12B had a problem with plumbing. Papi had to fix it. Papi could fix anything. Papi could fix the moon.

"Do you think he got any of the aspirin down?"

"Yeah, I think so. Alex, keep still. We're trying to make you better."

No one ever tried to make Carlos better. Carlos was just fine the way he was. He never had to work for anything. Neither did Bri or Julie because they were girls and no one expected anything from them. No, just Alex had to get better. Whatever he did was never good enough. Vice president. Assistant editor. Second in his class. Never good enough. How could he be president of the United States if he was only second in his class?

He was tired of being second best. He was tired of trying and failing. He was too hot. He must have died and gone to hell. Only hell could be this hot.

Monday, December 19

Mami washed his face with a cold washcloth. "Don't fall asleep, Alex," she said. "Stay awake now."

Sleep? How could he sleep? He was freezing. Why wasn't the radiator working? "Papi, I'm cold."

"Put another blanket on him," Bri said. "Take one of ours."

One of their what? Who threw him into a snowbank? Carlos must have. Carlos thought he was a big baby. He'd show Carlos. He'd climb out of the snowbank himself.

"Julie! He's trying to get up. Hold him down."

Julie couldn't hold him down. No one could hold him

down. Not even Chris Flynn could hold him down. He was the first Puerto Rican president of the United States. Chris Flynn wasn't. Carlos wasn't. Not even Papi was the first Puerto Rican president of the United States. Why would anyone throw the first Puerto Rican president of the United States into a snowbank? Why wasn't there any heat in the White House?

Kevin respected him. "Hello, Mr. President," Kevin said.

"Hello, Mr. Vice President," Alex said. That didn't seem right. Alex was vice president, not Kevin. What was Kevin? Was he Secretary of State? It was hard to remember.

"Heaven's not too bad," Kevin said. "Better than I'd imagined. Lots of copies of *Playboy* in heaven. Harvey gets me all the latest issues."

Harvey had opened a newsstand. "Wanna copy of *Playboy*?" he asked Alex with a leer. Harvey had lost all his teeth. "Two copies for a can of tomatoes and a spitfire."

Hell had been so hot, but heaven was even colder. Somehow Alex had thought heaven would always be at seventy-six degrees. Maybe warmer if you wanted to go swimming.

"You might as well die, Mr. President," Kevin said. "We're all going to die soon enough."

"Not I," said Father Mulrooney. "I will never die."

Alex was pleased to see Father Mulrooney. "I think you should be Chief Justice," he said to the elderly priest.

"I'd rather be ambassador to the Vatican," Father Mulrooney said, shooting his eyebrows so high they bounced against the ceiling of the Sistine Chapel.

"Want to go body shopping, Mr. President?" Kevin asked. "Look at this nice big pile."

Alex walked over to the pile of bodies. There must have been a hundred of them. Kevin brought him a ladder so he could climb all the way to the top to look for shoes and watches.

Papi was on top of the pile. Alex picked him up and threw him down to Kevin. "Good catch!" Alex cried.

Next came Mami. "Here we speak English," she said as he tossed her to Kevin.

Somehow Kevin himself had gotten to the top of the pile. He grinned at Alex and said, "I'm dead, Mr. President. Remember?"

"No you're not," Alex said. "I pulled the branch off of you. Kevin! Come back here! Kevin!"

"He's calling for Kevin," Bri said. "Do you know where he is, Julie? Maybe he could help calm Alex down."

"Kevin's dead," Julie said.

Alex laughed. Kevin was the only person on earth who hadn't been a fluicide. Kevin hadn't waited around to die of the flu. And he hadn't risked his immortal soul by killing himself. No, Kevin was too smart for all that. He found a tree limb to stand under.

"Good thinking, Mr. Vice President," Alex said. "We need more men like you at Vincent de Paul."

Vincent de Paul. It was a school day. Even the president of the United States had to go to school if he wanted to get into Georgetown.

"Bri, help me. He's trying to get up."

"Alex, lie still. Don't struggle so. Alex, it'll be all right. Just relax."

Relax. Like the leader of the free world could relax when he was being held down on a snowbank. Where were the Marines when you needed them?

"Here we are!" Carlos said, looking very handsome in his Marine uniform. Aunt Lorraine was standing by his side, sobbing hysterically, but Carlos didn't seem to mind. "Stay where you are, Mr. President. I'll take care of Bri and Julie. You're just a baby."

"Am not," the president of the United States protested. "Mami, Carlos is teasing me. Mami!"

"A real man doesn't need a mother," Papi said. "Look at me. I'm a real man. I don't need a mother."

"Mami!"

"Alex, it's me, Bri. I'm here and so's Julie. Alex, take another swallow. Do it for us."

"No! I'm the president of the United States. I don't have to swallow."

"Julie, stop laughing. Alex's delirious."

"I know," Julie said. "I just think he's funny."

Funny? The president of the United States funny? She should be arrested for treason. Alex decided to make a list of all the reasons why Julie should be arrested for treason, but he was too cold to look for a pencil. He'd take a nap instead. Maybe when he woke up, he'd be warm again.

"Alex. Just one more swallow," Bri said.

But the president didn't hear her.

Tuesday, December 20

"Bri! Come here. I can't get Alex to wake up! Alex! Alex!"

Wednesday, December 21

"What?" Alex said, struggling to sit up.

"Julie, wake up. I think Alex is awake."

"Of course I'm awake," Alex said, but he had a feeling all that came out was "Wugga wugga."

"Alex, look at me," Bri said. "Do you know where you are?"

That was a tough question, but he'd answered harder ones at school. "Home," he said. That didn't sound like "wugga wugga" at all.

Bri smiled. Alex could see Bri smile. Alex smiled back.

"Alex, we want you to drink some of this soup," Julie said. "Here, take a sip. It's split pea soup. It's your favorite."

Alex was too polite to tell Julie that minestrone was his favorite. He took a sip of the soup. It tasted awful. "You're a lousy cook," he said.

"Take another sip," Bri said. "It's yummy."

Alex did as he was told, but the soup was anything but yummy. "Where are my arms?" he asked.

"They're right by your sides," Bri said. "You're in the sleeping bag."

That made sense, he supposed. "The sun is shining in my eyes," he said.

"The sun doesn't shine anymore, Alex," Julie said.

"*Santa Madre de Dios,*" Bri said. "The electricity's back on."

Thursday, December 22

"What time is it?" Alex asked. "What day is it?"

Julie laughed. "It's close to three," she said. "And it's your birthday."

His birthday. There was a reason why that was important, but Alex couldn't concentrate enough to think why. "How long have I been sleeping?" he asked.

"You got sick days ago," Julie replied. "Saturday night. Today's Thursday, so you've been sleeping all week. You were delirious at first, but since yesterday I guess you've been more normal."

"Fluicide," Alex said.

"What?" Julie asked.

"The flu," Alex said. "I must have had the flu."

"You still have it," Julie said. "But now I don't think you'll die."

"Was I that sick?" Alex asked.

Julie nodded. "Especially Sunday and Monday," she said. "You were really crazy on Monday. Then you went to sleep and we couldn't wake you up and we were terrified. But you woke up on your own, and you've been awake a little bit at a time ever since."

"Did I eat soup?" Alex asked. "I seem to remember soup."

"We found a bottle of aspirin, so we dissolved pills in the soup," Julie said. "You hated it, but we got some of it down each time. How do you feel?"

"Awful," Alex said. "Like a truck ran over me. And I'm wet. How come I'm wet?"

"Well, you sweated a lot," Julie said. "And you wet yourself. You were in the sleeping bag, and we figured it was better to keep you in it, because you kept trying to get up. When you're stronger, you can get out of it, and we'll let it dry."

Something about the sleeping bag made Alex think of Kevin. "Kevin?" he said.

"He's dead," Julie said. "That's what you told me on Friday."

Yeah, that was right. Harvey was dead, too.

"I'll be better soon," Alex said. "I promise. I'll be strong enough to take care of you soon."

And with those words, he fell back asleep.

When he woke up again, it was dark, the only illumination coming from a single candle. "What's happening?" he asked.

"Nothing," Julie said. "Go back to sleep."

But Alex felt more awake than he had in days. "What time is it?" he asked.

"I don't know," Julie said. "It's not that late. It's just dark in here, that's all."

"I'm hungry," Alex said.

"You haven't eaten very much the past few days," Julie said. "We still have food, if you want some. Would you like some spinach?"

Alex thought about it and shook his head. "I want something sweet," he said. "Do we have anything sweet in the house?"

"I don't think so," Julie said.

Alex tried to focus. His whole body ached and the throbbing in his head was close to unbearable. "Could you blow the candle out?" he asked. "It hurts my eyes."

"I don't think I should," Julie said. "It's the only light we have. But I can move it farther away." She got up and carried the candle to a table behind the sofa so Alex's back was to it. "Is that better?"

"Yes, thank you," Alex said. "I know this is crazy, but did the sun start shining while I was sick?"

"You thought it did," Julie said. "That was yesterday. The electricity came on. It was on today, too, but you slept through it."

"Electricity," Alex said. "That's a good sign."

"I guess," Julie said. "The microwave sure made things easier."

"I don't suppose Mami or Papi came back," Alex said. It felt like he'd spent a lot of time with them lately.

"No," Julie said. "It's just us. Same as always."

"Where's Bri?" Alex asked. "Is she all right?"

"Bri was great," Julie said. "She and I took turns watching after you. She was really amazing. It's like she didn't even care she had asthma. She said we just had to keep our faith that the Holy Mother would watch over you, and she did."

"And today's my birthday?" Alex asked. "I'm eighteen?"

"Yeah," Julie said. "Happy birthday. Sorry there's no party."

Alex closed his eyes, trying to remember why his birthday was so important. But before he could come up with an answer, he'd fallen back asleep.

Friday, December 23

His throat was parched. He groped for the glass of water he always kept on the end table, but he couldn't find it.

"Julie!" he said. "Julie, I'm thirsty."

"I'll get you some water," she said. "And a couple of aspirin."

Alex waited for her to bring the water to him. When she did, he took a gulp, then swallowed the two aspirin, washing them down with more water. There wasn't enough water in the world, he thought. Or maybe there was too much. Whatever, he was still thirsty.

"Could I have some more?" he asked. "Please?"

"I guess," Julie said. She went back to the kitchen and returned with a full glass. "Don't gulp," she said. "Are you hungry?"

"I don't know," Alex said. "I think I will be. I feel better than yesterday, but I still ache all over."

"The aspirin should help," Julie said.

"What time is it?" Alex asked.

"I wish you'd stop asking that," Julie snapped. "What difference does it make?"

Alex considered telling Julie not to use that tone with him, but it wasn't worth the effort. "Where's Bri?" he asked instead. "Is she still sleeping?"

"Maybe you should go back to sleep," Julie said. "It's still pretty early."

That seemed like a very good idea. He'd go back to sleep and let the aspirin work its magic. When he woke up next, he was sure he'd feel much better.

He woke up with a smile on his face. He'd had a very pleasant dream, although he couldn't quite remember the details. Something about living in a small town, like the ones where he'd spent his Fresh Air Fund summers. People walked around smiling. He remembered the smiles.

"It's daytime, isn't it?" he said to Julie. She was sitting in the easy chair, facing him, but she seemed to be concentrating on the front door. Alex turned around to see what might be interesting there, but it looked the same as always.

"Yeah," Julie said. "It's daytime."

"I remember drinking some water," Alex said. "How long ago was that?"

"Maybe three hours ago," Julie said. "Do you want some aspirin?"

Alex shook his head, and found he got dizzy doing so. "Not just yet," he said. "I hope you and Bri don't get sick. Is there much aspirin left?"

"Enough," Julie said. "And we're not going to get sick. We would have by now if we were going to."

"Why are you so interested in the door?" Alex asked. "Are you expecting company?"

"No, of course not," Julie said. "I'm just tired of looking at you."

"I don't blame you," Alex said. "Is Bri sleeping?"

Julie turned away from the door. "Bri isn't here," she said.

"What do you mean she isn't here?" Alex asked. "Where is she?"

"I don't know," Julie said.

Alex struggled to free his arms from the wet and smelly sleeping bag. "Where do you think she is?" he asked.

"I don't know," Julie said. "Look, I'm sure she's okay. Why don't you go back to sleep. Maybe she'll be back when you wake up."

"I'm not sleepy," Alex said. "Where the hell is Bri?"

"I told you, I don't know," Julie said. "Yesterday, when there was electricity, she decided to go to St. Margaret's. It was your birthday and she wanted to light a candle and thank the Holy Virgin for saving your life. I told her not to. I really did, Alex. I told her the Holy Virgin knew how grateful we were, she didn't have to go to church to tell her. But Bri said it was a miracle that you got well and besides it was your birthday and Mami always lights candles on our birthdays."

"You idiot," Alex said. "Why didn't you stop her?"

"Because I couldn't!" Julie cried. "Bri's just like Papi. When she gets an idea, she can't be talked out of it. I told her I'd go and she should stay here, but she said she wanted to make confession so she could take communion on Christmas. And she looked so much better. You have no idea how much she did while you were sick. I thought maybe the Holy Mother had made a second miracle and healed Bri. And the electricity was running. All she had to do was go to church and then take the elevator back up."

"Why didn't you go with her?" Alex demanded. "You could have watched out for her."

"I watched out for you instead," Julie said.

Alex fumbled around trying to find the sleeping bag zipper. "How long has she been gone?" he asked. "What time is it?"

"It's about one," Julie said. "She's been gone almost twenty-four hours."

"Oh my God," Alex said. "She could be anywhere. Have you even looked for her?"

"I couldn't leave you," Julie said.

"Well, you can now," Alex said. "Take the candle and check the stairwell. Maybe Bri got home last night after the electricity went off and spent the night in the stairwell."

"Will you be okay alone?" Julie asked.

"I'm fine," Alex snapped. "Find Bri."

Julie nodded. She grabbed the candle and left the apartment.

Alex managed to free himself from the sleeping bag. He stripped, then put on clean clothes. He still stank, but that didn't matter.

He walked to the kitchen and washed his face with cold water. His entire body shook as he found the aspirin bottle and swallowed two more. He wasn't at all sure he could make it back to the living room, but he knew he had to. Each step felt like he was climbing Everest, and by the time he fell back onto the sofa, his heart was pounding.

I haven't eaten in days, he reminded himself. The problem was he didn't think he could make it back to the kitchen to get himself something to eat. He wasn't sure he'd ever be able to stand up again.

Something made him get on all fours and crawl to the girls' bedroom. He couldn't imagine either Bri or Julie playing such a horrific practical joke on him, but he had to be sure Bri truly was gone.

The bedroom was empty.

"Bri?" he called. Maybe she was hiding in the closet. But there was no answer.

Alex tried to crawl back to the living room, but it was miles away. He remembered something about smiling faces before he passed out on the bedroom floor.

Saturday, December 24

"Alex! Don't hog the bathroom."

Alex woke up with a start. But it wasn't really Bri's voice. For a moment he couldn't remember where he was. Then he saw Julie sleeping in the easy chair in the living room and it came back to him. Apartment 12B. Mami and Papi had been gone for seven months, Bri for two days.

He looked at his little sister and tried to allocate blame so it all fell on her, but he couldn't. He'd spent seven months unable to talk Bri out of her obsession that Mami and Papi would be coming home any minute now. How could he expect Julie to keep Bri from going to St. Margaret's if she had her mind set on it?

Julie had found him on the bedroom floor. Somehow she'd gotten some food into him, and with her help, he'd been able to make it back onto the sofa. He'd wanted to go out and look for Bri, but he couldn't walk ten feet without collapsing. And the last thing Julie needed was for him to wind up in the fourth floor stairwell, unable to climb another step.

Still, he felt better today, better than he could remember feeling in days. He rose carefully and was pleased to find his head wasn't spinning. The kitchen didn't seem a million miles away, and he made it there without incident. He drank some water, swallowed a couple of aspirin for no particular reason, and opened one of the cans of red beans. Judging from the amount of food still remaining, Bri and Julie hadn't eaten much more than he had the past week.

Bri had been gone for two days and what had he done besides sleep? Had he even prayed for her safe return? He couldn't remember.

"Heavenly Father, look after her," he whispered. It was the one prayer he could think of that God might accept from him.

He walked back to the sofa and tried to think. Bri had gone to St. Margaret's two days ago. The only thing he knew was Julie hadn't found her in the stairwell. He rubbed his forehead. If she wasn't in the stairwell, where was she?

At St. Margaret's, maybe? Suppose she got there and stayed so long that it was dark when she was ready to leave and Father Franco told her to spend the night there. Alex liked that idea, although he couldn't understand why Father Franco hadn't sent her home the next day.

Except there was no electricity the next day. Maybe Father Franco told her to stay at the church until she could take the elevator up to 12B. Bri could be alive and well, better off there than at home, since the church still had some heat, or at least it had the last time Alex had been there, before the snowstorm. If Father Franco had any food, he'd share it with

Bri. And Bri had her inhaler with her, so really she would be just as well off at St. Margaret's as she would be at home.

It would be easy enough to find out if Bri was at St. Margaret's. All he had to do was walk over there. Think of Julie's reaction when he and Bri walked back into 12B together. What a Christmas present that would be.

Alex decided to practice walking. He strolled from the sofa to the girls' bedroom, then back again to the kitchen. He ate two more spoonfuls of frozen red beans, then walked back to the bedroom. No dizziness. Sure he was a bit weak, but that was to be expected. But there was no hurry. If Bri was at St. Margaret's she was being taken care of. She'd be worried, though, worried about him and about Julie. Better he should get going.

"Alex?"

"Go back to sleep," Alex said. "I'm fine. I'm just going out for a walk."

Julie sat bolt upright. "What are you talking about?" she said. "You can't go for a walk."

"Just to St. Margaret's," Alex said. "I think Bri might be there."

"She isn't," Julie said. "Yesterday, after I checked the stairwell, I walked over and asked. Father Franco saw her on Thursday, but she left the church. He said he figured she'd be okay since the electricity was still running."

Alex collapsed back onto the sofa. "Why didn't you tell me?" he demanded, as though Bri's fate would be different if Julie had only had the good sense to tell him.

"Because you were sprawled out on the floor when I got back," Julie said.

"I'm not sprawled out now," Alex said. "Bri might be wandering around the streets. We need to look for her."

"Alex," Julie said.

"What?" he said.

Julie looked miserable. "If some guy grabbed her," she said. "Like that guy, you know . . . Well, Bri couldn't fight back. I know she felt a lot stronger because she'd helped you so much, but I couldn't even get away from that guy. Bri's hardly eaten in days and it's so hard for her to breathe. I don't think she's wandering around the streets."

"We won't know until we look," Alex said. "If you don't want to go, I'll go by myself."

"Can you make it back up the stairs?" Julie asked.

"I'll make it," Alex said angrily. "Are you coming with me or not?"

"Of course I'm coming," she said.

The two of them left 12B and began the long walk to the lobby. Alex was startled at how much energy it took simply to walk down a flight of stairs. Julie's question about his ability to walk back up seemed more and more reasonable. But he'd worry about that when the time came.

It had been over a week since he'd been outside. Everything was the same, except the snow was now charcoal gray. The cold cut into his lungs, and he began coughing.

"This is such a mistake," Julie said.

"I need to look," Alex said. "I can't just let her disappear."

"Don't you think I feel the same way?" Julie cried. "But what if you get sick again? What will I do then?"

Alex ignored her. He took two steps onto the sidewalk and asked himself what the hell he thought he was doing.

"Wait," Julie said. "I have an idea."

"Yeah, what?" Alex asked.

"Let's get the sled," Julie said. "You can sit on it and I can pull you around."

"Are you strong enough?" Alex asked.

"I'd better be," Julie said. "You aren't going anyplace on your own. The sled's in our old apartment, isn't it? You didn't barter it with Harvey?"

"No," Alex said. "It's there." He stood absolutely still, and then his eyes lit up. "Bri!" he said. "I bet she's in the basement. She came home after church on Thursday and the electricity was off so she decided to stay there. Come on. I bet she's been waiting for us to rescue her for two days now."

"You really think so?" Julie asked, but she raced back into the lobby. Alex could barely keep up with her, but adrenalin pumped him up and he walked down the single flight of stairs almost as fast as his little sister.

"Bri?" Julie cried. "Bri, are you in there?"

There was no answer.

"Wait a second," Alex said, searching for the key to their old home. With fumbling fingers he got it into the lock and pushed the door open. "Bri? Bri, are you all right?"

Julie ran through the apartment, yelling for her sister. "She isn't here," she said.

"Maybe Papi's office," Alex said. "Maybe she went there."

They walked down the hallway to Papi's office. Alex put the key in the door, but when he opened it, he saw the room was empty.

"Get the sled," he said to Julie. "We'll check the streets."

Julie did as she was told. She brought out the sled and carried it up the stairs. Once they were outside, Alex got on it and let her pull him around. He instructed her to stop at every pile of bodies, but there were no new ones. If people were still dying in their neighborhood, they were doing it alone in their apartments.

They went to St. Margaret's, just to check again, but

Father Franco said he hadn't seen Bri since Thursday. "I'll keep praying for her," he said, so Alex thanked him and said if he heard anything, they were in 12B and they'd be very grateful if he got the news to them.

He and Julie circled West Eighty-eighth, going as far north as Ninety-second and as far south as Eighty-second. Some of the distance he walked, and some he rode on the sled. They called Bri's name wherever they walked, but there was no sound in return except that of the wind howling and the rats scurrying.

She was gone. Like Mami and Papi, she had just disappeared.

Sunday, December 25

He woke up with a fever. Julie refused to let him out, not to look for Bri, not even to go to church. Alex felt too weak to argue.

"Do you want to go to Mass?" he asked, in spite of his terror that Julie might vanish on the streets as Bri had.

Julie shook her head. "There'll be other Christmases," she said.

They both knew that was unlikely. Neither said so. Instead they sat still, looking at the door, praying for a miracle.

Monday, December 26

Julie had fallen asleep in the chair. Alex got up and lit a candle so he could look at his watch. It was almost 8:30 in the morning.

He walked over to Julie and shook her awake. "Get up," he said. "Now."

Julie stared at him. "Is it Bri?" she asked. "Do you know where she is?"

"No," Alex said. "But it's the twenty-sixth. You have to get to Port Authority for the convoy."

"You woke me up for that?" Julie asked. "We don't even know if there is a convoy. And what about Bri?"

"I'll stay here and look for her," Alex said. "But at least you'll be safe."

Julie shook her head. "I'm not going anywhere without you and Bri."

"You have to," Alex said. "That's an order."

"Order someone else," Julie said. "I'm going back to sleep. It hurts less when I'm sleeping."

chapter 19

Tuesday, December 27

It was the sound of the refrigerator rumbling back to life that galvanized Alex.

"Come on," he said to Julie. "The electricity's back."

"So?" she said.

"I want you to eat something," he said. "When was the last time you ate?"

"I don't know," Julie replied. "Yesterday, I guess."

"I'm going to heat some water in the microwave to wash with," Alex said. "Then we'll eat something hot while we can."

"And then what?" Julie asked.

"Then we'll go out and look some more for Bri," Alex said.

"How?" Julie said. "You think half a can of beans is going to make you strong again?"

"We'll use the sled," Alex said. "Julie, we can't quit looking. Maybe she got back to St. Margaret's for Christmas. Maybe she got back to the basement."

The voice he'd grown to hate within him said that maybe whoever had taken Bri had disposed of her body somewhere and that was what they really were looking for. He knew Julie was thinking the same thing, but she also knew not to say so.

"Can I clean myself, too?" Julie asked. "Before we go?"

"Good idea," Alex said. "But let's get a move on while there's still electricity. We can take the service elevator to the basement to get the sled."

"Luxury," Julie grumbled, but she left the chair and went with Alex to the kitchen.

Half an hour later, the two of them were as clean as they were ever going to be, and as well fed. There was still some rice, and reheated with the beans, it almost tasted like real food. Alex was tempted to open the can of sardines, but he figured that could wait for a day with no microwave. They needed to be very careful with the little food they had left, in case there were no more food handouts and Vincent de Paul didn't reopen. There was still a chance Julie could get onto the January 9 convoy, if they could both stay alive until then. The possibility that he might die first and then Julie killing herself filled him with terror.

Twelve more days, he told himself. After everything they'd been through, what was twelve more days.

Julie rinsed off the dishes, then put her gloves back on. "I'm ready," she said.

Alex nodded. He felt stronger than he had in days and didn't think he'd need the sled. But if they found Bri on the street, they could carry her home on it. He wouldn't leave her as he'd left Kevin. She belonged at home.

They walked silently down the corridor to the service elevator. Alex pressed the button. He could hear the elevator slowly churning its way up to the twelfth floor.

"That's funny," Julie said. "It should be on twelve. We're the only ones left in the building."

In a flash Alex realized what had happened. "Don't look!" he said to Julie, but it was too late. The elevator doors pulled open, and the all-too-familiar stench of death greeted them before they saw the body of their sister curled up in a ball on the elevator floor.

"Bri?" Julie said, her voice childish and shrill. "Bri, wake up." She bent down by Bri and began to shake her. "Wake up! Wake up!"

"Julie, stop," Alex said. "It's too late."

"It can't be!" Julie cried. "We've got to try harder. Bri! Get up, Bri. Now. Please. Now . . ."

Alex knelt next to Julie. Bri had been dead for days. By one hand was her inhaler, in the other her rosary beads.

"She died in a state of grace," he said. "That's the best we can really hope for."

"But why?" Julie asked. "Why did she even go to the basement?"

"I don't know," Alex said. He bent over and kissed Bri's cheek. Her eyes were closed. Maybe she'd been asleep when she died, he told himself. Maybe God had proved merciful to someone who loved Him so much.

"I don't understand," Julie persisted, as though understanding would somehow make things right. "Did she die in the elevator? Is that what happened?"

"I guess so," Alex said. "Last Thursday." My birthday, he thought. Bri died on my birthday after thanking God that I was still alive. "She went to the basement for some reason, then took the elevator up, only the electricity went out while she was in it."

Julie turned around to stare at him in horror. "How long did it take?" she asked. "Did she know she was going to die? Was she waiting for us to rescue her?"

"Julie, it doesn't matter," Alex said, although he'd been asking himself the same questions. "Look at her. Look at how peaceful she is. She's in heaven now, with our *dolce Virgen María,* watching over us."

"She is," Julie said. "I know she is. But she's here, Alex, and I miss her so much I think I'll die."

Alex swallowed hard. "Go back to twelve B," he said. "Get a blanket. No, that quilt Bri liked so much. Bring it back here. We'll wrap her up in it and take her back home."

Julie nodded. She bent over, kissed Bri's hand, then straightened up and left the elevator.

Alex stroked Bri's hair and prayed for strength. He told himself it was better this way. Bri hadn't died at the hands of another, her body carelessly discarded after it had served its purpose. The moon had killed her, not man. He made the sign of the cross and thanked Christ for what Bri had been spared.

Julie came back carrying the quilt. Alex took it from her and wrapped it around Bri.

"We're going to have to take the elevator," he said. "We're not strong enough to carry her down the stairs."

"I know," Julie said. "I've already prayed the electricity will last long enough. It'll be okay."

"It's where she'd want to be," Alex said, his fingers trembling as he pressed the elevator button for the basement. "We'll put her on her bunk bed."

"No, put her on mine," Julie said. "It's higher. It's closer to heaven."

Alex nodded. They rode in silence until they reached the basement and the elevator doors opened. He was uncertain that he'd have the strength to carry Bri by himself, but without his asking, Julie leaned over and helped pick her up. When they got to their home, Alex told Julie to take the keys from his pocket while he held Bri. Then together, they moved her to the girls' bedroom, and lifted her to the upper bed.

Alex left her face uncovered while they prayed. When he thought Julie could handle it, he kissed Bri's eyes, then pulled the quilt over her.

"No," Julie said. "Not yet."

Alex knew he had to give Julie as much time as she needed. "I'm going to the living room," he said. "I'll be there when you're ready."

Julie nodded. Alex left his sisters and went to the living room. He needed the time alone, he realized. He needed to find whatever it was that had made Bri go back to the basement.

Everything looked the same as it had when he'd brought the sled there weeks before. What was it that Bri went for? he asked himself.

He went to Mami and Papi's bedroom, thinking it might be something there, but he found nothing out of order.

Maybe she went to the kitchen, searching for food, he thought. Of course there wasn't any, but maybe she thought they'd left something behind. There was no place else to look, so he might as well check in there.

The cupboards were empty, just as he knew they would be. Alex glanced over the counter and saw the note he'd left.

His entire body began to shake as he picked it up. On the top of the paper, it said that they were living in 12B. But the rest of the paper was overflowing with Bri's handwriting.

Dear Mami and Papi,
I'm so happy you're home. Every day I've prayed for you.

 Alex sent me to a convent this summer, and even though the sisters were very kind, I prayed day and night that I could go home. Santa María, Madre de Dios, *answered my prayers.*

*Two weeks ago, Alex said we had to leave New York. Don't
ever tell him, but I prayed even harder that we wouldn't have to go
and the Holy Virgin kept the bus from leaving.*

*I know in my heart that God let us stay in New York so we'd
be here when you came home. It will be His Christmas gift to us.*

*You'll be so proud of Alex and Julie. They've been wonderful
to me. Alex was sick, but he's getting better now. When he and Julie
see you, they'll believe once again in God's mercy, and love Him as
I do.*

    Your loving daughter,
    Briana

P.S. It's okay that we're staying in 12B. Mr. Dunlap said we could.

Alex stared at the piece of paper in horror. Bri had died
because she'd refused to believe Mami and Papi were dead. If
she hadn't written the note, she could have gotten back to
the building, taken the elevator up to twelve, and been in
their apartment before the electricity went out. Her delusions
had led to her death.

But was he any better? Until that moment, until seeing
Bri's body and reading her final words, hadn't he held out
hope that Mami or Papi would somehow miraculously return? He had never told Bri otherwise because he had never
been able to accept that their parents really were both dead.
Bri's false belief had been his also. She just believed it more.

Bri was gone now. No, she was dead. Dead like Kevin.
Dead like Mami and Papi. But Julie was still alive and there
had to be a way to save her. Christ, in His mercy, couldn't possibly condemn Julie to death just because her older brother
was stubborn and stupid.

Alex folded Bri's note, unable to part with it. He was putting it in his coat pocket as Julie came out of the bedroom. "I left that postcard with her," she said.

"What postcard?" Alex asked.

"The one of the painting," Julie said. "*Starry Night.* I had to look for it, but I found it and left it by her side. Do you think that's okay? She really loved it."

"I think that was a very good idea," Alex said. "You were smart to think of it."

Julie looked at him. "Will we be safe on the elevator?" she asked.

Alex knew there was no place on earth that they would be safe. "Yeah, sure," he said. "But we'd better get going. Are you ready?"

Julie nodded. "She'll be all right here?" she asked.

"She'll be all right," Alex said. "Mami and Papi will look out for her."

Wednesday, December 28

He slept fitfully and whenever he awoke, he heard Julie sobbing in the bedroom she'd shared with Bri. He was glad she still knew how to cry, and he made no effort to comfort her.

Eventually he got off the sofa bed and went into the kitchen to check on their supplies. A couple of cups of cooked rice, two cans of red beans, one of spinach, one of mixed vegetables, and the sardines. He remembered a time when that wouldn't have been enough food for him for a single day.

I was so spoiled, he thought. I had so much and I didn't appreciate it. I always wanted more.

It didn't matter. All that mattered was getting Julie to a

safe place. If he succeeded at that, he could die knowing he'd done one thing right and that would be enough.

He knew he had to leave a note for Julie, but just putting pen to paper made him shake. He forced himself to stop thinking of Bri's final moments, and wrote, "I've gone to St. Margaret's about a Mass for Bri."

There was so much else he wanted to put in the note, but there was no point. Instead he went to the bedroom to check on his sister. She'd finally fallen asleep, he was relieved to see. She might even sleep through his time away. When he got back, he'd make sure she ate.

He walked down the twelve flights slowly, not wanting to waste more strength than he had. Neither he nor Julie had felt like eating after they'd gotten back the day before, so it was close to twenty-four hours since he'd last had food. He was pretty sure he was over the flu, but he knew it wouldn't take much for him to collapse.

Julie's all that matters, he told himself as he walked to St. Margaret's. Carlos might be alive, but there was no way of knowing. Julie *was* alive and she was tough and strong and she deserved to live. Father Franco would surely see that and help Alex find a way to save her.

But when he got to St. Margaret's, Alex found a sign on the door.

ST. MARGARET'S IS NOW CLOSED
DOMINUS VOBISCUM

In spite of the sign, Alex tried opening the door, but it was bolted shut. He walked to the side door and tried that one with no luck. The church was deserted. Father Franco had told him that would happen, but Alex had never quite believed him.

Not knowing where else to go, Alex began the walk to Vincent de Paul. He'd long since given up believing in miracles, but he prayed that the chapel would be open and he'd at least be able to light a candle for Bri.

The walk was long and hard, and Alex was almost surprised that the tears he shed didn't freeze on his cheeks. His lungs ached from the ash in the air, and his mind filled with pictures of Bri trapped in the elevator, dying slowly and alone.

Not Julie, he repeated. I won't let Julie die also.

There was no sign on the door of Vincent de Paul, not even one about the quarantine. Alex turned the knob and the door opened.

He entered the school. He heard nothing and saw nobody. But the door to the chapel was open. He walked in, found it empty, also, genuflected before the cross, then went to the pew in the section for seniors, knelt, and began to pray. He begged the Lord's mercy and forgiveness, prayed for the souls of all he loved and for Christ to find it in His heart to let Julie live.

"Alex?"

Alex turned around and saw Sister Rita standing in the doorway.

"Alex, is that really you? I thought you and your sisters had gone."

For a moment Alex was confused. Then he remembered the note he'd left Father Mulrooney to let him know they were leaving.

"No," he said. "We never got to go."

"Are you all right?" Sister Rita asked. "How are Briana and Julie?"

"Bri died," Alex said. "St. Margaret's is closed. I didn't know where else to go."

"Bri?" Sister Rita said. "Oh, Alex, I'm so sorry. I had her in eighth-grade English. She was a lovely girl."

Alex thought of Bri in eighth grade, but couldn't make himself speak.

"Is Julie all right?" Sister Rita asked.

Alex nodded.

"Thank Christ," Sister Rita said. "Come with me, Alex. We'll talk to Father Mulrooney."

Alex followed her out of the chapel to the father's office. Father Mulrooney was sitting at his desk, silently praying. They waited until he was finished and then Sister Rita knocked on the door to get his attention.

"Mr. Morales?" Father Mulrooney said. "We thought you were gone."

"I know," Alex said. "We tried to go, but the convoy didn't leave because of the quarantine."

"How are your sisters?" Father Mulrooney asked.

"Julie's all right," Alex said. "Bri died because of me."

"Sit down," Father Mulrooney said. "How are you responsible for your sister's death, Alex?"

Alex told them the whole story. He remembered when he'd asked Father Mulrooney to hear his confession because he'd felt Father Franco would be too soft on him. He knew there was no penance Father Mulrooney could demand that would ease the guilt he felt, but he didn't care. It was better that Father Mulrooney and Sister Rita see how inadequate he was. They'd be more likely to be merciful to Julie that way.

When he finished, Father Mulrooney cleared his throat. "I don't know what to say," he began.

"May I say something?" Sister Rita asked. "If you don't mind, Father."

"Please," Father Mulrooney replied.

Sister Rita turned to Alex. He'd forgotten how kind her eyes were. "I know you feel responsible for Briana's death," she said. "You feel you should have acknowledged your parents' deaths, and forced Bri to do so. If you had, she wouldn't have been so foolhardy and she'd still be alive. That's it, isn't it?"

Alex choked back a sob and nodded.

"I think it was that very faith that kept Bri alive for so long," Sister Rita said. "If she hadn't had that, then all the sacrifices you made for her, all the care and protection you gave her, wouldn't have been enough. Bri needed to believe her parents would come back. And you loved her enough and respected her enough not to kill her hope, or your own. If she'd known you'd given up, she might have also, and that would have destroyed her."

"Would it really have mattered?" Alex asked. "She suffered so much the past few months."

"She kept you alive," Sister Rita replied. "Julie couldn't have done that alone. Your life is Bri's gift to you." She took Alex's hand and held it between her own. "She was lucky to have you for a brother," she said. "She knew it and you should, too."

He couldn't stop crying. He felt like a fool, a baby, but the tears knew no end.

"Enough," Father Mulrooney finally said. "I suppose you don't have a clean handkerchief on you, Mr. Morales."

In spite of himself, Alex laughed.

"Neither do I, as it happens," Father Mulrooney said. "Very well, use your sleeve, but wipe your nose dry. We have decisions to make."

Alex did as he was told. "I need to find a safe place for Julie," he said.

"Not just for Julie," Father Mulrooney said. "For yourself also Mr. Morales."

"I don't matter," Alex replied. "Just Julie."

Father Mulrooney shook his head with fierce disapproval. "How old are you, Mr. Morales?" he asked.

"Eighteen," Alex said.

"In the forty years I taught at St. Vincent de Paul Academy, I never once encountered an eighteen-year-old saint," Father Mulrooney declared. "And I sincerely doubt that I have now. Sister Rita, when is the bus coming to get you? Tomorrow afternoon?"

"At one," Sister Rita replied. "Although we shouldn't count on it being on time."

"What bus?" Alex asked.

"I believe it's the last one, too," Father Mulrooney said. "Your timing, Mr. Morales, is impeccable. I cannot say the same about your appearance."

"Father Mulrooney," Sister Rita said.

"You're right," Father Mulrooney said. "The question is under what guise should the young Moraleses take the bus."

Alex took a deep breath. "What bus?" he said. "Isn't there a quarantine?"

"The flu is everywhere," Father Mulrooney replied. "There's no point in a quarantine if the entire world is ill."

"I'm sure you'll be all right," Sister Rita said. "And Julie must have a strong immunity if she was with you all that time and never got sick. How can we do this, Father?"

"Do what?" Alex demanded. "I won't let Julie go to an evacuation center. Can't you just take her in here?"

"Who said anything about an evacuation center?" Father Mulrooney asked. "Do you think a bus is stopping here tomorrow at one to take Sister Rita to an evacuation center?"

"Father Mulrooney, please," Sister Rita said. "Alex, the church has evacuated almost all of the religious. A handful, including Father Mulrooney, are choosing to stay on, to minister to the needs of those who can't leave. But at his insistence, I'll be going tomorrow on a bus to the campus of Saint Ursula College, in Georgia. The church is using it as a kind of holding station for its religious, until it knows where to send us to do its work."

"But Julie and I haven't taken any vows," Alex said. "How can we go there?"

"That's what we're trying to figure out," Sister Rita said.

Father Mulrooney looked thoughtful. "Christ is merciful," he said. "I'm sure He won't mind if we simply claim Mr. Morales is a seminarian. Who knows, one day he might be. We'll give him Mr. Kim's identification papers. That should suffice to get him to St. Ursula's, and once there, I'm sure he'll be allowed to stay until he can find a more suitable location."

"My aunt and uncle moved to Tulsa," Alex said.

"Excellent," Father Mulrooney said. "Surely, Sister Rita, your order could stand a young postulant?"

"A very young postulant," Sister Rita said with a laugh. "And I doubt Julie will ever take holy vows. But I do still have Sister Joanne's papers and clothing. As long as I'm with her to vouch for her, I don't think anyone will question Julie too carefully."

"You would do this?" Alex asked. "You'll be breaking the rules."

"Sometimes the rules don't work," Father Mulrooney replied. "Now you and your sister must return tomorrow morning, first thing. Do you still have food in your home?"

"A little," Alex said.

"Excellent," Father Mulrooney said. "If need be, we can bribe the driver with a can or two. Save some for yourselves, though, since the drive will be long and no food will be supplied. Take only the most essential items. Everyone is allowed one bag, and we'll give you each one, so you'll look less like students."

"Julie can sit next to me for the whole ride," Sister Rita said. "We'll be on the same bus together, but it will cause less suspicion if you don't sit together."

Alex nodded. "I can't thank you enough," he said.

"Your future is our thanks," Father Mulrooney replied. "Now go home and tell your sister what needs to be done. Be here first thing in the morning. Chapel is, of course, mandatory."

Thursday, December 29

"Hurry up," Alex said to Julie. "We don't have all day."

"I'm hurrying," Julie grumbled. "You sure you have everything?"

Alex went through the plastic bag one more time. Two changes of underwear, rigorously scrubbed the day before and still a little damp. All remaining cans of food and a can opener, two forks. Whatever information he could find about Carlos's regiment. The photograph Uncle Jimmy had taken of all of them, the papers from Mr. Flynn, and all their birth and baptismal certificates, which he planned on putting in a pocket once he changed at Vincent de Paul. Bri's note he carried in his shirt pocket.

"Oh," he said. "My St. Christopher medal." Mami had given it to him before his first summer with the Fresh Air Fund family. He raced around the living room trying to find it.

"I have it," Julie said, coming out of her bedroom. "Bri put it on you when you were sick, but it kept falling off, so I took it and put it away. Here."

"Thanks," he said. "You have everything?"

Julie nodded. "I'm taking the lipstick Kevin gave me," she said. "I don't care if postulants don't wear lipstick. I want it."

Kevin would like that, Alex thought. "Do you have something of Bri's?" he asked. "Something to remember her by?"

"I have Bri," Julie said. "In my heart. I don't need anything else." She paused. "Except you," she said. "I need you."

Alex nodded. "I need you, too," he said. "Come on. It's time for us to go."

LIFE AS WE KNEW IT

BY SUSAN BETH PFEFFER

When Miranda first hears the warnings that an asteroid is headed on a collision path with the moon, they just sound like an excuse for extra homework assignments. But her disbelief turns to fear in a split second as the entire world witnesses a lunar impact that knocks the moon closer in orbit, catastrophically altering the earth's climate.

Everything else in Miranda's life fades away as supermarkets run out of food, gas goes up to more than ten dollars a gallon, and school is closed indefinitely.

But what Miranda and her family don't realize is that the worst is yet to come.

Told in Miranda's diary entries, *Life As We Knew It* is a heart-pounding account of her struggle to hold on to the most important resource of all—hope—in an increasingly desperate and unfamiliar time.

May 18

Sometimes when Mom is getting ready to write a book she says she doesn't know where to start, that the ending is so clear to her that the beginning doesn't seem important anymore. I feel that way now only I don't know what the ending is, not even what the ending is tonight. We've been trying to get Dad on his land line and cell phone for hours and all we get are the kind of rapid-paced busy signals that mean the circuits are tied up. I don't know how much longer Mom'll keep trying or whether we'll talk to him before I fall asleep. If I fall asleep.

This morning seems like a million years ago. I remember seeing the moon in the sunrise sky. It was a half moon, but it was clearly visible and I looked at it and thought about how tonight the meteor was going to hit it and how exciting that would be.

But it wasn't like we talked about it on the bus going to school. Sammi was complaining about the dress code for the prom, nothing strapless, nothing too short, and how she wanted a dress she could wear when she went clubbing.

Megan got on the bus with some of her church friends and they sat together. Maybe they talked about the meteor, but I think they just prayed. They do that on the bus sometimes or read Bible verses.

The whole school day was just normal.

I remember being bored in French class.

I stayed for swim practice after school, and then Mom picked me up. She said she'd invited Mrs. Nesbitt to watch the meteor along with us but Mrs. Nesbitt had said she'd be more comfortable watching at home. So it was just going to be Jonny and Mom and me for the big event. That's what she called it: the big event.

She also told me to finish my homework early so we could make a party of it after supper. So that's what I did. I finished two of my moon assignments and did my math homework and then we ate supper and watched CNN until around 8:30.

All CNN talked about was the moon. They had a bunch of astronomers on and you could see how excited they were.

"Maybe after I'm through playing second for the Yankees, I'll be an astronomer," Jonny said.

I'd been thinking the exact same thing (well, not about playing second for the Yankees). The astronomers looked like they loved what they were doing. You could see how excited they were that this asteroid was going to make a direct hit on the moon. They had charts and computer projections and graphics, but basically they looked like big kids at Christmas.

Mom had gotten out Matt's telescope and she'd found the really good pair of binoculars that had somehow hidden themselves last summer. She'd even baked chocolate chip cookies for the event, so we carried a plate out and napkins. We decided to watch from the road, since we figured we'd have a better view from up front. Mom and I brought out lawn chairs, but Jonny decided to use the telescope. We didn't know exactly how long the hit was going to take or if there'd be something exciting to see afterward.

It seemed like everyone on the road was out tonight. Some of the people were on their decks having late barbecues, but most everyone else was in front of their houses, like we were. The only one I didn't see was Mr. Hopkins, but I could tell from the glow in his living room that he was watching on TV.

It was like a big block party. The houses are so widespread on our road, you couldn't really hear anything, just a general happy buzz.

When it got closer to 9:30, things got really quiet. You could sense how we were all craning our necks, looking toward the sky. Jonny was at the telescope, and he was the first one who shouted that the asteroid was coming. He could see it in the night sky, and then we all could, the biggest shooting star you could imagine. It was a lot smaller than the moon, but bigger than anything else I'd ever seen in the sky. It looked like it was blazing and we all cheered when we saw it.

For a moment I thought about all the people throughout history who saw Halley's Comet and didn't know what it was, just that it was there and frightening and awe inspiring. For the briefest flick of a second, I could have been a 16-year-old in the Middle Ages looking up at the sky, marveling at its mysteries, or an Aztec or an Apache. For that tiny instant, I was every 16-year-old in history, not knowing what the skies foretold about my future.

And then it hit. Even though we knew it was going to, we were still shocked when the asteroid actually made contact with the moon. With our moon. At that second, I think we all realized that it was Our Moon and if it was attacked, then we were attacked.

Or maybe nobody thought that. I know most of the people on the road cheered, but then we all stopped cheering and a woman a few houses down screamed and then a man screamed, "Oh my God!" and people were yelling "What? What?" like one of us knew the answer.

I know all those astronomers I'd watched an hour earlier on CNN can explain just what happened and how and why and they'll be explaining on CNN tonight and tomorrow and I guess until the next big story happens. I know I can't explain, because I don't really know what happened and I sure don't know why.

But the moon wasn't a half moon anymore. It was tilted and wrong and a three-quarter moon and it got larger, way larger, large like a moon rising on the horizon, only it wasn't rising. It was smack in the middle of the sky, way too big, way too visible. You could see details on the craters even without the binoculars that before I'd seen with Matt's telescope.

It wasn't like a big chunk of it flew off into space. It wasn't like we could hear the sound of the impact, or even that the asteroid hit the moon dead center. It was like if you're playing marbles and one marble hits another on its side and pushes it diagonally.

It was still our moon and it was still just a big dead rock in the sky, but it wasn't benign anymore. It was terrifying, and you could feel the panic swell all around us. Some people raced to their cars and started speeding away. Others began praying or weeping. One household began singing "The Star Spangled Banner."

"I'm going to call Matt," Mom said, like that was the most

natural thing in the world to do. "Come on in, kids. We'll see what CNN has to say about all this."

"Mom, is the world coming to an end?" Jonny asked, picking up the plate of cookies and ramming one into his mouth.

"No, it isn't," Mom said, folding her lawn chair and carrying it to the front of the house. "And yes, you do have to go to school tomorrow."

We laughed at that. I'd been wondering the same thing.

Jonny put the cookies away and I turned the TV back on. Only there was no CNN.

"Maybe I'm wrong," Mom said. "Maybe the world really is coming to an end."

"Should I try Fox News?" I asked.

Mom shuddered. "We're not that desperate," she said. "Try one of the networks. They'll have their own set of astronomers."

Most of the networks were off, but our local channel seemed to be carrying NBC out of Philly. Even that was weird, because we get New York City feeds.

Mom kept trying to get Matt's cell phone, but without any luck. The Philly news broadcasters didn't seem to know much more than we did, although they were reporting some looting and general panic in the streets.

"Go check how things are outside," Mom told me, so I went back out. I could see the glow from Mrs. Nesbitt's TV set. There was still some praying going on in someone's backyard, but at least the screaming had stopped.

I forced myself to look at the moon. I think I was afraid I'd see it had grown even bigger, that it really was lumbering its way to earth to crush us all to death, but it didn't seem to have gotten any larger. It was still off, though, still tilted in a funny way, and still too large for the night sky. And it was still three quarters.

"My cell phone is out!" someone screamed a few doors down, and she sounded the way we'd felt when we saw CNN was gone. Civilization had ended.

"Check your cell phone," I told Mom when I came back in, so she did, and hers wasn't working, either.

"I guess cell phones are out in this part of the country," she said.

"I'm sure Matt's okay," I said. "Why don't I check e-mails? Maybe he sent us one from his laptop."

So I went online, or rather I tried to go online, because our Internet connection was dead.

"He's fine," Mom said when I told her. "There's no reason to think he isn't fine. The moon is right where it belongs. Matt'll call us when he has the chance."

And that was the one thing Mom said all evening that turned out to be true. Because about ten minutes later, the phone rang, and it was Matt.

"I can't talk long," he said. "I'm at a pay phone and there's a line of people waiting for me to finish. I just wanted to check in and let you know I'm okay."

"Where are you?" Mom asked.

"In town," he said. "When we realized our cells weren't working, some of us drove to town just so we could phone in. I'll talk to you tomorrow when things aren't so crazy."

"Be careful," Mom said and Matt promised he would be.

I guess it was around then Jonny asked if we could call Dad, and Mom started trying to reach him. But the phone lines were crazy all over. I asked her to call Grandma in Las Vegas, but we couldn't get through to her, either.

We sat down in front of the TV to see what was happening to the rest of the world. The funniest thing was that Mom and I both jumped up at the exact same moment to get the chocolate chip cookies from the kitchen. I beat her to it, and brought the plate in. We all started devouring them. Mom would eat a cookie, sit still for a few moments, then get up and try Dad or Grandma. Jonny, who's really good about limiting the number of sweets he eats, just kept ramming cookies into his mouth. I would have eaten an entire box of chocolates if there'd been any in the house.

The TV connection went in and out, but we never got cable back. Finally Jonny thought to bring out a radio, and we turned that on. We couldn't get any of the New York stations, but Philly was coming in strong.

At first they didn't seem to know much more than we did. The moon got hit, like we'd been told it would. Only something had been miscalculated.

But before some astronomer could come on and explain to the rest of us just what had gone wrong, there was a bulletin. First we heard it on the radio, and then we got enough TV reception to see it as well, so we turned the radio off.

Whoever was broadcasting the news must have heard it over his little earphone, because he actually turned pale and then said, "Are you sure? Has that been confirmed?" He paused for a moment to listen to the reply, and then he kind of turned to face the camera.

Mom grasped my hand and Jonny's. "It'll be all right," she said. "Whatever it is, we'll get through this."

The newsman cleared his throat, like taking an extra few seconds was going to change what he had to say. "We are receiving reports of widespread tsunamis," he said. "The tides. As most of you know, the moon controls the tides. And the moon, well, whatever happened this evening at nine thirty-seven PM—and we don't know just what really did happen, but whatever it was—the tides were affected. Yes, yes, I got that. The tides seem to have swelled far beyond their normal boundaries. The reports coming in are from people in airplanes who happened to be flying overhead at the time. Massive flooding has been reported all over the eastern seaboard. There has been some confirmation of this, but these reports are all preliminary. Sometimes you hear the worst and it doesn't prove that way at all. Wait a second."

I quickly thought about who I knew on the eastern seaboard. Matt's in Ithaca and Dad's in Springfield. Neither one was anywhere near the ocean.

"New York City," Mom said. "Boston." She has publishers in both cities and goes there on business.

"I'm sure everybody's fine," I said. "You'll go online tomorrow and send everybody e-mails and make sure they're okay."

"All right, we are getting some confirmation," the newsman said. "There are confirmed reports of tidal waves twenty feet or higher in New York City. All power there has been lost, so these are very sketchy reports. The tides don't seem to be stopping. AP is reporting that the Statue of Liberty has been washed out to sea."

Mom started crying. Jonny was just staring at the TV like it was broadcasting in a foreign language.

I got up and tried Dad again. Then I tried Grandma. But all I got was the busy-circuit signal.

"We're getting an unconfirmed report that all of Cape Cod has been flooded," the newsman said. "Again, this is unconfirmed. But the AP is reporting that Cape Cod,"—and he paused for a moment and swallowed—"that Cape Cod has been completely submerged. The same seems to be true of the barrier islands off the Carolina coast. Just gone." He stopped again to listen to whatever was being said through his earpiece. "All right. There is confirmation of massive damage to Miami. Many deaths, many casualties."

"We don't know what he's saying is true," Mom said. "Things get exaggerated. Tomorrow morning we may find out all this didn't really happen. Or if it did, it wasn't nearly as bad as they thought it was. Maybe we should just turn the TV off now and wait until tomorrow to see what really happened. We may be scaring ourselves for no reason whatsoever."

Only she didn't turn the TV off.

"There's no way of knowing the number of deaths," the newsman said. "Communication satellites are down. Telephone lines are down. We're trying to get an astronomer from Drexel to come to our studio and tell us what he thinks is happening, but as you can imagine, astronomers are pretty busy right now. All right. We seem to be getting a national feed again, so we're cutting to our national news bureau for a live update."

And there, suddenly, was the NBC anchorman, looking reassuring and professional and alive.

"We're expecting word from the White House momentarily," he said. "Early reports are of massive damage to all the major cities on the eastern seaboard. I'm coming to you from Washington, D.C. We have been unable to make contact with our New York City headquarters for the past hour. But here's the information as we have it. Everything I'm going to announce has been verified by two sources."

It was like one of those lists on the radio to let you know which schools were having snow days. Only instead of it being school districts in the area, it was whole cities, and it wasn't just snow.

"New York City has suffered massive damage," the anchor said. "Staten Island and the eastern section of Long Island are completely submerged. Cape Cod, Nantucket, and Martha's Vineyard are no longer visible. Providence, Rhode Island—in fact, most of Rhode Island—can no longer be seen. The islands off the coast of the Carolinas are gone. Miami and Fort Lauderdale are being battered. There seems to be no letting up. We've now had confirmation of massive flooding in New Haven and Atlantic City. Casualties on the eastern seaboard are believed to be in the hundreds of thousands. Naturally it is far too early to tell if that number is excessive. We can only pray that it is."

And then, out of nowhere, was the president. Mom hates him like she hates Fox News, but she sat there transfixed.

"I am broadcasting to you from my ranch in Texas," the president said. "The United States has suffered its worst tragedy. But we are a great people and we will place our faith in God and extend a helping hand to all who need us."

"Idiot," Mom muttered, and she sounded so normal we all laughed.

I got up again and tried the phone with no luck. By the time I got back, Mom had turned the TV off.

"We're fine," she said. "We're well inland. I'll keep the radio on, so if there's any call for evacuation, I'll hear it, but I don't think there will be. And yes, Jonny, you have to go to school tomorrow."

Only this time we didn't laugh.

I said good night and went to my bedroom. I've kept the clock radio on, and I keep hearing reports. The tides seem to have pulled back from the East Coast, but now they're saying the Pacific is being affected also. San Francisco, they say, and they're afraid for LA and San Diego. There was one report that Hawaii is gone and parts of Alaska, but no one knows that for sure yet.

I looked out my window just now. I tried to look at the moon, but it scares me.

JUL 2008

MAIN LIBRARY